"You're the last person to make judgments on someone else's character!" Molly snapped.

Jordan's jaw tightened. A muscle worked. He leaned toward her until they were eye-to-eye. Molly had to force herself to keep from backing away. "You didn't use to feel that way."

"I didn't know you then," she said.

"You *knew* me very well," he replied with unmistakable intent.

Nothing he might have said could have hurt her more. She fought it. She fought it hard. But a swelling, suffocating wave of emotion closed off her throat. Tears burned behind her eyes, but she forced them back. This was a battle she was determined to win.

His lips parted in surprise. He hadn't expected it to hurt, she realized. Not like that. Not that much.

When she spoke again, it was in a low tone vibrating with emotion. "You evil, rotten..."

Dear Reader,

Welcome to Silhouette **Special Edition** . . . welcome to romance.

Last year, I requested that you send me your opinions on the books that we publish, and on romances in general. Thank you so much for the many thoughtful letters. For the next couple of months, I'd like to share some quotes from these letters with you. This seemed very appropriate now while we are in the midst of the THAT SPECIAL WOMAN! promotion. Each one of our readers is a special woman, as heroic as the heroines in our books.

This September has some wonderful stories coming your way. *A Husband to Remember* by Lisa Jackson is our THAT SPECIAL WOMAN! selection for this month.

This month also has other special treats. For one, we've got *Bride Wanted* by Debbie Macomber coming your way. This is the second book in her FROM THIS DAY FORWARD series. *Night Jasmine* by Erica Spindler—one of the BLOSSOMS OF THE SOUTH series—is also on its way to happy readers, as is Laurie Paige's *A Place for Eagles,* the second tale in her WILD RIVER TRILOGY. And September brings more books from favorite authors Patricia Coughlin and Natalie Bishop.

I hope you enjoy this book, and all of the stories to come!

Sincerely,

Tara Gavin
Senior Editor
Silhouette Books

Quote of the Month: "All the Silhouettes I've read have believable characters and are easy to identify with. The pace of the story line is good, the books hold my interest. When I start a Silhouette, I know I'm in for a good time."
—P. Digney,
New Jersey

NATALIE BISHOP

A LOVE LIKE ROMEO AND JULIET

Published by Silhouette Books New York

America's Publisher of Contemporary Romance

SILHOUETTE BOOKS
300 East 42nd St., New York, N.Y. 10017

A LOVE LIKE ROMEO AND JULIET

Copyright © 1993 by Nancy Bush

ISBN: 0-373-09840-5

First Silhouette Books printing September 1993

All the characters in this book have no existence outside the imagination of the author and have no relation whatsoever to anyone bearing the same name or names. They are not even distantly inspired by any individual known or unknown to the author, and all incidents are pure invention.

®: Trademark used under license and registered in the United States Patent and Trademark Office and in other countries.

Printed in the U.S.A.

Books by Natalie Bishop

Silhouette Special Edition

Saturday's Child #178
Lover or Deceiver #198
Stolen Thunder #231
Trial by Fire #245
String of Pearls #280
Diamond in the Sky #300
Silver Thaw #329
Just a Kiss Away #352
Summertime Blues #401
Imaginary Lover #472
The Princess and the Pauper #545
Dear Diary #596
Downright Dangerous #651
Romancing Rachel #700
A Love Like Romeo and Juliet #840

NATALIE BISHOP

lives in Lake Oswego, Oregon, with her husband, Ken, and daughter, Kelly. Natalie began writing in 1981 along with her sister, Lisa Jackson, another Silhouette author. Though they write separate books, Natalie and Lisa work out most of their plots together. They live within shouting distance of each other and between them have published over thirty Silhouette novels. When Natalie isn't writing, she enjoys spending time at her mountain cabin at Black Butte Ranch, where she catches up on her reading.

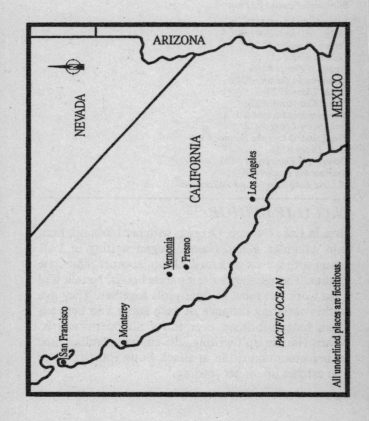

ARIZONA

NEVADA

MEXICO

CALIFORNIA

• Los Angeles

• Vernonia
• Fresno

• Monterey

•San Francisco

PACIFIC OCEAN

All underlined places are fictitious.

Prologue

Molly gripped her foam cup tightly between both hands. It offered little warmth, and she shivered uncontrollably as she stared blankly at the white walls behind Dr. Geddes's desk. The doctor herself stood in front of the desk, leaning her hips against it, watching Molly sympathetically. It was fifty degrees outside and because of the hospital's compliance with energy-conservation policy, it didn't feel much warmer inside. But Molly's chill was bone deep—emotional hypothermia, shock.

Without a word, Dr. Geddes took off her lab coat and draped it over Molly's shoulders. "Thank you," Molly managed to say. She glanced the doctor's way before fixing her eyes on the wall again.

"Take your time," Dr. Geddes said.

Molly inhaled deeply, tried to speak, failed, then subsided into silence. Fifteen seconds later, she tried again. "I don't want to talk to the police."

"That's why we're taping." Dr. Geddes pointed to the portable cassette recorder spinning silently away on the center of her desk.

"And I won't talk to Foster Montgomery or anyone from my family, either!"

"You don't have to do this now."

"Yes, I do," Molly countered bitterly, and this time when she met the doctor's gaze, determination burned in her eyes. "The man I love is fighting for his life, and it's all because of *them!* It's time to tell the truth. You're Jordan's doctor. You want to keep him alive almost as much as I do."

Dr. Geddes nodded, though she doubted anyone could be praying as fervently for his survival as the young woman in front of her.

"So, I'll tell you how this happened." She opened one fist and pressed a crumpled tissue to eyes too dry to cry. Her lips quivered. "It started over fifty years ago."

Dr. Geddes's brows shot up. "Fifty years?"

Molly nodded as she paced to the window and stared down at the parking lot, three stories below. She sent a faint, sardonic smile the doctor's way.

"It didn't just start with Jordan and me. During the Depression, Jordan's family managed to hang on to their money and make still more. You've met Foster Montgomery, Jordan's father."

"The tall man in the Emergency waiting room."

"Yes." Molly's jaw tightened. "The one I was arguing with."

"Go on."

"The Montgomerys had a lot of money during a time when nobody else had anything. My grandfather owned a small farm, and my father had a loan on a ranch nearby.

Both of them lost their property, and the Montgomerys bought the land from the bank at a tenth of its value."

"I see."

"My family never forgave them. And then Foster became head of the Montgomery family and he's such a..." She searched for the right word. "Bully. He doesn't care that his fortune was made on other people's misery. He considered it his due."

Molly rolled her shoulders back, attempting to ease the tension that tightened every muscle. "By the time I met Jordan, the die was already cast. My family hated his, and his hated mine. The feud had existed for decades, and my brother, Tyler, hated them with a learned passion." From beneath long black lashes Molly gave Dr. Geddes a look of irony. "Actually, I'd never thought much about the Montgomerys one way or the other. As far as I was concerned, the whole thing was ancient history. A fable. And since the Montgomerys went to Fairfield High, on the rich side of town, and we went to Central Valley, we didn't see them—apart from a rival football game or two...."

"Is that how you met Jordan?"

Molly paused, staring down at the now rain-slicked street. It had been raining that fateful night, as well. One of the few nights of rain during a sweltering fall when the temperature barely dropped below ninety during the day.

"It was homecoming my junior year," she explained. "We weren't even playing Fairfield. But some friends of Jordan's sneaked him into the dance. He was too old to be there, and much too bored. And I suppose that's what attracted me to him in the first place...." She paused. "If I'd known who he was, it never would have happened."

"*What* wouldn't have happened?"

She opened her mouth, shook her head, then admitted quietly, "Love at first sight." A spasm crossed her face, the pain surfacing from beneath her carefully composed exterior.

"Tell me about it," Dr. Geddes encouraged softly, but no further words were needed. Molly looked back into the past.

"It was raining, and I was soaking wet. I wanted to go home and change but my friend wouldn't let me and we were in her car...."

Chapter One

"Hurry up!" Charisse yelled, waving Molly impatiently toward the back door of the gymnasium. Above the misty rain the band's bass drum sounded like a heartbeat. The band itself, Temporary Insanity, had been selected by the teachers because they played golden-oldies from the fifties and sixties. The faculty could never trust the student body to hire a group. No way! The lyrics might condone *sex*, and God knew what could happen then!

Molly ran across the slippery grass. Her black hair whipped in wet, limp strands across her eyes. *Gross.* Temporary Insanity's lead singer screamed "Gloria" at the top of his lungs. Even outside, the sound was deafening.

"You could have taken me home to change," Molly complained to Charisse when they were both standing beneath the dripping gymnasium eaves. She was breathing hard; Charisse was examining her makeup in her compact mirror.

"Oh, for Pete's sake, everyone's soaked anyway." She snapped the compact closed and slipped it into her purse.

Except you, Molly thought, eyeing Charisse's lushly permed hair. The reason they were late was because Charisse had missed the game entirely. She'd spent the whole time primping. While Molly had cheered with the rest of the class from the uncovered student bleachers on the east side, Charisse had probably given herself a complete makeover.

It didn't seem quite fair.

"Lousy rain," Charisse complained, pouting.

"Yeah."

Normally rain wasn't a problem for the small town of Vernonia, California. Sunshine was practically a given. But tonight, of course, when the Central Valley Raiders should have chewed up and spit out Westside High's Black Bears, the rain had pelted down incessantly, turning the field into a squishy quagmire of grass and mud. The Raiders had slipped and goofed and screwed up all over the place. The final score: 21-7.

The side door to the gym was propped open by a molded orange plastic chair. Charisse peeked inside. "Jeremy's waving to us," she whispered. "Old man Gardner doesn't see. Come on."

"Why don't we just show our student cards and go in the front?" Molly suggested.

"Don't be a dweeb." Charisse glared at her and slipped through the door. After several seconds, Molly followed suit, half expecting a chaperon to grab her by the back of the neck and dump her outside again.

But the gym was too dark and too full of people for anyone to notice her enter. A mirrored ball rotated slowly above the crowd. Its silver squares refracted multicolored beams from the strings of leftover Christmas-tree lights that bordered every exit and zig-zagged across the wall above the bleachers.

Feeling self-conscious, Molly made a beeline for the girls' rest room. Dances weren't really for her. Besides, right now she felt like something the cat had dragged in—wet and ragged and pathetic.

Hazarding a glance in the mirror, she swore under her breath. What a disaster! Her forest-green sweater was nearly black with rain. And her hair!

Shuddering, she dragged a comb across her scalp, pulling the soaked strands into a lank ponytail. She grimaced. It looked more like a rattail than her "crowning glory." After attempting to fluff it out, she threw down the comb in disgust.

"Brother," she muttered, furious with Charisse and herself. Luckily her bangs, half dry, looked fairly decent, curling softly over her dark brows. She didn't have any makeup with her other than a broken tube of Peach-Raisin lipstick. With difficulty, she managed to add a bit of color to her mouth, sighing a little as she gazed at her reflection.

She wasn't Charisse. She would never be considered truly pretty. But she had high cheekbones, wide-set hazel eyes, thick black hair and a slim body that was the envy of her more-rounded friends. She had never learned to flirt, either, which, she'd discovered over the years, was a distinct disadvantage. Boys liked to be flirted with. Girls who felt awkward about it were considered awkward in every other way, as well.

What a cosmic joke.

Ten minutes later she returned to the gym floor, searching for Charisse, her sometimes best friend. Charisse was standing near the band, whispering something into the ear of one of the "coolest" senior boys. The boy whispered a response that made Charisse throw back her head and laugh.

Yeah, right, Molly thought, trying to picture herself playing that game. Not a chance.

"Wanna dance?"

Molly turned to the voice. Bernard Carleton, supernerd extraordinaire, was regarding her with anxious, bespectacled eyes. His nervousness was almost painful to behold.

"Sure," she said, just as anxious to alleviate his discomfort.

It was a slow song, and they stood at arm's length. Bernard moved so stiffly he could have been made of wood. He was desperate not to tread on her feet. She could almost hear him counting the steps in his head.

"How'd you do on the last algebra test?" he gushed out between sways.

"Not bad." She'd aced it. She was good with numbers.

"I thought I really blew the science exam, but I did better than I thought."

Molly smiled. Those were the only two classes she and Bernard had together. She searched her mind for further conversation. "Bad game, huh? Really disappointing."

"I only saw the first half. I went home to get out of the rain and change."

"Hmm..."

The song ended, and Molly thanked Bernard for the dance. As she drifted toward the punch bowl, red licorice whips and popcorn, Charisse yanked on her arm.

"Molly, that guy is a total loser! Why'd you dance with him?"

"Because he asked me."

"Well, Brian saw you and he made some crack about it. You know, if you want to stay with the cool group, you've got to wake up! Losers make you a loser, too."

Molly wanted to argue the point but Charisse was dragging her back to Brian, the senior class's resident Mr. I've-Got-It-All-Baby. Brian had never shown Molly any attention, unless it was a negative reminder of how stupid, clumsy or awkward she was. Molly, who'd once had a small crush on him, had gradually realized what a mean-spirited, insecure jerk he was. They'd stayed out of each other's way most of high school.

"Ooh, Molly!" Brian said, grinning. "Out on the dance floor with Bernard."

Rich McKinnon, a Brian wannabe, made retching noises. The boys laughed, and the girls giggled. Molly tried to smile but she felt like Benedict Arnold.

"Bernard's not so bad," she said with a shrug.

"Yeah, right. He can't get a girl, so he makes it with his calculator," remarked another Brian disciple. He gyrated his hips suggestively.

"Oh, how disgusting!" Charisse gasped.

"Yeah! Stay away from him. You could catch something contagious like a computer virus!"

They all roared with laughter. Even Molly could appreciate the humor, but she hated amusement at someone else's expense.

"I'm really thirsty," she inserted to change the subject. She was worse than a traitor. Why couldn't she just jump up and defend Bernard who'd been nothing but nice to her? But choosing his side would be "cool" suicide.

She escaped to the pop machine. She'd just gotten her drink when someone grabbed her sides and tickled her. With a shriek she dropped her paper cup, spewing soda everywhere. Sputtering, she whirled around, infuriated.

It was Brian. "Let's dance," he said, grabbing her hand and pulling her to the center of the gym.

She had cola splashed all over her pants and was steaming with fury inside. Luckily, the dance was a fast one. She didn't have to touch him. She didn't like one thing about him.

Charisse and Rich danced over next to them. "Nice moves," Charisse told Brian. She bumped her hip against his.

"Hey, Andy Collins and some of his buddies just crashed the dance. Look over there." Rich pointed to the bleacher side of the gym. A group of older boys was standing in a loose knot.

"What are they doing here?" Brian scowled.

"You wanna get rid of them?" Rich looked half scared, half excited.

"Just leave them alone," Molly said tiredly.

"Yeah, let the teachers take care of them," Charisse agreed. "Come on, Brian!" She wrapped her arms over his shoulders, squeezing between him and Molly. "Let's move."

Stuck with Rich, Molly hung around for a few seconds more, then decided the hell with it. She walked off the floor and back to the soda machine. This time she managed to get a full cup without someone making her spill it.

Glancing at the clock, she took a sip. It was ten-thirty, and she was thirsty and sticky. She drained half the cup, then brought it to her lips again. Near the back wall she noticed the older boys. One in particular seemed to be staring at her. She stared back, more out of belligerence than interest. Boys were an absolute mystery. They could be shy and bashful, charming and intelligent, then downright gross and stupid.

Bernard appeared at her side again. "Having a good time?"

"A blast."

"You wanna dance again?"

Molly sighed. "Not really. I'm kind of tired."

"Oh, okay." His shoulders hunched as he started to walk away.

"Wait a minute . . ." Molly inclined her head in the direction of the dance floor. "Can I change my mind?"

Bernard brightened as if she'd offered him the world. Her guilt nagged deeper. She was a fraud and a coward, not wanting to be with him because it might pull her down a few rungs on the social ladder.

They danced to a fast song, and Bernard was all wild legs and flapping arms. Molly determined she would not be embarrassed. She'd made her stand. She wouldn't falter now.

Nevertheless, when it was over she was glad to escape, and she half ran to the far side of the gym, then leaned against one of the pillars that supported the gym's main dome.

"You don't look like this is your idea of real fun," a masculine voice observed.

She glanced around the pillar. He was standing behind her, near the wall. The shadows were deep at this end but she could see he was smiling; his teeth flashed brightly.

"It's not," she admitted. "Who are you?"

"One of the uninvited." He shrugged. "Who are you?"

"A member of the student body."

"So sorry."

"You and me both."

Temporary Insanity slid into a slow ballad that Molly thought sounded vaguely familiar. The lead singer began to belt a solo that made Molly want to cover her ears.

"He could use a vocal-chord transplant," the stranger said.

"You said it." Molly cringed. "What *is* this?"

"'A Time For Us.'"

He stepped out of the shadows, and Molly got her first good look at him. His hair was dark brown, maybe black, and it brushed the collar of his shirt, a blue cotton chambray that peeked out beneath a black leather jacket. He wore blue jeans that hung low and sexily on lean hips. They were smudged with dirt at the knees but she could still see a crease, as if someone had bothered to iron them.

His face had lost its extreme youth; it bore the planes and angles of a man's. She couldn't tell the color of his eyes. Not as dark as hers, she guessed—maybe blue. Thick, spiky lashes framed them. He half smiled at her and his somewhat-forbidding countenance lightened.

"Come here," he said, pulling her into his arms. Molly stiffened, taken aback, but all he did was sway

with her to the music—a slow dance in the corner of
the gym.

"Would someone put that guy out of his misery?"
she murmured as the singer missed another note.

He laughed silently. She felt the movement in his
shoulders. His scent was a mixture of rain, men's cologne and musky leather. He held her surprisingly
close, his chest pressed to hers. She'd always hated
slow dancing, been afraid she'd step on toes or breathe
in someone's face, or a million other things. But he
made it seem easy and natural and right. She relaxed,
wishing she could rest her head on his shoulder,
knowing that was inviting more than she was willing
to give.

The song ended on a long note that the singer
couldn't hold. He broke off in a strangled gasp. As
bad as it was, Molly was sorry it was over.

Her partner shifted slightly so she could back up.
"Er...thanks," she said awkwardly.

"Are you from Vernonia?" he asked.

"All my life. And you?"

"The same."

"You didn't go to Central."

"Fairfield," he admitted.

Fairfield, Molly absorbed. The rich side of town.
"When did you graduate?"

"Four years ago."

Molly groaned. "I knew it."

"What?"

"You're too old for me."

He grinned—a slash of white in his face. "Give me
a break. Four years? My father's fifteen years older
than my mother."

Molly was delighted that he brought up his family. It made him seen less remote, more approachable, more real. "Are you going to give me a first name?" she asked him.

"Jordan. You?"

"Molly."

"You want to go somewhere?" he asked, glancing over her head to his buddies who'd meandered to the opposite side of the gym. "A friend of mine has the hots for one of your cheerleaders. That's why we're here. But I'd like to leave."

"I'm here with a friend. I can't just take off...." Molly felt like a child. He was used to being on his own, doing what he wanted to do, but she had curfews and rules and responsibilities.

He gazed at her thoughtfully. "This dance is going on for a while. We could just go outside and walk around."

She hesitated. What harm could it do? "Okay."

They slipped out the side door into the rain. Jordan grabbed her hand and they walked rapidly, heads bent, in the direction of the football field.

The place was empty now, and a bit lonely. Popcorn and mashed cardboard containers and cigarette packs littered the trampled grass through the gates. The concession stands were shut and locked. The rain still fell in steady drops. Jordan led her to the shelter of the covered bleachers, and they climbed to the uppermost row, then sat looking down on the dark, muddy field, with the rain softly tapping on the roof above their heads.

"You're kind of trusting," he said, after a minute, as if he'd suddenly realized her position.

"I'm a good judge of character."

"Yeah?" His eyes met hers. They *were* blue. A gorgeous, deep shade.

"Yeah." Molly smiled. She loved looking at him. Good grief, they'd just met, and she couldn't take her eyes off him! And wonder of wonders, he seemed to feel the same way.

"How do you know I didn't lure you out here to attack you?" There was lazy amusement in his tone.

"How do you know I didn't do the same?"

He laughed—a deep, rich laugh. She laughed, too. It felt great. Fabulous. She couldn't remember when she'd felt so happy and free.

The moment passed, and they remained looking at each other. His gaze drifted briefly to her mouth, then back to her eyes. "They had to drag me to that dance," he admitted. "A high-school dance!" He snorted in disbelief. "And now, here I am, with you. A *high-school* student!"

"I'm a senior. Does that help?"

"Not a lot," he admitted with a smile.

"I'm employed."

"Yeah? Where?"

Molly hesitated. "Burger Hutt." He gave a whoop of laughter. Tongue in cheek, she added, "Only part-time, but I've moved from general cleanup to sales."

"Now, I'm impressed." Curving his arm around her, he pulled her close to his chest.

"Do you have a girlfriend?" she forced herself to ask.

He shook his head. Molly shivered even though she wasn't cold. "You?" he asked.

"No *steady* girlfriends," she said, hiding a smile. "A few on the side."

This time instead of laughing he tilted her chin up with his fingers, staring down at her with an expression she couldn't quite read. Then a moment later he kissed her, lightly, his lips cool and smooth. Molly, who'd thought she hated kissing, responded with a surprising rush of desire. She eagerly kissed him back, loving the feel of the strong arms that surrounded her, holding her as if he never wanted to let her go.

He kissed her again and again, until Molly was lying half-atop him and he was stretched out on the hard wood of the top bleacher. The rhythm of the rain, the squeak of leather, the sensual feel of hard muscles and firm lips, the earthy, masculine scent enveloping her— Molly was lost to pleasures she'd only dreamed about.

He shifted, groaning a little, and she found herself pushed away from him by reluctant, but determined arms. They stared at each other for several long moments, then slowly, intimately, he untangled her wet ponytail until her tousled hair fell about her face. She held her breath and waited.

"I don't know what the hell we're doing," he muttered, sounding suddenly alarmed. "How old are you?"

"Seventeen."

"Oh, God!" Now, he started to laugh. "I must be out of my mind."

Molly smiled in relief. He wasn't mad at her. *Love at first sight,* she realized with a start. She loved him. Just like that. And she'd thought it only happened in romantic fantasies.

"Come on," he said, struggling to sit up. She moved away from him with utmost reluctance, sensing their interlude was over, wishing it weren't. His fingers curled around the edge of the bleacher, but he turned his head to look at her. "Molly," he said unsteadily, then stopped, as if he'd forgotten the next words.

She waited, never taking her eyes from him. With another groan, he reached for her, twining his hands in her hair, dragging her mouth to his, kissing her hard. Molly responded immediately. She didn't want it to end. And when his tongue sought entry into her mouth, her lips parted willingly. She trembled at the wonderful titillating invasion. Currents of desire shot through her body, until she felt like wax, melting, fluid, molded by his touch.

This time he released her abruptly, jumping to his feet and turning away from her. Molly's breath was labored, her chest heaving. Alarmed, she straightened her sweater, feeling hurt, rejected.

"We'd better get back," he said, clearing his throat. "Your friend's probably looking for you."

"No, she isn't," she said, then felt like a fool. "I mean, well . . . Okay."

She wanted to apologize, to ask what she'd done wrong, to make it right somehow, but she was afraid of further rejection. Her love was too new, too raw, for her to risk losing it all in one short hour.

When he finally turned around to her, she couldn't read his expression, but her spirits lifted as he reached for her hand and led her back to the gym.

At the door, he stopped. "Aren't you coming in?" she asked anxiously.

"I don't know." He ran a hand through his hair and she watched the movement longingly, wanting to touch him again.

He caught her watching him. They stared at each other. With a muttered imprecation, he pulled her into his arms, gazing down at her with smoldering eyes.

"I have got to get away from you," he told her.

"Are we bad for each other?" She couldn't believe how easily she had teased him!

"What do you think?"

"If this is bad . . ." she began.

"I don't want to be good," he finished with a sensual grin.

They both laughed. She could feel the smile on his lips when he kissed her, but very quickly the kiss became more serious. She slid her arms inside his jacket, feeling his warmth, the texture of his shirt, the hard muscles beneath.

"Whoa-ho!" Charisse cried in surprise.

Jordan pulled back from Molly as if she'd burned him. They both turned guiltily toward the door where Charisse stood in shock and wonderment.

"My God." Charisse's eyes widened as she stared at Jordan.

Before Molly could react, Jordan's friends, along with several giggling cheerleaders, slipped outside, too. They looked from Jordan to Molly to Charisse.

"We're out of here, Montgomery," one of them told Jordan and they walked toward the parking lot.

"I'll call you. What's your last name?" Jordan asked hurriedly as he started after them.

Molly went cold with shock. Montgomery? *Montgomery! Jordan Montgomery!*

"Capshaw," Charisse responded in a deadly voice when Molly couldn't find hers. "Molly Capshaw. So maybe you ought to vamoose with the rest of your gang, Montgomery. Molly doesn't want you to call her...ever."

Chapter Two

"You don't have to talk for me, Charisse!" Molly declared for the third time. "I can handle myself!"

"Well, sorr-eee." Charisse glared through the windshield, squinting at the slapping wipers as she maneuvered out of town. "I thought the last person I'd ever see you kissing was Jordan Montgomery!"

"I didn't know who he was! How did *you* know who he was?"

Charisse lifted one shoulder dismissively. "I've seen him before. He's been around."

"How come I didn't know?"

"Because you never look at men!" Charisse half laughed. "My God, Moll. Jordan *Montgomery!* I nearly fell over when I saw you kissing him. *Kissing!*"

"I know." Molly clenched her teeth together, then managed a faint laugh. "I can't believe it, either!"

"He didn't tell you who he was?"

Molly shook her head. "We never got past first names. He's probably as shocked as I am."

"He was dumbfounded! You should have seen the look on his face."

"I did."

Jordan had stared at her as if she were from another planet. Her own expression must have been very similar.

"Unbelievable," Charisse murmured, and they both lapsed into silence as Vernonia faded behind them and the car began winding through the rural farming area where Molly's parents still lived.

The Capshaws' home was on a section of land that had once been a hundred-acre farm but was now a jumble of housing developments, fig groves, strip malls and general California sprawl. Molly couldn't remember anything else, but her father was constantly reminiscing about how beautiful the area had been when he was a boy—until the Montgomerys ruined it.

The Montgomerys . . .

Molly had blindly believed every word spoken against them. Still, she'd never felt the same antipathy her family had. The feud was a fairy tale, a colorful distant part of Capshaw history, as substantial as the mining rights to nonexistent gold mines her great-great-grandfather had sold his soul for.

Now, with a new perspective, she realized Jordan's grandfather had only accomplished what some other eager entrepreneur would have if he'd had the opportunity first. The land would have been sold; the result would have been the same. The chance that some wealthy, farsighted philanthropist might have purchased the available land around Vernonia and turned it into parkland, or saved it all for farming, was a fool's dream.

But that didn't make the Montgomerys right, either.

"So, what are you going to do?" Charisse asked as they turned into Molly's drive.

"About?"

"About Jordan! What if he calls you? Or wants to see you, or something?"

"He won't."

"He might."

"I'm a Capshaw. He won't." Molly was positive.

Rain poured off the unguttered eaves, drenching the bougainvillea that hung limply above the double garage. Only one of the exterior light bulbs was working and it sent out a feeble, misty aureole of illumination around the front porch steps.

"Well, what if he does?" Charisse persisted as she threw the car into park and cut the engine. "I mean, the way he was kissing you. You could just tell what the guy wanted."

"Oh, Charisse!"

"I'm serious. Does he know where you live?"

"No! I don't know." She grimaced. "I suppose it's possible."

"Does he know you work at Burger Hutt?"

Molly didn't immediately respond, and Charisse sent her a knowing look. "I would bet a date with Brian that Jordan's going to find you. I *know* these things, Molly."

"Even if he did, I wouldn't have anything to do with him."

Charisse choked out a laugh. "I've never seen *you* kiss anybody—let alone like that!"

"That was before I knew who he was. Anyway, you bulldozed in and took care of things for me."

"If I'd had any idea that you might actually want to date that creep, I would have restrained myself."

"I *don't* want to date him!" Molly jumped from the car, ducking her head back inside and leaning on the door to keep from getting soaked. "Look, he thought I was too young for him anyway. He'll probably be as glad to be rid of me as I am of him."

"Maybe you're right." Charisse wanted to believe her, but her feminine receptors told her differently. "If he does call—hang up. That's the best way. Gets the point across real fast."

"Thank you, Ann Landers."

"He could be really dangerous," she added, her brow puckering thoughtfully.

"Charisse—"

"If he thinks you're interested in him, you might as well give it up right now. He's got lots of money, or at least his family does. He could seduce you with gifts and promises and oh, God, think about it, Moll!" She wrinkled her nose. "He *is* awfully cute."

"You can't talk me into Jordan Montgomery. Nobody—and nothing—can. It is simply not going to happen." With that, she slammed the door and started half-running, her head bent, toward the house. Rain poured around her.

Charisse leaned out her window. "Famous last words!" she yelled. "I just hope you mean that!"

Beneath the shelter of the eaves Molly watched Charisse back out of the gravel drive, then waited until her taillights were flickering red dots in the melting rain. Of course, she meant it. Jordan Montgomery? Good grief! She was lucky all they'd shared was one simple kiss.

Or two or three . . . or four.

She let herself in the front door, running her fingers through her wet hair and shaking water from her coat. The house was quiet apart from the beat of rain on the roof. A light was on in the kitchen. Molly walked like a robot toward the refrigerator, looked inside and leaned one arm on the door. She wasn't really hungry. Unseeingly, her eyes roved over foiled-wrapped leftovers and cans of soda.

Come here....

She shivered, shut the door, closed her eyes. The timbre of his voice had been low, husky. It had reached deep inside her soul, touched some vibrant, sleeping part of herself that was now awake and hungry.

Goose bumps appeared on her arms.

Come here....

She shook her head, shocked. She didn't want to remember. She couldn't!

Staring straight ahead, she didn't see the familiar maple table and chairs, or the flowered wallpaper, or the beat-up hardwood floor. She saw Jordan. Felt the strength of his muscles as he held her close. Relived those heart-shattering moments when firm lips crushed hers, tense arms enveloped her, hard hands wound in her hair—

"Molly?"

She screeched and jumped. "God, Mom! You scared the life out of me!"

Tina Capshaw frowned slightly. "Sorry. I didn't know you were home. Did you want something to eat?"

Stepping away from the refrigerator, Molly shook her head. "I was just . . . thinking."

"You were a hundred miles away. How was the dance?"

Her mother pulled out one of the kitchen chairs and looked like she was settling in for the next millenium. Molly panicked. She couldn't confide in her.

"The dance was a dance. What can I say? Kind of stupid and boring."

"How'd Charisse like it?"

"Better than I did." Her pulse was hammering as if she'd run a marathon. Taking a deep breath, Molly stretched, groaned and pretended a yawn. "Boy, I'm done in."

"Your father and I are driving to Bakersfield in the morning. We'll be home late tomorrow night or maybe Sunday. Try to keep an eye on Tyler for me, hmm? I know he's not your responsibility, but maybe if he gets out of line, you could just remind him about last time? I don't want to find beer bottles littering the front yard from his irresponsible friends again."

Molly met her mother's serious gaze. Two years older than Molly, Tyler was a volatile mix of resentment, high spirits, and a false belief in his own indestructibility. He pushed things to the limit, especially his parents' patience and faith. His crimes, though mostly small and familial—crunched fenders, punched holes in walls, lack of respect for other family members' rights, total disregard for the agreed-upon curfew—were numerous and still mounting. At nineteen, Tyler was less of an adult than Molly was at seventeen. He was a source of worry to both his mother and father, and an annoyance to Molly herself. Tyler invariably ruined every good thing that came her way. By trailblazing the path to adulthood for both of them—burning and pillaging as he went—he'd effectively shut down Molly's privileges; her parents had learned by experience that leniency planted the roots of evil.

Ha.

She could have told them she had no wish to be like Tyler. They *knew* she didn't approve of his antics. But once burned, twice shy. Molly was granted only the minimum of freedom: a school game and dance; a youth-group overnight with more chaperons than students; a trip in a car with scrupulously examined friends.

Luckily, Charisse was a bit of an Eddie Haskell: she only showed them her Goody Two-Shoes side. If Molly's parents suspected Charisse was as reckless as she was, the girls' friendship would be eliminated—*pronto*.

To Molly the situation was stifling and pointless, but not impossible to put up with. Not yet, anyway.

"If he does something stupid I'll sure let him know."

Tina smiled in relief. "He's talking about getting an apartment, but his job at the cannery isn't that secure."

"It isn't?" Molly dreaded to hear more.

"Some trouble with the foreman, I think." She sighed. "Anyway, I'm not sure how I feel about having him move out. Maybe in another year he might be more..." She trailed off, either unable or unwilling to complete her thought. Her comment about Tyler's irresponsible friends showed she knew what went on with Tyler but wanted to shift blame.

But Tina and Molly both knew Tyler drank and caroused with his buddies. Tyler's friends didn't take him with them just for his scintillating conversation.

"Good night," Molly murmured. She didn't want to think about Tyler. She had other, more pressing topics rolling around in her head. Her mother whispered a return good-night and Molly's last image of her was her straight-backed profile as she stared thoughtfully through the window to the black skies beyond.

In her room, Molly undressed in the dark and tossed an old Central Valley football jersey from Tyler's high-school days over her head. Sliding between the sheets, she clasped her hands behind her head and stared at the ceiling.

What a night! Jordan *Montgomery!*

"Well, at least I found out who he was before I did something totally stupid," she muttered, and, punching her pillow with resolve, reminded herself how unbelievably lucky she was that things had turned out as they had.

* * *

The rain broke at half-past midnight, the clouds parting to reveal a bright moon that sent a strip of white light across the glittering water-diamonds clinging to each blade of grass. Jordan stood with his hands in the back pockets of his jeans, following the line of illumination with his eyes to where it was broken by the dark shadow of the guesthouse and then trembled on the tile roof.

He tramped across the grass, soaking his sneakers, climbed onto the fence beside the guesthouse and jumped to the slippery tile roof, sliding squeakily halfway down before gaining purchase and climbing to the crest of the gable.

Sinking down there, he was oblivious to the wet tiles soaking through his jeans. It was a warm rain. A warm night. Hot, really.

He'd sat on this roof hundreds of times as a kid, but it had been a long time since the urge had gripped him. The last time had probably been when his brother, Michael, had broken his arm—a compound fracture that had sent the whole family scurrying to the hospital in a panic. They hadn't told him, hadn't had time. He'd waited on the roof, sensing something was desperately wrong, hurt that he was the one who'd been forgotten.

He'd been about fourteen at the time. Michael had survived with no serious aftereffects, and Mom and Dad had apologized profusely. Jordan had given up the sanctuary of the guesthouse roof. He'd never even thought about it again.

But tonight...

Turning his face to the sky, he closed his eyes and took a deep breath. He wished it was still raining. He felt... strange.

His mind's eye conjured up a vision of Molly Capshaw: wet black hair, serious hazel eyes, a dry sense of humor, lean hips, lush breasts, soft, pink lips....

He groaned in disbelief. The first girl who was even remotely interesting, and she was a *Capshaw!* Wait until his parents got a hold of this one. Wait until Michael found out. Jordan was sure he'd never hear the end of it.

Not that he cared. To hell with them. But it was funny. Hysterical, really. He hadn't known who she was, what her name was, who her parents were. But it wouldn't have mattered. He would still have been attracted to her.

Jordan opened his eyes and watched the clouds scudding across the black sky. She was too young for him. What was wrong with him that he was interested in a high-school girl? He was almost twenty-one himself and felt most high-school kids were as mature as two-year-olds, with interests to match. He'd been thinking the same of the co-eds at UCLA who'd shown him any interest. He'd dated one girl over a period of three months before he'd learned she was obsessive about her life to the point that she would eat cranberries every Wednesday morning, and if she couldn't get them, she would fast for a day because she felt it was the only way to stay "in tune" with her internal universe. He knew the cranberry scenario was merely a symptom of a larger problem, so he was out of there ASAP. Unfortunately, he'd been forced to change his phone number four times before she quit calling. He'd become part of her routine, and it had taken a while for her to change.

Luckily, she'd moved on to someone else and he'd been rid of her before the situation became ugly and dangerous. Still, it had cured him of trusting people, especially females.

But then, tonight, everything had fallen into place so naturally it had seemed heaven-sent. Good Karma. Serendipity. Call it what you will, it was incredible, and he'd be damned if he'd let Molly's last name affect how he felt about her. It had almost seemed like he'd been waiting for *something* and then tonight that something had happened.

With a seventeen-year-old high-school girl named Capshaw.

"Hell." Jordan shook his head. His brother, Michael, fell in and out of love—or maybe lust—with women on a daily basis. He'd accused Jordan of being too careful.

"Who gives a rip about what goes on in their heads?" Michael had advised Jordan one night after they'd both imbibed too freely from the short case Michael had brought home. "Women want one thing—security. And yeah, they like expensive junk like jewelry and clothes and stuff. But they really want to getcha, so the well doesn't run dry. Y'know what I mean? So don't trust 'em. Just take what you can get and have a good time. That's all there is, man. All there is . . ."

Now Jordan inhaled deeply, smelling the fresh, damp, slightly unpleasant scent of wet mud and grass. He wasn't quite the cynic Michael was, but he certainly wasn't trusting. He had met women who were more interested in a bank balance than in the man himself. Wincing, he recognized that his mother might even fall into that category.

But Molly Capshaw didn't. He'd bet his father's last million on that. She was pure and lovely with an uncomplicated, giving nature. Jordan hadn't wanted anyone, or anything, like he wanted Molly in a long, long time.

However, Molly had been stricken when she'd heard his name. The feud might be meaningless to him, but it sure as hell meant something to her.

The smart thing would be to forget tonight ever happened and move on.

But he couldn't. He just couldn't.

Chapter Three

"Two double cheeseburgers, a triple-bacon, two fries and four medium drinks. Is that it?" Molly's fingers hovered over the cash-register keys.

"Yeah, I think so." Her customer, a man in his thirties with a blond-haired boy by his side, kept squinting at the overhead menu, as if he felt certain there must be something *better* to order.

"That's twelve eighty-five."

As the man dug in his pockets for change, Molly glanced at the clock. Another hour until ten o'clock when she was off-duty. She hoped everything was still okay at home. Tyler had shown up at the Hutt about two hours ago with his friend, Peter Haas, and Molly had suspected they were both drunk. Her promise to her mom lay heavy on her chest. But she couldn't be Tyler's keeper! Why couldn't he just behave?

The door opened, and Molly glanced up from filling her order. Brian and Rich strolled in. Spying Molly, they pointed and laughed. All in the name of fun, of course. She wondered what she'd done to deserve this.

"Hey there," Brian greeted her, drumming his index fingers on the counter. "Gimme something good."

"What would you like?"

"How about a *teen* burger?" Rich grinned.

"You'll have to order what's on the menu."

Rich feigned disappointment. "Guess I'll just have to gulp down a triple-bacon-cheese."

"One triple-bacon-cheese. Anything to drink?"

"A triple margarita!" Brian grinned hugely. He and Rich both guffawed as if they were the comic team of the century.

"I'm sorry." Molly smiled. "We're fresh out."

Brian said, "Gimme the same as Rich. And a large root beer."

"Root beer for me, too," Rich agreed.

"Any fries?"

"Yeah. Large for both of us," Brian answered, digging in his jeans for some cash.

As Molly filled the tray, she reminded herself that these were the guys she was supposed to be interested in. Not Jordan Montgomery, heaven forbid. Not that she was interested in Jordan. No way.

"There you go. Two preteen burgers."

"Oooh." Brian made a face to Rich. "Fun-neee . . ."

Molly gazed expectantly over their heads to the next customer. It was a pregnant woman and her husband. A baby was in a stroller beside them, fussing slightly.

Brian and Rich looked down at the child. "Goochy, goochy, goo," Brian said. They both laughed uproariously as they swaggered to a table by the window, slouching into the attached chairs.

Through the window Molly saw a black-and-chrome motorcycle pull up to the bumper guard in front of the Hutt. Then her attention returned to the couple with the baby.

"Can I help you?"

"We're still thinking."

The door opened, and Molly glanced up. Her breath caught. Jordan Montgomery!

If he recognized her in her brown-and-orange striped uniform, he didn't act like it. But he did move into her line. Suddenly Molly was all thumbs. She could scarcely get through the order. The couple had to repeat themselves several times. By the time she'd filled the tray and collected the money, she was more in control, but her heart was racing double time.

"Hi," Jordan said as the couple moved away. "I wasn't sure if you'd be working tonight or not."

He'd come to see her! "Umm. Yeah. I'm working." *Brilliant! Positively brilliant!* "Do you want to order something?"

His blue eyes held hers. She couldn't tell what he was thinking. In her peripheral vision she saw Rich and Brian take note. Rich jabbed Brian, and they slid from their chairs to come up behind Jordan.

Jordan briefly scanned the menu. While his gaze was upturned, Molly focused somewhere near the base of his throat. He wore black leather again, and it looked good on him. She was glad he wasn't the preppy type. Not that there was anything wrong in that, but this way he was more appealing.

More appealing? She didn't care if he was more appealing! He was Jordan Montgomery and definitely off-limits.

"You know, I can't find anything to eat up there." He smiled faintly.

"How about a drink?"

"Was your friend right?"

"Pardon?" Molly's gaze jerked back to his in surprise. Behind him, Rich and Brian eavesdropped unabashedly.

"Last night. Your friend."

"Charisse?"

"Okay, Charisse. Was she right?"

He waited. When Molly couldn't think of a response, he grimaced as if in disgust. "Okay," he said, rapping the counter with his knuckles before turning around. He almost stumbled over Rich and Brian, giving them a long stare before heading back outside. She heard the muted roar of his motorcycle as he switched it on, then gracefully arced out of the Hutt's parking lot.

"You're talking to a Montgomery?" Brian's jaw dropped. Realizing how uncool he appeared, he snapped his mouth shut a moment later.

"Thinks he's something, doesn't he?" Rich sniffed.

"Did you guys want something else? I've got customers," Molly interjected shortly, directing her attention to the teenage guy and girl behind them who were hanging all over each other, kissing and chewing gum at the same time.

"When do you get off?" Brian called, stepping away.

Molly just shook her head, and after waiting a few seconds for an answer—and not getting one—he stomped out of the Hutt with Rich, his lapdog, at his heels.

Jordan Montgomery might not be the ideal guy, Molly decided, but she'd be damned if she'd date any of the losers from her class.

Sunday dawned fiercely hot. Friday's rain was a lingering memory, the last pools of water drying into caked mud by early morning. In cutoff jeans and a sleeveless green T-shirt, Molly sat in a chair in the backyard, pondering how to begin her writing assignment: The Earth: Love It Or Lose It. She wasn't especially good at writing and the topic, though worthy, wasn't exactly one to inspire the muse in her.

Her parents had called at midnight to tell her they were definitely spending the night in Bakersfield and would be back late the following afternoon. It was a blessing, really, since Tyler had roared home around two in the morning, blaring the horn to announce his fortuitous return, then slamming his way through the house before collapsing into a self-induced coma. Molly had picked up the one beer can he'd dropped on the front porch and tossed it out.

Sighing, she closed her eyes. Jordan Montgomery's face swam into her vision. Every taste, texture and shiver from Friday night came back in minutest detail. It was irritating. Infuriating, really. She wanted nothing to do with him.

But if her writing assignment were about Jordan she could think of dozens of things to say.

"Damn," she murmured, drifting off. Memories crowded her mind in a hazy montage: the rough yet gentle quality of his voice; the steel-blue intensity of his eyes; the breath-stopping feel of his fingers slowly discovering her flesh. Luscious thoughts. Thoughts that swung to and fro in her mind. Thoughts made more sensual beneath a grayish-blue sky and orange sun.

Cold water dripped on her leg. With a shriek, Molly jumped awake. "What? *Tyler!*" She glared at her brother whose beer can's melting condensation had dripped on her leg. "What are you doing?"

"I'm heading over to Pete's house. Wanna come?" He tipped back his head and drained his beer.

"Where'd you get that?"

Ignoring her question, Tyler replied, "Pete invited you. I don't care if you come or not." He crumpled the empty can in one fist.

"You're walking on thin ice with Mom and Dad. Leave that can lying around, and you're in serious trouble. I had to pick up last night's evidence."

"Ooh, I'm scared."

"I mean it, Tyler."

"Since when are you my conscience?"

"Don't you even care?" she practically screamed at him.

He stared her down. At length he asked, "So, what should I tell Pete?"

"Not interested. How many more beers have you got?"

"God, what a nag!" He stalked to the sliding-glass door, flinging over his shoulder, "Pete thinks you're a babe. What a joke!"

Molly gazed after him in astonishment. Pete? Tyler's delinquent friend thought she was a babe?

"Dream on," she muttered to the empty yard, listening to the rev of Tyler's engine as he backed his van into the street and roared away. Seconds later a new, throatier roar filled the air. A motorcycle.

Molly's heart jumped into her throat. She ran around the side of the house just in time to see the motorcycle, whose driver had long blond hair, disappear into the distance. Frustrated, Molly stood watching after it for long minutes before marching back to the house and calling Charisse.

"Any chance you can pick me up and we can go somewhere? I'm totally without wheels."

"Mmm." Charisse was munching on something. "I gotta buy my own car. Let me finish lunch, and I'll see what I can do."

Forty minutes later she appeared in the family car. Molly jumped inside. "Freed!" she exclaimed, grinning.

"Since when are you so anxious to be out and about?" Charisse grinned back. "It's always me pushing you."

"I just can't bear one more moment of jail," Molly answered.

"Jail?"

"The four walls feel like they're closing in. I've got this stupid writing assignment, and I just feel like screaming!"

Charisse threw her a puzzled look as they cruised toward Vernonia proper.

"Let's go to the Hutt," Molly suggested.

"You have to work?"

"Not today."

"You can't want the food?"

"No. Brian and Rich stopped by last night," she improvised. "Thought they might stop by again today."

Charisse gave her a hard look. "You got a thing for Brian?"

"Jeez, Charisse. Friday night it was Jordan Montgomery, now it's Brian. I'm not interested in either one of them!"

"Well, I know it's not Rich. He's such a dweeb." For all her grumbling, Charisse complied. They pulled into the Burger Hutt parking lot a few minutes later. "This isn't exactly a hot spot," she complained.

The Hutt was at the edge of town, and its food was just mediocre. But the management was good about accommodating Molly's erratic schedule. They made allowances the other establishments probably wouldn't have so that she could have a social life this last year of school.

"If Brian and Rich came here, it was because of you. Period. And now you want to see them, too!"

"I don't care if I ever see them again." Molly was adamant.

"Oh, yeah? So, what's the big attraction?"

"Nothing!"

Charisse slammed the car into park, and Molly jumped out. Inside the Hutt she chatted with some of the other employees and worked out her following weekend schedule. Charisse eyed the patrons and looked mildly disgusted.

It was hot, and sweat formed at Molly's temples. She felt restless and itchy. She could hear her own chatter and was embarrassed. What *was* she doing? What did she expect? That Jordan would roar in, sweep her up, and race off into the sunset with her?

"Let's go," she said shortly, heading for the door.

"Finally." Charisse sighed.

It was in the parking lot that it happened. One moment Molly was yanking open the passenger door, the next she was frozen like a statue, watching a motorcycle sweep into the lot.

But it wasn't Jordan. The guy who ripped off the black helmet was nearly his spitting image but fell just short of Jordan's appealing good looks. This man looked tough and angry. He stared Molly down with a fierce aggressiveness that made her quail inside.

Charisse sucked in a breath. "Is that who I think it is? It must be!"

"Who?" Molly choked out.

"Another Montgomery. The older one. What the hell is his name? Oh, God, Molly, he's coming over here! He's coming to see you!"

"No, he's not."

But he was. Or at least he appeared to be. His eyes weren't blue like Jordan's; they were darker, murkier. Instead of focusing his attention on Molly he went right for Charisse. "See anything you like?" he asked with arrogant superiority.

"No!" Charisse's aplomb had deserted her completely.

"Then stop staring."

He turned on his heel and slammed into the Hutt. Within seconds a car bounced into the lot. To Molly's intense surprise, Jordan jumped out, followed by a bunch of his friends. He did a double take on Molly, lifted one eyebrow in recognition, then strode after his brother.

"What's going on?" Charisse asked, enthralled.

"Let's get out of here."

"Forget it." She hurried after them, squeezing in with the crowd of Jordan's friends as they headed inside.

Reluctantly, Molly followed them.

"Sure as hell didn't leave it here," Jordan was saying through tight lips. "And if you hadn't ripped my engine completely apart, I wouldn't have taken the bike in the first place!"

"It's black and silver," his brother told the girl at the counter. "And if you don't have it, it was probably ripped off!"

"No one left a helmet here last night," the girl answered.

"How the hell do you know?"

"I know." She stood her ground.

"Why don't you go ask somebody else?" Jordan's brother suggested, nose-to-nose with her.

She glared at him, but it was no use. Molly took a step forward.

"He didn't have one on," Molly said.

All heads turned her way. She swallowed. She hadn't meant to just blurt it out like that. It just kind of popped out. "I waited on him, and he didn't have a helmet."

Jordan's look was unreadable. His brother frowned at her as if she were lying. "You work here?" he demanded.

Molly nodded.

He whirled on Jordan. "So, where the hell is it?"

"Maybe *you* lost it," Jordan pointed out.

"Bull."

He stormed back out of the Hutt. Jordan's friends followed at a slower pace, but Jordan waited. Charisse glanced from Molly to Jordan, wide-eyed.

"I'll be outside," she whispered, scurrying away.

Molly stood awkwardly to one side of him. Jordan's gaze was on the door, his jaw tense. Several moments later he slid her a look.

"My brother," he said.

She nodded.

"Thanks for getting him off my back."

He turned to leave. Desperate, Molly said, "Is he always so personable?"

Jordan hesitated, shooting her a sideways look that was calculated to send her pulse spiraling, she was sure. "Not always. Sometimes he's downright hostile."

"He doesn't know I'm a Capshaw, does he?"

"Not that I'm aware of."

They stared at each other. Molly wanted to hate him. Or at the very least dislike him...a little. She knew she didn't trust him. Who would be stupid enough to trust a stranger—especially one with such negative history with her family?

But she didn't hate him.

"Are you working today?" he asked, glancing back at the counter.

"No, I'm here with a friend."

"Oh, yeah. Charisse." His gaze narrowed through the window at Charisse who was hovering by her car, trying not to stare at Jordan's brother.

"Umm . . . yeah . . ."

Jordan looked as if he were going to answer, but instead he pushed through the door and walked into the baking heat. Molly hurried to catch up with him.

"I was surprised you stopped by last night," she said breathlessly.

He shrugged, his attention on the knot of his friends who were eyeing his brother who, in turn, was leaning against his motorcycle and glaring at all of them. "Michael decided to fix my car and tore the engine into a million pieces, so I took his bike." He smiled to himself, then shot her another look. "Wanna go for a ride?"

"On . . . on that? Now? Well, he won't— I mean, it's not yours. You don't mean ride *with him,* do you?"

"Not on your life." He strode to his brother and said something low and fast. Michael seemed to consider. He said something back, which made Jordan glance thoughtfully at Charisse.

"What's going on?" Charisse demanded, sidling close to Molly.

"I don't know."

"I don't like it," she hissed as Jordan came striding back. Today she wasn't as hostile. She just watched his every move like a hawk.

"Can your friend give Michael a ride home?" Jordan asked Molly.

Charisse gasped. "No way!"

"We can follow behind. It's not too far."

"But . . . you don't have a helmet. I don't have one," Molly sputtered.

"Oh, yes, we do. Michael's just missing his favorite one. Are you game?"

The challenge was evident in those sexy eyes. Charisse choked out a gasp and gazed at Molly helplessly. Michael waited, a half smile on his lips.

"I'm game," Molly said.

Ten minutes later they were whizzing down the highway. Molly leaned close to Jordan's back, her hair stinging her eyes as it whipped wildly around her head. She was wedged against his jeans, her thighs tucked behind his hips, conscious of the smell of his leather jacket, surrounded by heat and rushing wind.

Breathing deeply, she ignored the voice inside her head—that loud, shrill voice of reason—the one that demanded to know what she thought she was doing. Instead she hugged him tighter, succumbing purely to her senses, as if years of restraint and circumspection had never existed.

The pavement was a blur of gray. Molly closed her eyes and listened to the scream of the wind as they roared down the road. It felt as if they were traveling at the speed of light even though they were just keeping up with the traffic. At a stoplight, she glanced at the sedan next to her. A man in a bad toupee and a brown suit frowned his disapproval at her. She grinned back at him.

With a cock of his wrist, Jordan sent the motorcycle forward in a spurt, leaving the car in the dust. They raced past fig groves and fields and the beginnings of new housing developments. When they took a turn up the one small hill along Vernonia's west side, Molly realized they were entering the "rich" part of town.

Where Jordan lived.

They pulled into a drive lined by twelve-foot-high laurels, which disguised the grounds from the road. Charisse's car was parked just inside the gate.

Jordan killed the engine, and an unearthly silence followed. Charisse was standing on her side of the car; Michael Montgomery on his. They were regarding each other over the roof.

"Pervert!" Charisse snapped.

Michael just shook his head and strolled toward the huge Spanish-style home, whose red tile roof had faded to a salmon pink in those areas where umbrella-like oaks didn't provide shade.

"He tried to kiss me!" Charisse burst out, incensed.

"Michael doesn't have a lot of finesse with women," was Jordan's answer.

Charisse glared at him. "Come on, Molly. Let's get out of here."

Molly hadn't released her grip on Jordan. Now, reluctantly, she eased her arms back, sliding from the leather seat. "Thanks for the ride."

"Could you move that thing so I can back up?" Charisse demanded.

Jordan shrugged and dragged the bike to one side of the drive. "You want to go?" he asked Molly.

No! "Well ... Yeah ... I've got things to do."

"She doesn't want to get mixed up with a Montgomery!" Charisse burst out.

"Charisse!" Molly spat back.

Charisse held up her hands in supplication. "What are you doing?" she whispered.

Realizing how worried her friend was for her, Molly wished she could explain her behavior. But she couldn't. She didn't understand it herself.

But she wasn't about to quit now.

"I'm out of here," Charisse said, hesitating, waiting for Molly to make a move toward the car. "Your parents would kill you if they knew!"

"I can take care of myself, Charisse!"

"Come on, Molly. *Please!* This isn't smart."

"Goodbye, Charisse."

Charisse moaned and shook her head, but Molly refused to back down. Her shoulders slumped, Charisse slid into the driver's seat, then backed out of the drive with a furious screech of tires, and tore away.

In the aftermath, Molly didn't know what to say. She was in over her head, and she knew it. But she was powerless to do anything to change it.

"She was right, wasn't she?"

Molly gazed at Jordan uncomprehendingly.

"Your parents would kill you if they found out you were with a Montgomery," he clarified with shocking bluntness.

"Umm . . . no. No."

"Could you try to sound a little more like you believe it?" he asked humorously.

"I—I don't know what they'd do."

"Yes, you do."

He half smiled, and Molly's heart flipped over. Her feelings were still too raw from the other night, and every little movement he made seemed deep, intense, important.

And he was completely, utterly wrong for her.

"They'd think I'd lost my mind if they knew I'd been on a motorcycle with you. Motorcycles *are* dangerous," she hastened to explain.

He snorted. "Right."

"I really do have a lot to do. Maybe I should just go home."

Sucking air through his teeth, Jordan stretched and ran his hands through his thick black hair, frowning a bit. It was a rawly sensual gesture and Molly's heart responded with a painful little flip.

"How dangerous would a motorcycle be if someone else were driving it—someone besides a Montgomery?"

She opened her mouth to answer, thought a moment, and admitted shakily, "Not as dangerous."

His gaze narrowed thoughtfully. "So, how's it going to be when I take you home?"

"Oh, my parents aren't home. They're in Bakersfield. Won't be back until later this afternoon."

"So, you're safe. At least for today."

She shrugged. "I don't really care what they think."

"Oh, sure!" He gave a short bark of laughter.

"Okay, I do care. Sort of. I don't want to get mixed up with a Montgomery, either!"

The truth of that remark sliced through the air like a knife. Molly inwardly squeezed herself to stop the sudden shaking of her limbs.

"Don't you think," he drawled in that dangerous, sexy voice she was beginning to associate only with him, "that after the other night, we already are involved?"

"We were just kissing."

"I don't 'just kiss' everybody."

"Well, neither do I," she admitted.

"So...?"

He wasn't making this easy. She didn't expect it to be easy. She didn't know what she expected. "The other night I thought . . . you were someone else," she admitted. "I mean, it was great. Taking a walk. Being together. *I didn't know!*"

Silence followed her fractured outburst. He squinted against the sun, his thick lashes hiding his eyes and thoughts. Just when she thought he wouldn't respond, he said in a low voice, "If you hadn't found out, what would we be doing now?"

"What do you mean?" she asked automatically.

"I don't think we'd be standing here like this. I think we'd be doing something else."

What? she wanted to ask, but she had a hazy idea already. Her heart jerked. Dragging her eyes from his sensual lips, she asked herself helplessly what the hell she was supposed to do now.

"I don't care that you're a Capshaw," he bit out, as if the confession were dragged from deep inside him.

She wanted to return the compliment. That she didn't care that he was a Montgomery. But she *did* care. She *should* care!

"I'll take you back," he said, swinging the bike around. "Hop on."

With sharp regret, she slid behind him, wrapping her arms around his chest, feeling his heat. She glanced back to the house and saw Michael staring at them through the front windows.

Then they were on the road. The engine whined, air rushed past her in a deafening torrent, the landscape and sky melded into a blur of tan and blue. They drove for what felt like endless miles, and she decided he must be lost. He didn't know where she lived.

But then he turned the right way and she held her tongue, enjoying the long, spinning moments until he pulled into her own driveway.

"I'd like to go to the mountains sometime," he said as he cut the engine, glancing toward the horizon and the gray, faraway Sierra Nevadas.

She wanted to respond to the unspoken invitation, but responsibility had a choke hold on her. Responsibility and fear. "My brother's here."

"I guess that's my cue to leave."

"No . . ." Molly realized belatedly that Tyler's van was gone.

He waited, watching her closely.

"Want a lemonade? I made some fresh this morning."

"What about your brother?"

She felt like an idiot. If Tyler really were home, she wouldn't dream of inviting Jordan to stay.

"Actually, I think he's gone. His van isn't here."

"Oh."

Color swept up her neck and face. "Come on out to the backyard," she invited, leading the way before he had a chance to turn her down.

She made a stop at the kitchen, poured them both drinks, then stepped outside to the grouping of lawn chairs where she'd earlier tried to get her mind on her writing assignment. Jordan was standing by a well-used chaise longue whose plastic straps were beginning to pull free. He was staring past the peeling, white-painted fence to the empty lot beyond.

Remembering his palatial home, she cringed to think of how beautiful his own backyard must be.

She handed him a glass. "Never thought I'd have a Montgomery over," she said nervously.

"I'll bet."

"Does your family. . . feel the same way about us?"

Jordan was silent for so long she thought he wouldn't answer her. "I don't know what my family thinks. Yours, apparently, has a definite opinion about us."

She bobbed her head in nervous agreement.

"Tell me," he said.

"I don't think you want to hear."

"Yeah, I do."

Grimacing, Molly sighed. "Well, all the Montgomerys are—bad news."

"That isn't so far from the truth," he said with a silent laugh.

"They'll kick you when you're down."

He tossed her an ironic look.

"They'll steal your last cent and laugh all the way to the bank," she hurried on, burying her nose in her glass of lemonade.

He reacted with an involuntary jerk, and she kicked herself for being so blunt. She sensed, though it was a murky, indistinct feeling she didn't quite understand, that she was deliberately keeping him at arm's length.

"Your turn," she reminded him.

"What?"

"Your family must have some opinion about the Capshaws."

"Nothing that matters," he said softly.

"Oh, come on. I told you."

"My family. . ." His lips tightened. "My father would certainly. . ." He drew a deep breath and tossed back the rest of his lemonade. "My father doesn't have the right to criticize anyone," he finished bitterly. "Thanks," he added, setting the empty glass down on a table.

"You're leaving?" she asked quickly.

"Yeah. I've—got to go."

"Why?"

He made a harsh sound. "Because I don't know what the hell I'm doing here."

She was standing several feet away, as tense as he was. She knew how he felt. She felt the same. But she couldn't let this slip away. It was too important. One of life's moments that happen when they're least expected and have such lasting repercussions. Tiny ripples that turn into tidal waves.

"I don't want you to leave," she whispered in an uncertain voice.

"If I stay..." He left the thought unfinished, his hands clenched.

"It doesn't have to be bad," she blurted out.

"Oh yeah?"

He was facing the weed-choked fields beyond, focused with such intensity on the rampant Queen Anne's lace and dandelions, Molly thought they might catch fire from his searing gaze. Her own eyes searched the contours of his profile, loving every detail, memorizing it all.

"I don't care," she said defiantly.

His head turned. He stared at her. "Neither do I."

His blue eyes simmered. In them she saw the reflection of her own wild fears and desires. Whatever was going on, it was powerful. She wanted it very badly.

Swallowing, she took a step toward him. He didn't move. He was utterly still. Stonelike.

They stood like that for several seconds. Charged. The air thick with expectancy.

He slowly reached up and touched her face. His thumb marked a path down her cheekbone to her jaw. Her body thrummed like a hot wire. When he bent down to kiss her she stood on her toes. He groaned, his mouth slanting over hers, lips hard, arms surrounding her, crushing her. Kisses swarmed over her face and cheeks and the curve of her jaw. He gripped a tangle of her hair in his fist.

Molly gasped. Her heart beat hard in her throat. Hunger was like a living animal inside her. She matched his hard kisses with searing intensity. Her body wanted to wrap itself around him. When his hand stole down her back to the curve of her spine, she pressed closer. The groan that came from his lips left her breathless, limp and willing.

He released her mouth long enough to trail hot kisses down her throat. Molly's head lolled back, her eyes closed, her body burning with desire. This was sheer lunacy, yet Molly, who'd never been the least interested in any boy, suddenly wanted to stretch out on the grass and make wild, passionate love to him!

Sanity slowly reasserted itself. She opened her eyes to see the dusky blue sky while Jordan's mouth plundered the hollow of her throat, his hand sliding beneath her blouse and upward, to the lacy edge of her bra. His thighs were close to hers. She felt the rigidity of his desire, recognized it for what it was. A thrill shot through her even as she gulped out a moan of resistance.

Jordan froze. He took a long breath through his teeth. Agonizingly slowly he stopped his passionate assault, pulling back to stare at her through eyes that mirrored her own confusion.

"What *is* this?" he asked hoarsely.

She shook her head. "I don't know."

His hand trembled as he shoved it through his hair. She stared at those silky black strands and longed intensely to do the same.

"I have never felt this way," he bit out, angry in his disbelief.

"Me, neither."

"It's crazy. It's nuts."

She couldn't answer.

"Your parents *would* kill you if they knew," he added passionately.

Molly had no defense.

"My father would have a few words to say, too, but hell . . ."

Sighing, he half turned to her. As if compelled, he reached for a lock of her hair, examining its luster as it slid through this fingers. "I want to be with you, and that's all I can think about."

"I want to be with you, too," Molly admitted.

Jordan drew a steadying breath. "You're only seventeen, and I'm not that crazy."

"You're not?"

He laughed. "God, I hope not! Molly, Molly. . ." He hugged her tightly. She could feel the slight tremor that ran through him. "You've still got a year of high school left."

She didn't want to talk about this. It was too mundane and didn't matter. She just wanted this moment, these feelings, to go on and on. To consume her. "I'm going to be eighteen in a few weeks."

His answering look did dangerous things to her pulse. "You're still in school."

"So are you."

"College," he pointed out.

"I'll be there next fall."

He nodded, as if she'd finally said what he wanted to hear. His hand slid restlessly down her back. "What do you plan to study?"

She swallowed. His hand lay lightly on her hip. "Sex ed?"

Jordan threw back his head and laughed. "No, I mean for real."

"I'm good with numbers. Accounting, I guess." She grinned. "And you?"

"I'm in Business at UCLA."

"Really?" She was impressed. For just a moment she'd forgotten how wealthy he was. She'd been thinking about a community college. Something she could almost afford. "How do you like it?"

"Boring as hell," he admitted with a grin. "But one more year, and I'm outta there."

"Then what?"

"I'm not sure. I'd like to build something."

"You mean, like a building?"

He gazed at her lips. "Yeah, I guess."

"So, you're just home for the weekend?" She was inordinately depressed.

"I might be coming home a lot of weekends."

For a charged moment she thought he was going to drag her into another fiery embrace and kiss her senseless. Instead, he made a sound of self-disgust and reluctantly pushed her away.

"I'd better get going," he said. "I'll call you later, okay?"

"Do you have the number?"

"I tore it out of the phone book this morning."

His answer left her slightly light-headed. It was amazing to imagine that he felt just as compelled as she did. Yet, the evidence was there. He wanted her as much as she wanted him.

She watched him leave, still smelling the musky leather jacket and hearing its sensual squeak whenever he moved; still tasting the heat of his lips, feeling his hard muscles beneath her fingertips and seeing the glint of humor in his eyes long after he was a dark speck on the horizon.

Chapter Four

An hour later Molly was still feeling somewhat dazed when Ty's friend, Pete, bounced into the driveway in his junky sedan. Molly looked up from watering the flowers in the front planter box to see Pete's face through the open driver's window. A closer look revealed that the window was missing, and the car sported a crushed back fender and taillights made from red plastic taped over new bulbs. A real piece of work, Pete's car. It rattled to a wheezing stop about twenty yards from her.

"Molly!" Peter called. "Hey, we missed you. Come on. The party's just gotten started."

"What party?"

"At the Pendletons'. They got that new above-ground pool and the beer's ice-cold."

"Is that where Ty is?"

"Yep. Come on. Jump in."

Molly had no interest in Pete, or any other friend of Ty's. Their one common denominator seemed to be a lack of direction and responsibility. She didn't trust any of them, and Pete's newfound interest in her was bound to be trouble.

"I don't like beer, Pete. Thanks anyway."

"Wait, wait, wait," he said quickly when Molly turned off the hose and prepared to go inside. "Don't run off mad."

"Tell Tyler that Mom and Dad are going to be home soon and I'm not going to lie for him. He'd better be sober when he shows up."

Grinning, Pete climbed from the car, slamming the door behind him. Molly was certain a dozen bolts, nuts and maybe a fan belt and spark plug or two, fell from beneath the vehicle's dented frame. "You're really tough, aren't ya? Tyler said you'd be hard to convince."

She backed up several paces. "Look, Pete..."

"Now, what do I have to do? Throw you over my shoulder and carry you? Come on, Molly. It's party time."

"I'm really not interested." This was getting out of hand. She opened her mouth to say more, then gasped as he crossed the last few yards between them and grabbed her arm. "What are you doing?"

"Looks like it's got to be the fireman's carry for you!"

"Let go of me! I've—I've got a boyfriend!"

"Oh, sure."

"I do. And he's the jealous type," she embellished quickly.

He stopped. "I don't believe you. Who is he?"

Molly pulled his fingers off her arm. "No one you know."

"You're afraid of me," he announced, letting out a whoop of delight. "Oh, come on, Molly. I don't bite."

He grabbed at her again, and she reflexively slapped his hands away. "I mean it, Peter! Get the hell out of here and tell Tyler to come home!"

With that, she ran for the front door, slamming it hard and locking it behind her. Glancing down, she realized with mild shock that her hands were shaking.

Why is it so right with Jordan, and so wrong with anyone else?

She hugged herself. She knew the answer: She loved him.

"Molly!" Pete yelled on the opposite side of the door. "Stop playing games, or I'm leaving."

"Hurt me some more," she muttered under her breath. A warm feeling enveloped her. She was in love with Jordan, and nothing else mattered.

Pete rattled the door and swore under his breath before stomping away. Even after his stuttering engine faded into the distance Molly leaned against the door, holding her feelings close. Excitement bubbled inside her like a volcano. "I love him," she whispered softly, grinning.

She hoped he felt the same.

"So, what's with the girl?" Michael demanded over the wild roar of the motorcycle as Jordan pulled into the side garage.

"You took my car," Jordan yelled, cutting the engine.

"The transmission needed some work."

"Did I ask you to work on it?"

"Oh, relax." Michael swatted a greasy towel his way as Jordan climbed off the bike. They were standing to one side of a dark pool of oil. Car parts lay in neat piles along the perimeter of the room. Jordan's car, a red Mustang in prime condition, sat on blocks.

"If Dad sees this mess, he'll kill us both," Jordan predicted.

"He won't." Michael smiled confidently. "He's gone for the weekend."

"With Mom?" A bad feeling stole over Jordan.

"No, she's here."

"Who's he with?"

"It's a business trip."

Silence fell between them. No words needed to be spoken. Their father's business trips were generally spent in the company of a beautiful younger woman. Foster Montgomery was arrogant, autocratic and selfish, but his bank balance made up for a lot of weaknesses. Especially with the opposite sex.

Jordan's mother had only once confronted Foster with his infidelities, at least to Jordan's knowledge, and the verbal abuse that followed had singed his young ears. He'd prayed at night that there wouldn't be any more fights. He'd gotten his wish, apparently, but though the symptoms had been cured, the real ailment remained.

Throughout high school Jordan had been uncomfortable bringing a date home. Part of him expected her to fall under his father's spell. Michael had had the bad luck to actually care about a woman a few years older than himself who had subsequently dumped him for his father.

No one in the Montgomery house talked about it, and Jordan's mother preferred to pretend she had a perfect life. She might cry alone, but appearances were everything. She was no easier to communicate with than Foster was.

"I hope you don't have my car in a zillion pieces," Jordan said, shaking off his thoughts, "because I need it tonight."

"It's working. Better than ever."

"Yeah, right."

"Where're you going?"

Jordan shrugged. "I don't know."

"That girl with the dark hair causing a tickle in your pants?" He chuckled like a lecher. Jordan's skin crawled. Michael could be a little too much like his father sometimes.

But apparently Molly's friend hadn't blabbed that she was a Capshaw.

"I like the little blond one myself. But God, what a prude!"

"She's still in high school."

"Jesus! You're kidding!"

Jordan shook his head.

"And the one you like?" Michael demanded.

"Aren't those parts supposed to be *in* the car?" Jordan pointed to the greasy pile of metal under the right fender. "You won't have it together by tonight!"

"Yes, I will. Get off my back. I'm doing you a favor." Michael shouldered past Jordan and returned his attention to the Mustang. In truth, he was a master mechanic, but Foster wouldn't have a son with such blue-collar ambitions. Michael was being forced to take economics courses at a community college.

Jordan smiled grimly to himself. For the moment he'd diverted Michael from Molly. He had no intention of tackling that sticky issue along with everything else, especially since Michael and Tyler Capshaw, Molly's older brother, knew each other by sight and had engaged in some serious shoving around and name-calling on more than one occasion. In truth, the fault was really more Tyler's than Michael's; Michael could care less about defending the Montgomery "good name." But Michael had no love for Tyler on principle. If he knew about Jordan's involvement with Molly, all hell would break loose.

Watching Michael work, Jordan commented, "I've been thinking a lot about when you and Kitty had that thing going."

Michael snorted. "Don't make me sick."

"You cared a lot about her."

He shrugged. "You can't trust women. They're users."

"I'm talking about Kitty, not Janine."

Michael stiffened. "Kitty might not have had the hots for Dad, but she was just as bad! Always whining, wanting me to take her somewhere, spend money. I tell ya, they're all the same."

"That's not the way I remember it."

"Well, you got a wire loose, brother. No connection here." He pointed to his head.

"I always thought you two would get back together."

"True love? Is that what I'm hearing?" Michael mocked. "Listen to me, kid. Keep your hand on your wallet, and don't let your you-know-what do the thinking for you. There isn't a good woman left in this world. And that includes Mom!"

Jordan's teeth clenched. "That's not fair."

"She shoulda left him years ago." He shoved his hand in front of Jordan's face, rubbing his fingers together as if feeling money. "We both know why she stayed."

Jordan had no answer for that. He, too, felt Michael's bitterness. "Not every woman's a gold digger. Kitty really cared about you."

"Kitty's getting married," Michael declared bluntly, shoving a dolly under the Mustang's front axle, pumping the handle with repressed fury. "The guy's loaded. I went to see her. Told her what I thought of her. So much for true love, kid. You wouldn't know it if it jumped up and bit you in the butt...."

* * *

"My God, is that real?"

Molly's voice was a strangled whisper. Pete had dropped off a very loud, very drunk Tyler who was now swaying against the stairway rail. His backpack had slipped from one hand. The butt of a handgun poked through the zipper.

"Naw. It's a squirt gun."

"No, it's not." Molly could tell it was real. She didn't have the nerve to touch it. "Get it out of here. So help me, Tyler. If you keep that thing in the house, I'll go straight to Mom and Dad as soon as they walk through the door!"

"Okay, okay! Jeez. It's Pete's dad's. We were just doin' a little target practice. Forgot I had it."

"Get a grip, Tyler!"

"I'll call Pete back—" He lurched for the door.

"No!" Molly grabbed his arm. She could hear the frenzied roar of Pete's engine and knew Ty's friend wasn't in any better shape than he was. Neither of them should have a dangerous weapon in their hands. "Let him go. I don't want him here, either."

"Too good for him, are ya? Molly, he could have any girl he wants. Any girl."

This was certainly overstating the issue, but she didn't argue. "I know about guys who can have any girl," she bit out, thinking of Brian. "They've got swelled heads and egos. I'm not interested in Pete."

Tyler squinted at her. "He said y'got a new boyfriend. That right?"

"Just give me the gun, and I'll put it somewhere safe."

"It can go in the locked cupboard in the garage," Tyler answered, heading for the back door off the kitchen.

"Is it loaded?" Molly asked fearfully.

"You think I'm nuts?" Tyler snorted, as Molly followed behind him, resisting the urge to grab his arm and help him to walk steadily. Tyler stumbled forward, clanging the backpack against the wall as Molly switched on the garage light.

She jumped, half expecting a rain of bullets. Tyler threw back his head and laughed. "I'm not stupid, Moll."

"Just put the gun away."

Tyler dug behind the shelf of paint cans to the little hook on the wall where the key for the cupboard hung. Unlocking the cupboard, he shoved the whole backpack inside. "Pete can pick it up tomorrow. I'm going to bed."

Molly guarded the garage as Tyler turned back, banging his shoulder on the doorjamb as he swayed inside. She listened to him climb the stairs. When the house was quiet she slipped into his room to check on him. Tyler, in one regard, was as good as his word: he was flopped across his bed fully clothed, snoring like a buffalo.

Relieved, Molly returned to the kitchen, but she couldn't shake the sensation that something terrible was about to happen. Tyler was out of control. His aimlessness was fast becoming something worse—something she couldn't name. She wished she could talk to somebody about it, but who would listen? Her mom seemed to be aware, but Molly knew Tina didn't want to hear bad things about her son.

Sighing, Molly closed her eyes and pushed back her hair. Maybe she was making too much of this. Target shooting was common enough, she rationalized. Maybe it was just as Tyler had said. He'd given up the gun willingly enough.

The sun had set, leaving a bright streak of fluorescent pink staining the horizon. Molly checked the clock. Her parents should be back any minute. She chewed on a fingernail. If she brought up the gun, Tyler would be in big trouble. Maybe she should think about it for a while.

The phone jangled. Gasping, Molly nearly jumped out of her skin, her heart racing into instant overdrive. She reached for the receiver. "Hello?"

"Molly."

It was Jordan. She thrilled to his low, intense voice. Then suddenly she was shy. Her throat closed. She had to cough lightly to clear it and felt like an idiot. "Hi."

"Want to go somewhere? I know it's kind of late, but I had to get my car running after Michael screwed it up."

"I...can't."

"You can't."

She could hear the questions in his voice. "My parents are due home anytime...." The memory of the gun slid across her vision. She couldn't leave. She didn't dare.

"I'm not sure I can get home next weekend," Jordan said, as if thinking aloud. "There's no way you can get away, just for a little while?"

Molly ached to be with him. Why were Tyler's problems hers, anyway? It wasn't fair. As she bit her lip, her mind whirled. She could take the key to the cupboard and Tyler wouldn't be able to get to the gun even if he wanted to. And she could leave a note for her parents, saying she had to work.

It was a lie. But it could work.

"Don't you have to be back at school?" she asked. Counting traffic, the commute took nearly four hours.

"I should be there already," he admitted wryly.

"Are you sure you want to see me?"

"I wouldn't be talking to you if I wasn't."

Reassured, Molly drew a tight breath. "If I could be back by nine?"

"I'll pick you up in twenty minutes."

"Okay..."

It was dark, the moonlight pale and soft as they sat on the hood of his car, parked near the small pond at Kellerman Park. The pond had all but dried up this summer but now was a puddle of water left over from Friday's rain. It glimmered dully in the blue-white light. Jordan's arm lay lightly across Molly's shoulders. They didn't speak. They'd already talked and talked. Molly didn't even really remember what they'd discussed. Jordan's dreams. Hers. Theirs together. It didn't matter. All that mattered was being together, understanding they were on the threshold of something deep and monumental.

He leaned down to kiss her, with a feather-light brush across her mouth. Her hand slid down his face, encountering stubbly growth. She grinned. He kissed harder, and she felt his lips curve into a smile.

Sensations shivered inside her. When he broke contact, she fought back a moan of regret. "I'd better take you back," he murmured hoarsely.

"I don't want to go."

"Neither do I."

Molly stretched out on the hot metal hood, staring at the sky. She flung her arms wide and giggled. Jordan lay on one elbow beside her, kissing her while he pulled her resisting body off the car.

"Don't go," she whispered.

He groaned, his mouth finding her ear, his teeth lightly teasing on her lobe. Her knees were water. He had to hold her up. They both laughed.

"Come on," he said, and Molly reluctantly slid in beside him, ignoring the gearshift and brake and climbing onto the console so she could be close to him.

Her parents' car was sitting in the open garage when they pulled into the driveway. "Uh-oh," Molly said, knowing they'd left the garage door up so that she could let herself in through the back.

"Uh-oh?"

"I lied about where I was. Now I've got to lie some more." She wrinkled her nose.

"You could tell them the truth."

"Maybe later."

"*Maybe* later?" Jordan questioned.

She shook her head and opened the door. He followed suit and crunched across the gravel with her to the garage, then stood to one side of the light. In the darkness his expression was unreadable.

"You don't want your parents to see me, do you?"

She sighed. "I don't want—to deal with it. Yet."

"It's going to be that bad?"

She nodded. "Won't it be for you, when you tell?"

"I don't care what happens."

He was lying. Or deluding himself, which amounted to the same thing. "It's not going to be fun."

"No."

Molly glanced toward the upstairs windows. "My brother came home drunk tonight. And he was doing some stupid stuff. It's all a real mess, and I don't want to make things worse right now."

Jordan nodded, but Molly could tell he didn't completely agree. He would be direct and damn the consequences, whereas she wanted to wait for better timing.

"I'll see you later," he said, dropping a light kiss on her lips before turning back.

Feeling suddenly anxious, Molly followed him, waiting as he rolled his window down. He looked up at her and she leaned her elbows on the warm metal door. With a groan,

Jordan pulled her face close and kissed her longingly, passionately. She melted against the car. When he finally released her, he laughed softly, in disbelief. "If I don't leave now, I won't!"

"I wish you didn't have to."

"I'll call you," he said tensely.

"Good."

She waved after him, watching his taillights wink out. The door to the garage creaked open. Her father stood in the aperture. Molly's heart jumped into her throat.

"Who was that?" he asked.

"Umm...a friend from work stopped by." She hated lying. Her tongue felt fat and sluggish, as if it resented performing the dirty deed.

"Well, come on in now. It's late." He motioned her to the door and Molly hurried to comply. "Tyler's already in bed."

"Oh. Good."

"No trouble while we were gone?"

"No." She forced her face into a smile.

Her father nodded and after kissing her mom goodnight, Molly ran upstairs, feeling more like a Benedict Arnold than she ever had in her life.

Three weeks later she turned eighteen. And three weeks after that, almost to the day, she and Jordan drove into the Sierra Nevadas, equipped with backpacks, sleeping bags and a tent. The Capshaws thought Molly was with Charisse, who'd been sworn to secrecy. The Montgomerys didn't know their son was in town.

The lie was growing. A necessary evil. A weight on Molly's heart.

It had been pure hell keeping the identity of her new "boyfriend" a secret from both her parents and Tyler.

Tyler had spilled the beans that she was seeing someone, and the questions had come thick and fast. She'd bobbed and weaved, but the very fact that she was being mysterious piqued her family's interest all the more.

However, when it didn't seem like any young man was calling on her, Tyler stopped believing there was any truth to her claim. Her parents ceased asking questions. As far as anyone knew, she was spending all her free time with Charisse, and Molly did everything in her power to perpetuate that myth.

Jordan didn't like it much, though. Molly knew he half hoped her machinations would fail one day, and they'd be forced to tell the truth. He hated the deception and said he was prepared to face her family head-on.

But he didn't know the depth of their anger and animosity. He couldn't. To the Montgomerys, the Capshaws were just a nuisance, a grousing bunch of losers who couldn't get over the fact that the Montgomerys had prospered during a time when they'd lost everything. The Capshaws felt the Montgomerys were worse than mere opportunists: they were the reason for their failure! It wasn't fair. It wasn't right. But it *was*.

Jordan just didn't understand. He believed everything would be okay as soon as the shock wore off. He thought she was overstating the situation, letting her imagination run away with her.

It would all work out, he assured her time and again.

Molly knew differently. And if Jordan checked with his own family, he might realize the truth. The problem was he didn't seem to have the same family closeness that Molly enjoyed. He rarely spoke of his mother, and he always referred to his father with undercurrents of bitterness. He only seemed to really feel something for his brother, Michael. Communication in the Montgomery household had ground to a halt or had never existed in the first place.

Molly knew revealing her love for Jordan would be a disaster. As soon as the truth was on the table, she would be forced to make a choice: Jordan, or her family. For the Capshaws, there would be no other answer. She knew it, because she'd already tried.

It had been one quiet evening when her father and mother had decided to sit on the back porch with cups of coffee and enjoy the last warmth of fall. Off work and finished with her homework, Molly had curled up in the porch swing, her thoughts on Jordan.

And then her father had mentioned something about the Montgomerys....

"The old man swallowed up as much of Vernonia as he could without a burp. Now he's moving on to Los Angeles. Good riddance."

"Are they moving?" Tina asked.

"I'd sell everything I own to make that happen! Nope. They just keep buying and buying. In my prayers, I hope the old man overextends." John Capshaw chuckled. "Wouldn't I love to see him fail, though!"

"Isn't the feud kind of silly?" Molly asked lightly.

There was silence. Tina glanced anxiously at her husband. John turned to his only daughter.

"Maybe you're too young to appreciate what happened," he offered as a way out.

"It's all over, though. It was over a long time ago."

The sliding-glass door opened, and Tyler stepped out. He hadn't heard the conversation, but it didn't matter. Molly's father enlightened him with one sharp, furious retort.

"Those Montgomerys stole our land away from us and then spat on us! It won't ever be over, Molly. Just you remember that!"

"I'd like to kill 'em all," Tyler snarled.

"Don't talk nonsense," Tina said quickly. "The whole thing is ridiculous."

John turned on his wife. "This is Capshaw history we're talking about. You married into it, for better or worse. So don't tell me what's ridiculous!"

Tina had subsided into injured silence. The congenial atmosphere had disintegrated into something ugly and deep and never-to-be-resolved.

Now, as she made her way up the steep trail behind Jordan, the weight on Molly's heart nearly crushed her. Charisse, who'd picked her up earlier and dropped her off at the Burger Hutt, had also been full of unsolicited advice and opinions.

"This thing with Jordan is a time bomb," she'd hissed. "You're going to be blown into tiny little pieces! Your parents are going to kill you. He isn't worth it, Molly! You have completely lost your mind. Listen to me! All those years, you told me how crazy I am. How stupid and foolhardy. Well, this is way, way beyond anything *I've* ever done. Give him up *now!* God only knows why he's seeing you, anyway. Think about that!"

"He's seeing me because he cares about me. Because he...loves me," Molly had answered furiously, crossing her fingers hopefully. He hadn't actually said he loved her, but she knew he did.

"He's using you. He wouldn't fall for a Capshaw if you were his age and loaded with bucks!"

"Then why is he seeing me?"

"I don't know." Charisse had shaken her head emphatically. "But there's another reason. Maybe he's rebelling.

What better way to make his family mad than date a Cap-shaw?''

Now Molly gritted her teeth, pushing the thought an-grily away. Charisse didn't know anything about her and Jordan. Molly knew he loved her. When people loved each other as much as she and Jordan did, it didn't have to be stated in words.

Jordan stopped abruptly and Molly bumped into him.

''Sorry,'' he said, turning around and steadying her arms with his hands.

''Are we there?'' she asked, brought out of her reverie.

He grinned and nodded. ''We're here.''

A brisk breeze swept her hair in front of her eyes. Pushing the strands away, Molly drew in her breath at the sight of a small clearing where a pure stream trickled down a series of stones in bright, sweet song. She shivered, hunching her shoulders inside her down parka. It was still hot in the valley, but here, in the mountain foothills, the air was thinner, clearer, and sharp with fall's crispness.

''It's gorgeous,'' she said.

He wrapped his arms around her. Molly's lips trem-bled. She was fearful. She knew what this night meant. Stolen moments of sweet, anxious desire were about to be fulfilled; and though she wanted to make love to Jordan more than anything, she couldn't help being afraid.

''Come on,'' he said, clasping her hand and pulling her forward.

They pitched the tent together and laid out twin sleep-ing bags. Molly's gaze hung there, as if drawn by a mag-net. This was the first time they'd been somewhere special together. Somewhere private. Neither one of them had had any interest in making love in the sordid confines of a back seat. They'd wanted to wait until everything was perfect.

This spot, surrounded by the serenity of the mountains, the music of the stream and the warmth and security of each other, was as close to heaven as they could hope to find.

Jordan had shed his backpack and was pulling sandwiches and drinks from an insulated pouch. No campfire. The woods were far too dry. It didn't matter. Molly suspected they'd generate their own heat.

"Want something to eat?" he asked.

"No, thanks."

"A soda?" He held out a can of cola.

She took it, gingerly sitting down beside him on a fallen log.

He munched on a sandwich. She sipped her drink. Moments stretched. Tension thrummed. She could almost hear her nerves tighten.

"You know, nothing'll happen that you don't want to happen," Jordan said slowly.

Molly nodded. "I know." She heard how terrified she sounded and cleared her throat. "I know you've done this before," she said, trying to sound sophisticated and unconcerned.

Jordan's sideways look said she wasn't fooling him. "I've never brought anyone to the Sierras. And not for lack of trying," he added. "Most girls don't feel like camping."

"You know what I mean." She hugged her knees.

"Molly..."

"I— I need you to tell me. I don't know why. It's dumb. But I need to know how you felt and how many there were." Her voice trailed into a barely audible whisper.

For the first time since she'd known him, Jordan was at a loss. He opened his mouth, half laughed, then fell silent. After several moments he tried again.

"There haven't been that many," he managed.

"More than one, though?"

"Yes..."

"Did you love her...them...?" Molly felt like an idiot.

Jordan's brows drew together. "Look, Molly. I cared about the girls I was with. It just wasn't enough, and as soon as I figured that out, it was over."

"That's reassuring," she murmured through a tight throat.

"This is different. We both know this is different."

She nodded jerkily. "Yes, yes."

"You sound like you're trying to convince yourself."

"I am," she choked out.

"Molly." His hand cupped the downy curve of her jaw. He drew her face close until her anxious eyes looked into the deep blue irises regarding her with desire and affection. Leaning toward her, he grazed his lips across hers.

She responded with the natural ease she'd discovered these past few weeks in Jordan's arms. He caressed her throat and ran kisses down the side of her neck. Her heart thudded, hard, painfully.

She clung to him, feeling his urgency, conscious of her own. Long kisses passed. Passionate, questioning kisses. When he pulled back, Molly stared at him. Swallowing, she couldn't help a glance toward the tent. His gaze followed hers, stayed on the tent. Clasping her hand he drew her to her feet and led her to that intimate sanctuary.

Inside, Molly shivered. But it was warm in the tent, protected from the mountain breezes. Jordan sat down on a sleeping bag, his arm balanced on one bent knee. Molly slowly sank to the other bag, tucking her legs beneath her.

"Remember, nothing's going to happen if you don't want it to," he repeated.

"I know," she returned.

He shook his head and smiled. Molly forced out an answering smile. Lord, she felt strange! Maybe this was wrong. Wrong timing. Wrong place. It was too soon—too *important!* She wasn't ready. She needed more time!

Jordan leaned forward. Molly opened her mouth. Before any words came out, his mouth closed over hers. Her tongue touched his lips, unconsciously inciting. Jordan groaned. Molly whimpered in response. It was all the invitation he needed. His kisses turned hard, demanding, the pressure of his mouth bearing her backward until she half lay on her side, Jordan's legs and arms tangled with hers. Her head roared with desire and belated warnings, but his possessiveness stole her breath away.

"Molly," he murmured in a strained voice.

Resistance melted. She cradled him close, thrilling to the deep thrust of his tongue. This was familiar and delicious, and when he lay full length atop her, her bones all but melted.

His shirt separated from his jeans. Tentatively, her hands explored the taut muscles of his back. He shifted his weight, moving against her in a way that had her panting for more. When he pulled back, she moaned.

"Don't stop."

His answer was a shake of his head, amusement mixed with desire. Belatedly she realized he was unbuttoning her shirt, pulling it off her shoulders before nearly ripping off his own.

He unclasped her bra with a deftness that set off warning bells in her mind. But then he lay his bare torso against hers. The feel of his hot skin was too wonderful to resist. When he bent his head downward, she braced herself, but it was *her* sigh of need that hung in the air at the heat of his mouth on her trembling nipple, *her* hands that snarled in the silk of his hair, *her* back that arched upward.

As his hips fit tightly against hers, the friction of jeans was too much to bear. She helped him yank off both pairs and then they were naked, staring at each other intensely.

If there was a moment to turn back, it was now. Jordan's whole body was tense, waiting. He stared at her through smoldering eyes, his jaw taut. Everywhere their bodies touched, her flesh burned with desire.

He kissed her again. He tasted good...so good. And he smelled of pine and that indefinable masculine scent she associated only with him. His hand kneaded her breast and she moved sinuously against him.

The time for turning back melted away like last winter's snow—gone, forgotten, over.

Then his hand foraged lower, and lower still, until he touched her with such gentle inquiry that she gasped. Lost to sensation, she barely registered when his fingers' exploration ended, was replaced by a hard, masculine part that slowly rubbed against her.

"Jordan..." she whispered in a choked breath.

With infinite slowness, almost as if it was painful, he pulled back enough to stare into her eyes. Sweat moistened his brow. Restraint, she realized with awe.

"I love you," she said on a swallow.

"Molly..." He hesitated and she tightened up. "I love you, too," he answered softly and she relaxed, relieved. "I don't want to hurt you."

"You're not."

He made a strangled sound. "Oh, Molly."

"I love you," she whispered again, in an anguish of need.

He pushed against her, harder, giving in to his own raging desire. Molly strained to meet him, then suddenly he plunged deep inside her. Pain shot through her. Molly cried out, clinging to him, stiff with tension.

"I'm sorry," he murmured. "Sorry."

"It's okay," she said shakily.

"No..."

She expected him to pull back, but he did just the opposite. He pushed forward, then back, then forward. Molly's breath swept in and out. She wanted to cry out, but no sound came. Instead she gritted her teeth, fighting back a swelling tide that frightened her.

The motion continued, grew steadier, stronger. Taut as wire, Molly resisted. But that deep, swelling, sweet sensation grew inside her. Her body moved *with* him of its own accord! Little moans issued past her lips. She quivered. Her body arched like a bow. She felt sweat dotting her brow. Her fingers dug into Jordan's back. She eagerly met his thrusting tongue with her own. Wine-dark hunger burned inside her, and she wrapped herself around him, whimpers of desire falling from her lips.

And just when she thought she couldn't stand it one more second, ecstasy burst inside her like a rush of roaring flames. She cried out.

"Molly..." Jordan stiffened and groaned, pushing deep within her, his mouth covering hers, demanding every ounce of her surrender as he reached his own climax.

Molly hadn't believed such sensation existed. She floated, a smile on her face. Discovery was as beautiful as love.

"I love you," she said again, sated and happy. Faintly she realized Jordan was kissing her softly, their hearts thudding as one.

"No one is going to take you away from me," he said fiercely, staring down at her possessively.

She wrapped her arms around his neck, amazed at the sweat that dampened her brow and his. "No one can," she answered.

With a growl, he swarmed kisses over her face and Molly laughed and cried out and held him close and loved him for all she was worth.

Chapter Five

"Can't talk now, Charisse," Molly murmured into the receiver. "I've got to get to work."

"What did the doctor say?" Charisse demanded. "For God's sake, Molly. *Tell me!*"

Glancing over her shoulder, Molly could see her mother at the far end of the kitchen. Tina was setting the table for dinner. "Stop by the Hutt," she said tersely.

"Oh, God, Molly. It was positive, wasn't it? The test was positive."

"I didn't go to the doctor, all right?" she hissed through her teeth.

"How long's it been since you had a period? Three months? There might still be time, but you've got to do something!" Charisse was practically shrieking.

Molly turned her back to her mother, whispering fiercely, "I don't know for sure that I'm pregnant."

"Then go see the doctor!"

"I took a home test." She glanced at her mother again. Her pulse was pounding so hard she could scarcely think.

"And?"

Molly swallowed hard. "Positive."

"Oh, God . . . Oh, God . . ."

"Don't panic. I'm going to see Jordan tonight."

"Molly . . ." Charisse moaned in empathetic pain.

"It'll be okay. I know it will."

She knew nothing of the kind. The thought of telling Jordan she was pregnant scared her so much she felt lightheaded. She hadn't believed it at first. These things didn't happen to her. But she knew it was possible. Sure, they'd taken precautions. Most of the time, anyway. But those stolen weekends with Jordan were sometimes such a last-minute escape that, well, she'd been stupid. *They'd* been stupid.

And God help her, she hadn't really believed it could happen to *her!*

"Have you told your parents about Jordan?" Charisse blubbered.

"That I've been seeing a Montgomery? *No!* I didn't want to say anything until the time was right." She choked out a laugh. "Oh, God. Looks like Jordan and I will be telling them together."

"Don't tell Jordan. Molly, there are other ways to deal with this."

"Not for me. I've gotta go."

"Don't hang up!"

"No, listen, I told Mom and Dad I was meeting you after work. This'll be the last time you have to cover for me."

"Molly . . ."

"I've *got* to go!"

"Call me later," Charisse pleaded as Molly cradled the receiver.

The hairs on the back of her neck lifted. She whirled around. Tyler stood at the top of the stairs, his eyes boring into her. Her heart jumped.

"You're pregnant?" he asked in a dangerous voice. "By a *Montgomery?*"

The world stopped. She stared in white-faced shock at her stunned brother. She was in a nightmare. This wasn't happening!

But it was. Tyler's skin was mottled with rage. Molly struggled to speak. It was the second-worst moment of her life. The first was earlier that day when the home pregnancy test she'd smuggled into the house had been resoundingly positive.

She stretched a shaking hand toward him. "Tyler, please. I'm taking care of this."

Tyler ignored her protests as he brushed past her, and she grabbed for his arm.

"Tyler, don't!"

He shook her off with repressed violence and headed toward the back door to the garage.

"Tyler, where are you going?" Tina Capshaw demanded.

He didn't answer.

"Dinner's almost on the table."

Molly stood frozen in the kitchen. Her mother stared at her in puzzlement. "Molly...?" she asked.

The engine of Tyler's van roared to life. Molly found her feet, racing to the garage. He was backing out.

"Where are you going?" she screamed.

"To Pete's," he snapped coldly, squealing away in a spew of gravel.

Molly's heart pounded. She swallowed three times. There was no spit in her mouth.

"What was all that about?" Tina demanded when Molly walked back inside.

"I don't know," she squeaked out.

She didn't taste dinner. Time truly stood still. The clock seemed stuck in a groove. The second hand ticked but nothing happened. It was endless.

Jordan was going to meet her at the Hutt. She knew she wouldn't be able to work. She would have to call in sick. It wasn't far from the truth. In fact, she felt like throwing up *right now!*

Racing from the table, she stumbled on the stairs, barely making it to the bathroom before her stomach heaved in endless spasms. Her mother pounded on the door.

"Are you all right, Molly?" she called.

Molly rinsed her face, washing out her mouth. Her image in the mirror was ghastly: green-tinged skin; wounded eyes; unhappy mouth. She prayed her mother would just go away.

"Molly?"

"I'm okay."

Maybe she should tell her the truth. Maybe that would end all these problems once and for all. Opening the door, she took one look at her mother's concerned face and lost her nerve. "I've been sick ever since I had that hot dog for lunch."

"Maybe you should skip work."

She had to get to the Hutt to see Jordan. "No, I feel okay. It just didn't settle right."

"Well, come straight home. If Charisse can't drop you off, I'll come get you."

This was a problem she hadn't foreseen. "I'll call you," she murmured vaguely.

Twenty minutes later she was at the Hutt, shivering in the cool January-night air as she stood outside, hoping

Jordan would appear. She'd already begged off work and had told them she would wait outside for her ride home. The manager had regarded her dubiously, but either her appearance had convinced him she really was ill, or he was too inured to irresponsible employees to care.

The wisping wind was chilly, and Molly hugged herself. She couldn't remember ever feeling more miserable. When she'd missed her first period she hadn't thought a thing of it. She was kind of irregular, anyway. But when the second month rolled around with no sign of her menstrual flow, Molly had been dry-mouthed—a perpetual state now.

The home pregnancy test had been a last-ditch hope. She'd hidden in the bathroom, her eyes glued to the colored solution, dizzy with fear and crushing disbelief when her worst fears were confirmed.

Stupid, stupid, stupid!

A life inside her. A baby. Jordan's baby.

Molly swallowed, aching. The stupidest part of all was that she wanted this baby. More than she would have believed. Or was there a part of her that had hoped for this, maybe even planned for it a little bit...?

Her parents wouldn't be so cruel as to tear her away from the father of her child.

Self-reproach was a load of bricks weighing her down. She was too confused and desperate to think clearly. She needed Jordan.

"Please, please," she murmured, stamping her feet to stay warm.

A loud rumble barreled down the road toward the Hutt. Molly looked up expectantly. A van appeared, screeching and swaying into the parking lot.

"Tyler!" Molly cried out, alarmed.

He pulled to a shuddering stop, slammed the door and headed purposefully for the Hutt's front door. Molly ran to him, grabbing his arm.

"What are you doing here?" she demanded, shaking him.

"Where is that bastard?" he growled.

"You're drunk!"

His head swung around. "Where is he? Where is the bastard?"

"Get out of here," Molly hissed.

"You come with me! Whad're you doin', anyway?"

"Tyler, just get in the van. I'll drive you home." Molly clamped down on her temper in an effort to restore reason.

"That bastard knocked you up." Tyler hiccuped, sounding like he was about to cry.

Molly led him toward the back of the van. He came reluctantly, stumbling a little. She opened the doors. He sat down with a thud, shoulders slumping, legs dangling out the back.

"Bastard," he muttered again, his expression ugly. "I'm gonna kill 'im. Shoulda done it before."

"You don't even know Jordan." Molly glanced at her watch and scanned the road. No sign of Jordan's Mustang.

"Know his brother," Tyler spat. "Michael Montgomery. Jeezus, how could you let that scum touch you?"

"I love Jordan," she told him squarely, sitting down beside him.

Tyler shook his head. "Won't let you do it. Won't..."

Molly looked at her watch again. "Hurry," she whispered. "Please, hurry...."

* * *

"You don't know Molly," Jordan said calmly, through his teeth.

Jordan glared at his brother through the open window of his car. The engine was running and exhaust tainted the air of the garage. Michael stared at him in pure fury. "She's a teenage gold-digging *Capshaw!* You think she loves you? You're nuts! I can't believe you're so stupid!"

Jaw tight, Jordan shifted into reverse, peeling backward. Michael's hand gripped around the open window, his glare fierce. Jordan glared right back. He'd made a mistake in telling Michael. A huge mistake. Months of hiding their affair had frustrated him to the breaking point, and he'd decided if Molly wouldn't tell her family, he'd start by telling his.

Now he knew what she'd been fearing. And it made him furious.

"Where the hell are you going?" Michael demanded, moving with the Mustang as it slid backward.

"Let go of the car."

Michael clung on. "You're meeting her. You lovesick moron. You're meeting her!"

"Janine really did a number on you."

"This isn't about Janine!"

Jordan stamped on the accelerator. The Mustang jerked back with a sharp squeal. Michael pounded a furious fist on the hood. Jordan wheeled onto the road, tires screeching in reproach as he tore away. Away from Michael and his family. To Molly...

Molly regarded her brother anxiously. He'd reluctantly moved inside, and now his head was leaning against the wall of the van, eyes closed. "Are you all right?" she asked.

Running a hand over his face, Tyler drew a deep breath. The back doors were shut and Molly sat cross-legged in the center of the cluttered carpeted interior. Tyler had bottles and clothes and cannery junk everywhere.

"Either I can drive you home, or you can stay here and wait until you're sober."

"I'm not drunk!" His eyes snapped open.

"Okay, okay." Molly held up her hands.

Tyler sighed. "I'm going to get something to eat."

"That's a great idea."

"Stay here," he ordered, when she scrambled to her feet. "I don't need a jailer following me around." With that, he slammed out of the van. Molly watched from the window until he actually entered the Hutt, then she shot another glance at her watch.

"Come on, Jordan," she murmured.

The whole evening had an unreal quality about it. She could smell spilled oil and stale potato chips, both buried under the mounds of stuff in Tyler's van. It made her slightly sick and she examined the back window, seeking some air.

Jordan's red Mustang suddenly peeled into the lot with a shriek of tires. He jumped out and slammed the door. Molly pounded on the window but he didn't hear her. Seconds later another, louder, meaner roar filled the air, and Michael Montgomery's motorcycle came to a skidding stop beside Jordan's Mustang. Molly stared in surprise. What was going on?

Her answer came a moment later as Michael hurled himself at Jordan.

"Oh, no," she moaned. She knew instinctively this had something to do with her.

Jordan and Michael began yelling at each other. Grabbing Michael by the lapel of his black leather jacket, Jordan propelled him to the far end of the lot so that Molly scrambled to the other side of the van for a good view.

They were several dozen yards from the Hutt on a graveled side-lot, half in shadow, away from the road and the asphalt parking area. She raised her hand to bang on the window again, then turned to reach for the back door latches. In her peripheral vision she saw a flash of movement. Glancing back she saw Tyler, at a dead run from the Hutt, hurl himself on Jordan.

"No!" she screamed, her eyes glued to the scene through the window.

Tyler tackled Jordan, and Michael roared out a scream, jumping at Ty. The force knocked Michael and Ty sideways, away from Jordan, who was also yelling at the top of his lungs.

"Stop it! *Stop It!*" Molly cried hysterically.

Jordan fought his way between them. Tyler's right hand hit him an undercut to the jaw, and he went down. Michael jabbed a vicious kick at Tyler who saw it coming and feinted backward.

Molly was frozen between the back doors and the window. The scene was fast. Fragmented. Warp-speed quick. There was scarcely time to take a breath.

"You're trash, Capshaw!" Michael taunted. Tyler swore a stream of ear-stinging insults. Jordan staggered to his feet, massaging his jaw. Michael lunged for Tyler, but Jordan caught his arm.

And then Molly saw the gun Tyler yanked from inside his coat. Pete's handgun. She screamed, covering her eyes with her hands.

"Dammit," Jordan whispered, his bones cold with fear. "Put that thing away, Capshaw." The pain in his jaw disappeared, forgotten, as he looked down the barrel of Tyler's gun. The barrel of Tyler's *gun!* he repeated in his mind, stunned with disbelief.

"Stay 'way from my sister," Tyler choked, half sobbing. "Bastard. Damn bastard."

"She's a lying bitch. A—" Michael screamed. The four-letter word he spat was meant to provoke bloodshed.

Jordan moved on instinct. He grabbed Michael by the waist, hauling him backward while Michael flailed against him in fury. "Let go of me!"

"Wait! God, wait! Think! Think!" Jordan yelled. Michael was tearing at his fingers, bending them back. Jordan lost his grip, snatched at Michael's shirt, heard fabric rend.

Michael lunged forward. Ty's hand was shaking, his face white. Jordan tackled his brother and fell between Ty and Michael. They were packed together. Struggling.

Blam! A shot echoed dully. Gunsmoke stung Jordan's nose like a bite. Michael growled. Tyler shook with hysterical silent sobs.

Jordan looked down at his shirt. Blood began to soak through it. *His* blood. There was no pain.

Then Michael crumpled and lay still. His shirt was red. His eyes were glassy, his mouth open, his breath coming in fractured sobs.

"Michael," Jordan whispered.

"He shot me," Michael murmured. "He shot me. Under your arm."

"No. No. No..." Tyler stumbled backward. He dropped the gun with a clatter, broke away and ran for the van. Blackness blotted out Jordan's peripheral vision. People were screaming. Someone was calling his name. An authoritative voice yelled he would call 911.

Jordan leaned over his brother. Michael's head lay in the gravel. "Michael," he whispered, holding his brother's head up.

Michael's breath whooshed out in a long, protracted sigh. Then nothing. In dulled wonder and anguish, Jordan realized his brother had stopped breathing.

Someone pulled him up by the arms, thunked Michael's chest with a hammy fist. There was blood everywhere. There couldn't be any more left inside him.

"He's dead," Jordan said matter-of-factly at the same moment he heard the wild roar of Tyler Capshaw's van as it tore out of the parking lot.

"Tyler!" Molly screamed, clutching the back seat as the van rocked on its tires. "Stop! Stop! Please stop!"

The van skidded to the right. Molly was slammed against the side wall. She tried to brace herself. Her palm connected with a sharp object. Pain shot through her hand. Blood welled.

"Tyler!"

"Shut up!"

"Tyler!"

"Dammit, Molly!" he yelled through his teeth, yanking the wheel to the right. Tires squealed. Molly tumbled to the other side, her head slamming into the wall.

She started crying. Jordan was dead. She knew he was dead. Tyler had killed him. She pounded on the back seat. Tears of pure fear blinded her.

She'd opened her eyes to witness Jordan step between Michael and Tyler. She'd heard vicious, ugly, crazed words. Seen a flash of yellow-orange light. Seen Jordan and Michael sway, stumble, fall....

"No!"

Sobs hiccuped in her chest.

The van zigzagged as if drunk itself. Molly was past feeling. She was cold. Numb.

Headlights flashed across the back of the van. Dull-eyed, she glanced back. A Mustang was following them.

With hope fighting its way to life inside her, she crawled to the back, crying so hard she couldn't hear anything but the roar of anguish inside her own head. A red Mustang. Jordan's car?

"Tyler, slow down!" Molly yelled, struggling to hold on as he took another corner so fast she was certain they lifted off two wheels.

Jordan, she thought, hanging on to the back seat. *Jordan's alive. He's alive!*

Slam!

The jolt sent her flying forward, cracking her chin on the back seat.

Tyler screamed. The van shimmied and swayed, turning in a slow-motion spiral, its wheels locked. Dazed, Molly wondered what had happened. Dimly she realized the car behind them had purposely hit them. They spun full circle, then tipped. The top of the van turned over her head, and Molly scrambled for a hold in a dizzying whirl of motion and fear.

With blood-crazed exultation, Jordan watched the van slide off the road. He would smash and kill Tyler Capshaw with his bare hands. Revenge was a hard, aching lust throbbing inside him.

The van slid, and slid, and turned. Nose first, it bucked off the road, slammed forward, then flipped on its back like a pathetic insect, tires spinning, headlights weakening streams of light focused toward the horizon.

Adrenaline pumped through his blood, a scary, vital drug that worked magic to Jordan's way of thinking. He pulled off the road and jumped out, fury, not empathy, driving him to the scene of the accident.

"Damn you, Tyler. Damn you. Damn you..." The oaths poured from his lips as he ran through the moonless night. He was going to drag him by his collar. Smash his fist into his face. Kill him himself.

The side doors of the van were dented and sprung. Upside down, Jordan swung them back. They screeched as if in pain.

But the body he saw wasn't Tyler's. It took a moment for this fact to burn through his homicidal rage.

"Molly?" His voice cracked.

Touching her blood-streaked face, Jordan slowly surfaced from the nightmare. Molly? *Molly?*

"Oh, God..." he choked, reason returning with the force of a sledgehammer. He reached forward. He felt drugged, sluggish.

"Molly," he whispered, pulling her raglike body to safety with infinite tenderness and regret. Silent tears rained down on her white face as sirens split the air. His tears. And he waited in an agony of remorse as carnival-bright red-and-blue globes flashed through the darkness—a snaking line of police cars arriving in droves.

Floor wax and that peculiar mixture of disinfectant and illness that pervades every hospital were the odors that awakened Molly. The rattle of gurneys and the low hum of distant conversation penetrated. She felt weightless, senseless, swathed in a cocoon with no sensation of touch and feeling. It ached to open her eyes, but she managed a small squint. Yes, it was a hospital. She was a patient.

"Hello there," a friendly voice greeted her.

Memory returned in soul-hurting fragments. "Tyler?" she whispered.

"Now, you just relax. You've been asleep awhile."

"He alive?" she managed past a sluggish tongue.

"Yes, he is. I'll get the doctor...."

Memory jabbed her sharply. "My baby!"

She thought she'd uttered the words, but no sound passed her lips. She moved her hands to cover her stomach. Pain jerked through her and she gasped.

The doctor appeared, talked to her, examined her eyes and body but Molly lapsed into a semiconscious fog. *My baby's gone,* she realized. Pain caught in her throat. "My baby...?"

"Shh, now."

"Tell me!" she demanded in a croak.

He hesitated. It was answer enough. With a moan Molly turned her head aside. Tears welled, sliding down her cheeks and nose.

"I know it's inadequate," the doctor said kindly, "but we're lucky to still have you."

"Go 'way."

The silence said he'd obeyed her. She cried in small whimpers. Drifted off. Came to again. The pain was sharper this time, her memory clearer.

Voices sounded in desultory conversation. Familiar voices. Her mother and father. Some self-protective instinct warned her to stay quiet and listen.

"...never walk again." Her mother sounded bitter, almost hateful. Unlike herself. Molly shivered uncontrollably. "Jordan Montgomery crippled my son, and he's getting off!" Tina broke into noisy, angry sobs.

"He'll pay. I'll make certain of it." Her father was grimly determined.

"No. It won't happen. His brother's dead. And it—was—Tyler who—"

"Attempted murder," her father spat. "Ran him off the road. I'd kill him myself if I could."

"The judge will never take the Montgomerys' only living son away from them."

"We're pressing charges. Don't worry. He'll be put away until he's old and gray. . . ."

Old and gray. Molly moaned in anguish and subsided into a fretful sleep.

When she awakened again it was to cold reality. She was alone. It was dark. A nurse bustled in to take her temperature and blood pressure.

"What day is it?"

"Thursday."

"I've been here almost a week?"

The nurse nodded.

"My brother was crippled in the accident?"

She frowned.

"I overheard my parents talking. Will he ever walk again?"

"I think you should save your questions for the doctor."

"You just answered them," Molly said, swallowing hard.

Later that afternoon her parents returned to the hospital, overjoyed to see her awake and quietly thoughtful. "Is Jordan in jail?" she cut in as soon as she was able.

"Jordan? You know him?" Tina asked, uncomprehending.

"You know that bastard?" her father reiterated.

The stunned looks on her parents' faces told Molly they hadn't connected him as the father of her child. Slowly, the truth dawned, and her father's face turned brick red. "You were pregnant by a Montgomery?" he asked in a dangerous voice.

"Is he in jail?"

"Not yet!" her father roared. "But you can bet he will be!"

"John," Tina Capshaw murmured, touching his arm.

"How could you?" he demanded, his voice breaking as he gazed at his daughter. "How could you?"

The recriminations ended with the arrival of the doctor—but only temporarily. Her parents considered her involvement with Jordan a major breach of trust, just as she'd known they would. But she hadn't really expected them to blame her so completely.

Nor had she anticipated the cold shoulder they gave her, even during her recuperation at home. Tyler was still in the hospital, and the specter of prison lay over him like a dark shroud. He'd shot and killed Michael Montgomery. Molly had found one of the newspapers they'd tried to hide from her in the hospital and read the obituary. A part of her still didn't believe it. These events hadn't really happened. They *couldn't* have.

And there had been no word from Jordan, though she knew for a fact that he was out on bail.

On the fifth day after her release from the hospital she called Jordan's house. It took all her courage. He hadn't called her, but then, he must know she'd been in the hospital and it would be unlikely her parents would let him visit her.

A man answered the phone, his voice stern and deep. "Is—is Jordan there?" she asked in a voice that shook slightly.

"Who's calling?"

"It's—Molly."

The silence roared. "He's not here," the voice told her with acid fury.

He hung up.

Molly was incensed. She burst into tears. Crying was too easy, these days. It felt like it was all she did.

But then the worst moment came, and like most truly terrible life-shocks, it came out of left field—and hit hard.

Foster Montgomery paid her a visit.

He was tall and handsome, his hair graying at the temples, his blue eyes frigid as a glacier. He arrived in the middle of the day when her father was gone. Her mother let him in, looking stricken when she realized who he was, but Foster had already shouldered past her, stopping short when he encountered Molly who was seated on the living room couch, looking like the invalid she truly was at that point.

"Miss Capshaw," he said politely.

Molly quaked at the menace ringing through his phony politeness. Determined not to fall apart, she nodded carefully.

"You're acquainted with my son, Jordan."

Acquainted... "Yes."

Molly's mother stood by like a sentinel, a line drawn between her brows. She hadn't phoned Molly's father yet, but Molly could tell she was on the verge of flight to the phone, should Foster Montgomery do something threatening.

"This unfortunate accident has caused both our families immeasurable grief," Foster said. It was a canned speech, rehearsed carefully, Molly was sure, but she was too upset and unnerved to realize it until much, much later. "We all want to put it behind us and get our lives back on track." Pulling an envelope from his pocket, he frowned down on the white missive, tapping it gently against one hand. "Jordan asked me to give you this."

"Is he all right?" Molly burst out.

"No man is 'all right,' miss, when he's been accused of vehicular assault."

"My son will never walk again," Tina Capshaw whispered emotionally.

"Now I only have one son," Foster replied in a quiet, deadly voice.

Molly's gaze was riveted to the letter. Jordan hadn't been able to see her but he'd written her! Through the haze of pain and misery these past few weeks, there came a heart-jumping moment of hope.

Foster handed it to her. For a moment they made eye contact. Molly had to look away, confused. She didn't understand what she saw. It wasn't hatred. It was . . .

Foster showed himself out, and Molly opened the letter with shaking hands. It was short and to the point, so coldly dispassionate that Molly had to assure herself it was in Jordan's hand. She knew his signature. He'd sent her one silly love note from school. He'd indeed written the letter, and there was no mistaking how he felt about her.

He wanted her out of his life. He was glad she would recover, but there was too much water under the bridge, too much pain for either of them to be able to stand each other's company ever again. He hoped they could both put this behind them. He never wanted to see her, or any other Capshaw, again.

"Can you tell me what it says?" Tina asked.

Molly carefully refolded the letter, running her fingernail along the crease until it was razor thin.

"It says goodbye."

Brushing past her worried mother, Molly climbed the stairs to her room. She sat down at her desk and wrote Jordan a blistering letter in return, a missive chock full of the bitter passion his carefully worded letter had so clearly lacked. She hated him. She never wanted to see him again.

He'd killed their child and their love and sent her brother to a wheelchair, and she hoped he suffered over it for the rest of his life.

Only years of carefully practiced social skills kept her from penning what she really felt: *I wish* you *were dead instead.*

But anyone reading it couldn't miss the underlying message.

And Jordan never wrote, called, or tried to see her again, so apparently he understood. In mutual agreement, they closed the book on their ill-conceived, starcrossed love forever.

Chapter Six

"Well, almost forever," Molly finished. "Ten years, anyway." She smiled faintly at Dr. Geddes.

Dr. Geddes nodded. The tale was one of sorrow, the passion of youth and misguided good intentions. Everyone had a tale to tell, but this one was poignant in its intensity and misery.

Molly turned to the doctor, her eyes full of powerful memories. "I thought that was the end of it. I hated him, and I fed that hatred with all the real and imagined wrongs the Montgomerys had ever perpetrated against the Capshaws. Do you know how easy it is to make yourself believe something, simply by telling yourself it's the truth over and over again?"

"Yes," Dr. Geddes said.

"After a while I really believed I hated Jordan. I convinced myself it had all been an elaborate plot against my family. I was glad to hate him. It made it all easier."

Sighing, she lifted her shoulders and collapsed in a seat on the other side of Dr. Geddes's desk. "But then..." Taking a deep breath, she shook her head. "I guess you can't fool yourself forever."

"Some people do an excellent job of it."

"Well, that's true. I sure did for a while. A long while. But then some things happened and I had to face the real reality, not the one I'd made for myself. Are you sure you want to hear the rest of this?"

The doctor nodded.

Running her hands around behind her neck, Molly leaned back, gathering her thoughts. Dr. Geddes watched the emotions that crossed her mobile face. "I'd gone to college—a small community college near Vernonia—and I'd earned a two-year degree in accounting. I moved to Los Angeles and bounced around in a few jobs before I settled at Westwind Construction, a commercial-construction firm. I'd worked there about a year when I started dating the owner of the company, Paul Sheffield. And we were talking about marriage. At least Paul was and then—Jordan showed up and—all hell broke loose...."

"Molly!"

Molly jumped, shocked out of her concentration. The papers on her desk scattered hither and yon. Annoyed, she glared in mock anger at the young assistant, Heather something-or-other, who'd yelled at her.

"Yes?"

"Ready for lunch?" Heather shouted.

Heather always spoke at top decibel level, even while ordering food from Anderssen's mobile lunch cart, which cruised down their street each day, offering outrageously priced so-so-tasting sandwiches and goodies. More often than not, Molly asked Heather to bring her something since she rarely took time to go out, but she cringed whenever she heard Heather shouting out her order as if Stanley Anderssen—who was more than a few years under thirty—were deaf.

"I guess so," Molly said, frowning at the pile of work in front of her.

"What d'ya want today? Chicken salad? Avocado and mozzarella? Green roast beef?"

"Ugh." Molly wrinkled her nose. "Tell Stanley I might have to start boycotting him if he can't come up with something more appetizing."

"He won't care," Heather predicted breezily. "So, what'll it be?"

"Avocado and mozzarella. Here..." She dug in her purse for a five-dollar bill. Heather still held her hand out after Molly passed it over. With a snort, Molly pulled out a few more dollars. "His sandwiches cost more than the national debt."

"Yeah, but they're delivered to your door."

Molly snorted again, amused and irritated at herself for falling into this trap, day after day. "Tell that bandit this is the last time!" she called after Heather.

Heather saluted and left. Chuckling, Molly stretched her arms over her head, thinking her diet was as bad as a teenager's these days. Breakfast this morning had been coffee. Lunch was going to be an Anderssen special, and dinner was bound to be something she could shove from freezer to microwave.

"Hey there. Whoa!" Paul ducked his head around the doorjamb, lifting his brows up and down at the tightened fabric across her breasts.

"Hey, yourself." She dropped her arms, a little embarrassed. She and Paul were on the verge of sleeping together but she'd been holding off, unsure. It had been a long, long time since her one and only physical relationship, and the longer it became, the more uncomfortable she grew about renewing that side of love.

"Want to go out for lunch?"

"No can do. I've already sent Heather out with my life savings."

"I don't know how you can eat that stuff. Throw whatever you bought in the garbage. I'm taking you out for a meal."

Molly tried to protest, but Paul could be downright bullheaded when he wanted his way. Though she would rather have stayed and finished her work, she wasn't all that eager for her sandwich, anyway. So, more to humor Paul than from any real want of companionship, she agreed to accompany him and she surprised herself—when they got to the restaurant she actually unwound and had a good time.

Only when she returned to the office nursing a headache from the glass of wine Paul had pressed upon her did the good feelings fade. She stared out the window, reflecting on the surprisingly aimless path of her life. Oh, sure, she'd gone on to college and picked a career that she'd followed for the past eight years. But where others were driven by passion, hunger and a desperate need for security or power, she'd simply bought time. Maybe she should seriously consider a life with Paul. Maybe it was time for a decision.

Picking up the documents on the latest project Westwind had signed on to build, she shook off her uncomfortable melancholy. "Okay, okay," she murmured distractedly, scanning the papers. A name jumped out at her.

Montgomery.

A stab of pure shock drove through her. Her pulse leaped painfully. "Idiot!" she swore through her teeth, annoyed that something so small and simple could affect her so radically. How juvenile!

She reread the paragraph to learn that Montgomery Industries had purchased a strip mall and planned to rebuild and renovate it, using Westwind Construction as the general contractor. Montgomery Industries' address was in Los Angeles, not too far away from Westwind's main offices. It was not in Vernonia.

"Coincidence," Molly said aloud, but she knew Foster Montgomery's company had also been named Montgomery Industries. Legally, there couldn't be two companies with the same name in the same state.

Dialing the number listed with the address on the contract, she got a bored-sounding receptionist on the other end. "Can you help me? My company, Westwind Construction, has been contracted to rebuild a strip mall for Montgomery Industries. The contract's signed by a Mr. Hornbarrin. Is Mr. Hornbarrin the CEO?"

Her fingers tightened around the receiver.

"Mr. Montgomery is the CEO," the voice replied.

Molly's heart pounded heavily. "Foster Montgomery?"

"No, Jordan Montgomery."

She nearly dropped the receiver. Pushing out a "Thank you," Molly hung up, hands shaking. It couldn't be! But it was!

Jordan! Head of Montgomery Industries!

A moan of protest passed her lips. Stricken, Molly couldn't seem to get her brain in gear. She sat like a statue. When her watch beeped gently three times, she jerked awake.

A red tide of anger swept over her. How could she let the past affect her like this? Hadn't she learned anything? Jordan Montgomery might be the head of his daddy's company, but he was still a first-class bastard who'd used her and tossed her aside, all in the name of the Capshaw-Montgomery feud.

The phone buzzed. "Yes?" she answered sharply.

"How're ya doing? Working hard?"

It was Tyler. Her brother's voice was another reminder, a stinging memory of bad times. "Hi there," Molly said gently. "I'm just checking over some new contracts. Are you in town?"

"I'm with Sharon."

Sharon was the woman Ty used and abused. An enabler, she seemed to think her life's mission was to take care of Ty. Not that Ty wasn't able to do most things for himself, but Sharon was his whipping girl. He heaped verbal abuse on her that she seemed to resent, but never did anything about.

"You going to be around tonight?"

"Sure. How about I make you both dinner?" Molly suggested.

"Sharon can just drop me off."

Molly hesitated. Her love for her brother was as familiar as the changing seasons, but years of Tyler's disillusionment and bitterness, coupled with his increasing use of alcohol had turned it into something harsh. "Sure..."

"I'll be there around seven."

Hanging up, Molly pushed her heavy tresses away from her face and closed her eyes. Jordan's image wavered before her: young, handsome, arrogant, sexy. Her eyes snapped open and she ground her teeth together.

Scooping up the contracts, she marched down the hall and swept into Paul's office. He glanced up in surprise.

"Well, hello, Molly. Uh-oh . . . Bad news?"

"Doing business with Montgomery Industries is a mistake. They're unscrupulous and ruthless, and I'm not convinced they're completely ethical."

Paul laughed in disbelief. "What?"

"I know the Montgomerys, Paul. We're from the same small town. They're not trustworthy. It's a family trait."

Paul looked at her as if she'd lost her mind. "I've never heard you talk like this about anyone."

"Then you know I'm not making it up," Molly pressed on.

"Molly, Montgomery Industries has a sterling record in business. I've been busting my butt trying to get them to use us on a project. You know how I finally broke in? One of the temps here has a step-uncle who works for them! Through him, she got us an interview with Montgomery himself. Believe me, he's not such an ogre."

"You met with—Jordan Montgomery?"

"Yes. And he was impressed enough with our work to put us on the job. Maybe you didn't like living next to the Montgomerys, but Westwind needs their business."

"I didn't live next to them," she said shortly, feeling like a chastised schoolgirl.

"I appreciate your interest in the business," he replied with growing amusement. "I promise I won't make you check out the job site."

"Don't patronize me, Paul!"

"Sorry." He held up his palms. "I just think you're being a little hysterical."

Was she? A flush crept up her neck and flamed her cheeks. Oh, Lord, she hadn't accomplished anything but prove to herself how much Jordan still affected her.

Not Jordan, she reminded herself grimly. *The Montgomerys.* For now she believed with all her heart that they were just as self-motivated, greedy and culpable as her father and brother had maintained all those years ago.

"No, I'm sorry," she apologized. "It's your company, and you know what's best."

Paul grinned. "I love it when you're contrite."

"Just make sure I don't have to deal with them. Where the Montgomerys are concerned, I don't trust myself to be fair."

"Deal."

She left work feeling marginally better, but an evening spent with her brother left her feeling guilty and depressed, with a nagging headache to boot. Whereas adversity seemed to bring out the best in some people, it merely helped Tyler wallow in self-pity and smoldering hatred....

"Sharon thinks I should go back to school," Tyler growled, wrapping spaghetti around his fork. "What for? I'm working for Dad, making enough money to get by. Who'd hire a man without legs?"

"A lot of people. There are all kinds of jobs for the disabled. I'm not telling you anything you don't know already."

"Disabled." He flung his fork down with frustration, shoving the plate to the edge of the table. Molly lunged to catch it, but it flipped end over end, landing with a messy plop on the floor. "Sorry," Tyler bit out.

"Learn to control your temper," she said, rising to clean up the mess. She'd learned years earlier that forgiving Tyler for his tantrums didn't work. Tough love was the only answer, and half the time it didn't work, either.

"That bastard put me in a wheelchair *for life!*"

"Griping about it isn't going to change things!"

"You're sure coldhearted, Molly," Tyler murmured, feigning hurt.

"You can do anything you want, Tyler. You just don't want to."

Hours later, lying in bed, she regretted how harsh she'd been, even though she knew it was the only way. She wished with all her heart Tyler would lay the past to rest. Maybe if he could, she could.

What would he do if he knew her company was doing business with Jordan's?

She decided she never wanted to know.

Three weeks later, Molly was frowning down at a series of compounded errors on the balance sheet when her phone purred. "Accounting Services," she answered distractedly.

"Molly, have you put through payment for Buzz Bentley?"

"Which job?" she asked, recognizing the voice of Jim Wright, one of Westwind's project managers.

"Montgomery's strip mall. I don't know the job number."

Annoyed at her jolt of recognition, she said without hesitation, "Partial payment's gone through, and I've just cut the final check."

"Don't send it! Montgomery's real unhappy with Buzz's interior demo. Buzz cut through a few wires he shouldn't have and I guess he left a bunch of tools around and some kid climbed over the fence and hurt himself."

"With one of Buzz's tools?"

"So he claims. Anyway, Buzz's gotta get back over there like yesterday and fix things. Otherwise we're in deep trouble."

"Okay, Jim. I'll hold payment."

"Thanks."

Wasn't it just like Jordan to blame a series of screwups totally on Westwind's subcontractor, denying the poor man payment when Buzz Bentley was struggling financially, trying to pay off his ex-wife and send his daughter to college all at one time? It just wasn't fair.

An hour later the phone rang again. "Accounting Services."

"Hey, Molly, it's Buzz. Can you get me that check this afternoon? I've gotta pay Karen's tuition today or she's out for the semester."

"Buzz, there seems to be some kind of problem—"

"I know, I know. Stupid kid climbs the fence, drops over the top and lands on my power saw. Damn thing wasn't plugged in, luckily, but he still sliced up his arm pretty badly. His parents want to sue Montgomery, Westwind and me. Can you believe it?"

"Is he going to be all right?"

"Oh, sure. He'll be back climbing fences before you know it. Damn kid's a thief. He wanted my tools! But they fought back," he added with a short laugh.

Molly smiled in spite of herself. "Buzz, I can't pay you until you go get those tools and fix whatever's wrong over there. Jim's orders."

"Damn that Montgomery. He's the one who got Jim all riled up! I said I'd fix it, and I will. In fact, I'm on my way."

"Jordan Montgomery?"

"The CEO himself. Came and looked over everything and didn't have a nice word to say about anything. I swear he wanted to find something wrong. I made a few mistakes, but nothing serious. You know me, Molly."

"Yeah, I know you, Buzz."

"He was totally unreasonable, but I'm heading over there today to make things right. On my way back, I'd like to stop by and pick up that check. I oughta have just enough time to get that payment made if I make it to your offices by three.''

Molly glanced at the clock. "It's already noon, Buzz."

"I'll be working right through lunch. How about it, Molly? Can you help me?"

Molly chewed on her lower lip. She'd never disobeyed a project manager's directive before, but if the work was completed there'd be no reason to withhold payment.

"I'll have it ready," she assured him.

Buzz stopped by the office right on schedule. His hair was full of dust and he looked beat. "Had to work like a dog to please everybody," he growled. "Montgomery was looking over my shoulder the whole time. What's the matter with him? Don't he have enough to do?"

"Apparently not," Molly answered crisply, handing him the check.

She was just slinging her purse over her shoulder and gathering some papers when she heard loud voices in the hallway. Jim Wright, the project manager, ducked his head inside her door. "Molly, you didn't pay Buzz the rest of his money, did you?"

He was certain she hadn't. His tone suggested the answer was meant to satisfy the man he was arguing with.

A cold feeling settled over her heart. "Buzz did the work, so I ordered out payment," she replied truthfully.

"I told you not to!" Jim was stunned.

"That was before the work was completed."

"The work still isn't completed," a harsh male voice retorted from the hallway.

Molly turned to the newcomer, some sixth sense warning her a heartbeat before Jordan himself strode into her office and glowered at her in a way that made her want to crawl into a hole.

He was just as she'd remembered him—and radically different at the same time. His hair was black, thick and about the same length as it had been when he was in college. His eyes were just as blue, just as heavily lashed. His mouth was just as sexy. But there were lines of disillusionment bracketing it, and his skin looked sleeker and tougher, more a man's than a boy's.

She stared in shock, her palms sweating, her heart in her throat, beating like a hammer. He stared right back, without the least flicker of recognition in his eyes. She wondered hysterically if there was a chance he might not know her.

He was dressed in a shirt and faded jeans, no sport jacket or tie. His shoulders were broad, stronger than she remembered, and his rolled-back shirt sleeves revealed deeply tanned, sinewy forearms. He looked as if he worked outdoors.

He did not look like the CEO of Montgomery Industries.

His expression changed from fury to shock to a kind of steely-eyed assessment she didn't immediately understand.

He made himself crystal clear a moment later.

"Molly Capshaw," he greeted her coldly, his gaze dropping to her nameplate for verification.

"Hello, Jordan." Her voice was incredibly controlled.

"You knew this sub hadn't completed the job to my satisfaction, so you chose a petty revenge."

Her mouth dropped. Jim, completely at sea, looked blankly at Molly, then at Jordan, and back to Molly.

"I paid a man who deserved to be paid. He finished the work today."

"Is that what he told you? Or did you just make that up?"

She gritted her teeth. "That's what he told me."

"Well, he didn't finish the work. In fact, all he did was tell me where I could stick the project."

Jim choked and coughed, turning slightly gray.

"He did, however, manage to pick up his tools," Jordan went on in a mocking tone. "I'd have to conclude from all this that he's not coming back to fix the mess he made. And thanks to you, he's been paid for it."

"He needed the money for his daughter's tuition," Molly said flatly, knowing it was a poor defense.

"If I felt like making a charitable donation to Mr. Bentley, I'd do it."

"Westwind will send someone else out right away," Jim cut in. "We'll make it right for you, Mr. Montgomery."

"You bet you will," Jordan replied, holding Molly's gaze grimly.

A moment passed between them. A nuclear blast of past memories and current hatred. Molly despised his intensity, his good looks, his damn virility. The man's masculine sex appeal radiated in waves. And he *knew* it, damn him! He did nothing to tone it down. If she'd ever been made to feel like the weaker sex it was right now, with Jordan Montgomery's power and anger directed at her, full force.

"I'll pay the cost out of my own pocket," she declared rashly, lifting her chin.

"Now, Molly, that's not necessary." Jim waved her off.

"Whatever you think is fair," Jordan told her.

Oh, he was a bastard! "Stay right there," she ordered, snatching her purse from her arm. With jerking motions, she dug for her checkbook, flipped it open and wrote a check for the exact amount she'd paid Buzz Bentley earlier that day. "That's what I gave Buzz."

"Molly..." Jim sounded sick. "That was for half Buzz's job. This is just a cleanup. A small fix-it. Westwind will pay and supply the subs until Mr. Montgomery's satisfied with our work. It's a matter of company pride."

"And this is a matter of personal pride," she told him, her hands shaking with reaction as she held out the check to Jordan. He glanced down at her outstretched hand and hesitated, showing the first glimpse of humanity beneath his harsh exterior. But then he met her gaze again.

They stood closer now, literally an arm's length apart. She saw the striations of blue in his irises, everything from azure to indigo—the aristocratic line of his nose, his slightly cruel mouth. He looked like Foster, she realized with a jerk of her heart. Not quite as cold, maybe. But a damned fine imitation, nonetheless.

He took the check without a flicker of remorse. Jim looked as if he was about to protest. Molly silenced him with a cold glare of warning.

"See that the work's done by the end of the week," were Jordan's final words.

Jim nodded. As soon as he and Molly were alone, he looked at her with a sick expression. "That's a lot of money. A *lot* of money. What in God's name were you trying to prove?"

"What an arrogant bastard Jordan Montgomery is. And I think I managed," she said around a catch in her throat.

Chapter Seven

Slam! Molly placed the saucepan back in the cupboard and reached for another. *Bang!* She set the new one carefully on a burner. *Clatter! Jingle! Slam!* She selected a spoon and closed the drawer.

Drawing a deep breath she counted to eleven. Ten just wasn't high enough, she realized, as she proceeded to stir the canned soup she'd dumped into the saucepan.

. . . knew this sub hadn't completed the job to my satisfaction, so you chose a petty revenge. . . .

"Arrogant, coldhearted humanoid," she murmured in disbelief.

. . . conclude from all this that he's not coming back to fix the mess. . . . Thanks to you, he's been paid for it. . . .

Molly gritted her teeth and growled, stirring in sharp, jerky motions. The soup boiled and she poured it into a bowl, spilling drops all over the counter.

If I felt like making a charitable donation to Mr. Bentley, I'd do it. See that the work's done by the end of the week....

Spooning scalding soup into her mouth, Molly narrowed her gaze on the snapshots of her mom and dad and Tyler that covered the front of her refrigerator. One photo was before Tyler's accident. He stood straight beside Molly, his arm loose over her shoulders, his smile smug with the invincibility of youth.

She thought of Jordan. How he'd been today. The churning feelings of anger and resentment that had burned through her blood like acid. If he were here right now she would hit him. As hard as she could. Right in the mouth.

Doubling up her fist, she thought about how that would feel, knowing even while she did it that she possessed neither the nerve nor the irresponsibility to physically strike another person. But oh, he deserved it!

If she could just get him in a position where he was the weaker one...

The doorbell rang. "Hello, hon," Jamie Lee Rogers greeted her as she swept in. "Oh, soup. Molly, you've gotta start eating healthier."

"Soup's healthy."

"Too much salt. Way too much salt. Turn your arteries brittle as my Aunt Verna's hair. You gotta watch that now, before real trouble starts."

"I like soup."

"What's the matter?" Molly's irrepressible neighbor asked, frowning.

"I'm in a bad mood, Jamie Lee."

"You? Miss Merry Sunshine?"

"I'm not Merry Sunshine." Molly stalked back to her soup, eating it defiantly as Jamie Lee perched herself on the other café chair at Molly's tiny kitchen table. Blond, petite, and just a cut above tacky, Jamie Lee was a character right out of a trashy novel. Half the time her barrel-straight-ahead-and-never-mind-the-fallout attitude frustrated Molly right down to the soles of her feet. The other half, her generous, upbeat nature was a refreshing antidote to life's ills.

Jamie Lee was Molly's new Charisse. The yin to her yang. Though the friends and acquaintances of Molly's youth were scattered to the ends of the cosmos, she always remembered them in bits and pieces of every new person she met. And if Jamie Lee was like Charisse, then Paul possessed a bit of her old nemesis, Brian, though she hated to admit it. And Stanley Anderssen looked enough like Bernard Carleton, supernerd, that Molly's guilt sent her back to the lunch cart time and time again.

And Jordan Montgomery was Foster in spades.

"Man trouble?" Jamie Lee guessed sympathetically.

Molly opened her mouth to deny it, then switched tactics. "Was there a movie about a woman who'd been relentlessly beaten by her husband and instead of going to the police, she tied him to the bed and walked all over him with a pair of cork boots?"

"If there wasn't, there should've been," Jamie Lee replied, wide-eyed.

"I know I've heard that story before. I just never understood the revenge angle like I do now."

"You want to walk over a man in cork boots?"

"And how!"

"Okay, what did he do, this black knight?"

"I really don't want to go into all that," Molly answered, depressed by the enormity of her past with Jordan. "I just want to think about fun things. Like the payoff a pair of cork boots would bring."

"Well, I once clobbered Donald with a Wiffle bat. It didn't really hurt him much, but he got the message."

Molly smiled in spite of herself. Donald was Jamie Lee's ex-husband. He was fairly mild-mannered. The marriage had broken up because he and Jamie Lee were just too opposite to attract for long.

"After that, things were better for a while," Jamie Lee revealed, "but they didn't really change. He went back to being a control freak anyway."

"Why did you hit him?"

"Because he wanted to know everywhere I'd been that day. When I mentioned I'd run into Suzy, an old girl-friend he disapproved of, he came unglued. Wanted to know how come I hadn't come right out and told him. Wanted to know if she'd moved to L.A. Would I try to keep the friendship going? Was Suzy still with that awful Ron, the musician?" Jamie Lee's lips tightened. "You know the drill . . . control stuff. He's lucky he got off with a Wiffle bat."

"Why are men such jerks?" Molly sighed.

"Now, honey. They all aren't. Just because you want to tar and feather one, doesn't mean Mr. Right isn't out there."

"Did you want something?" Molly remembered to ask.

"A diet cola, if you got one. I was just sick of staring at the four walls."

Molly cleaned up her dishes and poured Jamie Lee a soda.

"So, who is this man who's got you so riled?" she asked, leaning an elbow on one jeans-clad knee as if she were settling in for a good, long yarn.

"I really don't want to talk about it."

"Someone at work?"

"Sort of."

"Your boss?"

"No, Paul's great."

"Someone who wants your job," Jamie Lee said with sudden comprehension.

Molly half laughed. "No, not really. I just did something kind of stupid today, and this guy jumped all over me. So then I told him I'd pay for the whole thing, and I wrote him a check and practically flung it in his face."

Jamie Lee nodded her approval. "Bet that felt good."

"Yeah, except I don't have the money to cover it." Molly admitted the truth aloud for the first time. "Now, I don't know what I'm going to do. That check'll bounce all over the place when he cashes it."

"Will your bank cover it?"

She shrugged. "Even if they do, I still don't have the money to pay them back. It was a stupid thing to do. I just wanted to *win,* that's all!"

"How much is it?" Jamie Lee asked.

With a rush of affection and gratitude, Molly knew her friend was about to offer to help. "Too much," she answered gently. "But thanks for the thought."

"Can you borrow against your car? Or your credit card?"

"Maybe. But I've got to do something fast. I'm thinking about asking for a salary advance. It'll be tight for a while, but I'd rather eat bread and water for a year than give in."

Jamie Lee lifted her delicate brows but didn't point out that Molly was being incredibly unreasonable for her.

"Let me know if I can do anything to help," Jamie Lee said on her way out.

Molly changed into shorts and a T-shirt and headed out for a brisk walk. It was September, the same time of year when she'd met Jordan—nearly the exact same date, as a matter of fact.

She walked faster, sweat beading on her forehead. Another neighbor's dog, a black Lab with a lolling tongue and happy face, leaped over the fence and joined her on her walk, sniffing and zigzagging in front of her. Leash laws be damned, Molly thought, enjoying the company. The Lab's name was Dixie and she always made Molly feel safe.

They walked together. To entertain herself, Molly pictured Jordan strapped to a bed, helpless, vulnerable. She could almost hear his groans of pain and pleas for mercy as she stomped him with cork boots. It was a heady vision. She was tired of being bested by the Montgomerys. Always getting the short end of the stick. Always second best. Always losing. She was tired of Jordan winning.

Oh, true, if she really reflected on those terrible events that had led to Michael's death, she couldn't honestly say the Capshaws had been the only losers. The tragedy had devastated both families. But Jordan's uncaring, cut-your-losses attitude had driven a stake through Molly's heart. He'd taken the best of her—her innocence, her trust—and crushed it beneath the heel of his boot.

How could she have fallen in love with him?

She *hadn't* been in love, she reminded herself quickly, picking up her pace. Her breath came harder, faster. Puppy love, that's all it was. Adolescent infatuation. Maybe even hero worship. Those were the emotions she'd let herself drown in, believing them to be so much more. No teenager ever believes the deep love they feel is as empty as a politician's promise, as insubstantial as fairy dust, as forgettable as elevator music.

Luckily, she'd faced those facts early. She'd been jerked from that cocoon of adolescent fantasy before it had strangled her with its deceptive warmth and security. She'd never trusted another man with her heart since. It was too dangerous.

She'd never trusted another human being since.

She slowed down at the corner of Elm and Central, walking in place as she determined which street to choose. "Elm" was a misnomer. The once-stately trees had succumbed to Dutch elm disease and the little maples planted in their stead were looking dry and crackly. Too hot, not enough care, not strong enough to withstand life's cruel tricks— Molly knew she would never let herself fall prey to a similar malady.

Jordan leaned his elbows on the glossy mahogany table, barely tasting the delicate puff pastry Carmella had prepared for him that evening. He didn't have much appetite for food, anyway. He didn't have much appetite for anything but acquisition.

"She thinks it's your favorite," Julie said with a sideways smile.

Jordan gazed at her blankly. To Julie's lifted brow, he said, "Oh," realizing she meant Carmella.

"I think it's because it's the only thing you eat more than a few bites of." Her assessing gaze slid from the top of his head to his shoulders, chest and flat stomach. "You must be eating something somewhere, though. Otherwise you'd look like one of those starving people in Africa."

Her casual words grated hard. A lecture on the state of the world and the horror of famine in particular rose to the tip of his tongue, but he swallowed it back. Julie was from privilege. Beverly Hills-Rodeo Drive privilege. The total desperation, hopelessness and humankind suffering in drought-stricken Africa were merely a headline to Julie. She couldn't really understand the enormity of its desolation—not in the pit of her soul, the wellspring of her emotions. It just wasn't in her.

"I've been eating late lunches. Don't have an appetite for dinner."

"Mmm." She looked at him over the rim of her wineglass.

Julie Huntington was his fiancée.

Jordan rubbed a spot above his left eye. His stress point. He thought it again: *Julie Huntington is your fiancée.*

No.

He couldn't ask her. He couldn't marry her. He didn't fit with her.

"Are you really going on that male-bonding trip to those mountains in Oregon?"

"The Wallowas. No."

"I thought the L.A. office had planned a horseback-riding trip."

"Mac did," Jordan replied shortly, referring to his right-hand man and Montgomery Industries' second-in-command. Mac was his property-acquisition scout, and when he'd eagerly planned this horseback-riding trip, Jordan didn't have the heart to tell him there was no possible way he could join him.

"But the trip's off?" She couldn't really hide how pleased she was.

"The trip's on. I'm just too tied up to join them."

She pretended not to smile but it was in her eyes. Jordan managed a cynical smile of his own. Julie felt that if they spent more time together, that hoped-for wedding day would be moved up. Maybe she was right. It was time he got married. Time he thought about having a child.

A child.

His flesh broke out in goose bumps. The reaction brought him to instant fury. *Damn it all to hell!* He was sorry she'd miscarried. If he'd known... If he'd but known...

Dull pain speared through him—the kind of pain that's so familiar it almost seems like a friend.

"Jordan?" Julie asked, her blue eyes anxious.

He shoved his chair back. "I'm going to have a beer. Do you want something?"

"My wineglass is still fairly full," she murmured, pursing her lips.

He strode into the kitchen, shooting the only-Spanish-speaking Carmella a tight smile of thank-you as he headed for the refrigerator. He grabbed the first bottle of beer he spied, his glower almost comical when he realized it was a light.

"Who got this?" he said slowly to Carmella.

She responded in lightning Spanish. The only word he understood was "Julie."

Back in the dining room, he held up the bottle for Julie's inspection. She brightened. "You like it?"

"Love it," Jordan drawled.

"It's kind of a first step toward mineral water."

"Oh yeah? Who told you that?"

"Gloria."

Gloria was the self-appointed fashion guru of Julie's set. It appeared that this, then, was a fashion issue.

"I didn't realize beer drinkers were switching to light beer in order to wean themselves to mineral water."

Julie hesitated, her extraordinary social radar switching on. She knew Jordan wasn't on the level. "Gloria says that's what Al's doing."

"Either Al's lying, or Gloria's kidding herself. If I wanted a light beer, I'd get it myself."

If I felt like making a charitable donation... I'd do it....

This afternoon's face-off with Molly hit like a bullet between the eyes. Jordan sighed.

"Well, I'm sorry." Julie lifted her chin, more annoyed than hurt. "I was only trying to help."

"If I'd asked for a glass of wine, would you have doctored it with water?"

"That doesn't dignify an answer," she muttered, sweeping up her black clutch bag. "Good night, Jordan," she said coolly.

He let her go. He didn't even act like he wanted her to stay, though in truth, he wouldn't have minded a night of sex and self-deception. But Julie was too hungry for marriage for Jordan to really enjoy making love to her. Every time he touched her, he could feel the strings that he knew were attached to him wrap around his throat and strangle him. Nothing was free. And sex with Julie came with guilt and a drowning sense of self-hate.

He drank the light beer in record time, crushing the can in one hand. Water with a bite. He laughed aloud. If nothing else, Julie was funny. Not that she meant to be, but yes, she was funny.

Julie Huntington is your fiancée.

A pair of fury-darkened hazel eyes in a perfectly sculpted, ivory-skinned face glared at him. Soft pink lips, a sweetly rounded chin too stubborn for its own good, and, thick, lush, silken black hair.

And a voice that throbbed with hate.

Julie Huntington is your fiancée.

He nodded, tossing the can lightly into a wicker basket meant more for decoration than utility. Against his will, his gaze moved traitorously toward the yellow check he'd placed on the mantel earlier.

He had half a mind to cash it.

Muttering a sound of self-deprecation, he snatched it up, his eyes tracing the sharp line of fury that was her signature. Molly Capshaw. She'd bought him off in a gesture he suspected she'd been waiting to make for ten years.

The check blurred in front of his eyes. He saw Michael and Tyler, their angry, passionate faces. And he heard the echo of Molly's terrible, bitter words. The words she'd sent him in a letter that had changed the course of his life.

I hate you for what you did.... I never want to see you again.... You killed our baby...my baby....

Jordan closed his eyes, held his breath and counted to fifty. The pain of her fierce, accusing words had receded like the tide, but like the tide it always came back, sometimes at the most unexpected times. When he was stepping out of his car into a bright sun-drenched morning. At the end of a hurried meal at some fast-food restaurant. While he was at his desk, or midway through a sentence on the rising price of materials—or more often, when he was alone and lonely.

He growled an oath and opened his eyes, the muscles in his jaw taut.

Julie Huntington is your fiancée....

He was beginning to believe it.

Chapter Eight

"What's really going on with you and Jordan Montgomery?" Paul asked from the doorway of Molly's office.

Glancing up from her computer terminal, Molly managed to keep from reacting. "Nothing. He was just a little high-handed yesterday, and I let him know he couldn't treat people that way."

"By all accounts, he was completely in the right."

She was terse. "Jim thought so. I didn't."

"Uh-huh." Paul gave her a searching look. "Are you ever going to explain this animosity toward Mr. Montgomery?"

The back of her neck prickled with irritation. "I told you. We're both from Vernonia. My family and his had some business dealings that went bad."

"Jim said you could cut the tension with a knife."

"I don't like him. All right? It goes way back, and it's just a thing I've got to deal with."

"Okay...okay," Paul said slowly. "Let's just not let it become a *company* thing."

Molly's irritation exploded into full-blown anger. She turned her attention to the computer, hiding from Paul's scrutiny. *Aye, aye, Captain,* she thought, clicking the keys with righteous fury. "I promise to be good."

"I'll cover the check you wrote him," Paul flung over his shoulder as he left.

"Oh, no!" Molly swiveled her chair and bolted from behind the desk, surprising both Paul and herself with the force of her vehemence. But she'd heard the condemnation in his voice, and she wasn't going to stand for it. "I'll pay for yesterday's misunderstanding. It's my fault, and I'll take care of it."

"Now don't be a martyr. Everyone's temper gets away from them sometimes."

"I'm going to pay that bill," Molly said firmly.

Paul opened his mouth, glanced at her unsmiling face, clamped his teeth together and shook his head in disapproval.

"We'll talk about it later," he mumbled, sliding away from her before she could argue further.

Striding back to her desk, she pulled open a drawer, then slammed it shut again, too angry to concentrate on work. This was all Jordan's fault! Snatching up her keys from the pocket inside her purse, she stormed out of her office and down the hall.

"I'm cutting out early," she informed the receptionist, who blinked at her in surprise.

Molly didn't wait for an answer as she slammed open the front door. Outside, the air was cool and promised September rain. Running her hands through her hair, she took a deep breath to calm herself, remembering with an uncomfortable jolt that Tyler was stopping by to see her again tonight.

Lord! She seemed to be bouncing from one minor disaster to another. Sighing, she drove off in a blue funk. She had to get out of this downward spiral and put some fun back in her life.

"And sitting around thinking about the past isn't *fun*," she muttered, stamping on the accelerator.

An hour later she was tossing a Caesar salad and munching on extra croutons when the front bell rang. Molly opened the door. Tyler wheeled himself inside with a grunted, "Hello," and Sharon, who'd been standing behind him, gazed at Molly uncertainly.

"Come in. Come in," Molly invited, sweeping her arm forward. "I'm glad you're here. I've made enough salad to feed an army and I've got some garlic bread—"

"Sharon can't stay," Tyler interrupted.

Horrified, Molly twisted to glare at Tyler, but not before she'd caught the hurt look that crossed Sharon's face.

"I've got some things to do," Sharon murmured quickly. "I'll be back later to pick Tyler up."

Molly sputtered, "Are you sure? I mean, can't it wait?"

"No," Sharon said softly and disappeared out the front door, closing it behind her.

"That was a rotten thing to do!" Molly exclaimed to Tyler. "Really rotten! Don't you care about her feelings at all?"

"She said she had things to do."

"Oh, sure."

Tyler scowled, wheeling himself furiously into the living room. He looked as if he wanted to growl something back. Molly waited, boiling, and her anger must have gotten through because he hesitated, then wound up saying nothing at all.

Molly fought her own need to hurl accusations, grabbing the handle of the oven door and pulling out the foil-wrapped garlic bread. She sawed off steaming hunks of it and clamped down on her feelings.

"I talked to Mom today," she managed to grit out between tight lips. "She said you're not working for Dad's refrigeration business anymore. Have you decided to go back to school?"

"Nope. I'm just sick of pushing papers and answering the phone for him."

"So, what are your plans?"

"Don't worry." He barked out a harsh laugh. "I'm not going to dump myself on you. Sharon and I are moving to L.A., but we'll stay out of your space."

"Oh, for God's sake, Tyler!" Molly thumped the bowl of salad on the table. "Whenever you say things like that you just make everybody miserable, especially yourself."

"Don't lecture me, Molly. You don't know what's it like, being in this chair!"

She met his gaze. "I should. You tell me often enough."

Tyler shook his head, seemingly appalled at her callousness. In the old days, Molly would never have been so blunt. But she'd learned how to deal with her brother, and stoking his self-pity was like arming a nuclear bomb.

"So, you think I should go back to school?"

"It's a thought." She grabbed the bread, then filled two glasses with ice. Pulling out a chair, she gestured for Tyler to come to the table. Almost reluctantly, he moved himself to a position opposite her and watched as she filled their plates.

"You think education's the answer to my problems?"

"I don't know." She shoveled a bite of salad into her mouth and didn't look at him.

"Maybe I could become a therapist. You know, help other cripples like myself." His mocking tone raised gooseflesh on her arms. "We'll work out our problems together. Look for that silver lining. What do you think?"

Molly didn't answer. The weight on her chest nearly suffocated her. Silently, she handed him the garlic bread and willed herself not to break down and cry.

So much for trying to find some fun in life.

The doorbell rang again just as they were finishing up. Molly swept in a surprised breath at the sight of Paul on the front stoop, looking sheepish and holding a bouquet of flowers.

"I didn't mean to get all over you about Jordan Montgomery. These are for you."

Molly accepted the flowers, jerking a glance at her brother, wondering if he'd heard. Her heart sank. Tyler's eyes were wide with disbelief and betrayal. He wheeled himself to her right side.

"Jordan *Montgomery?*" he boomed. "The bastard that cut off my legs?"

"Tyler," Molly protested faintly. A roar sounded in her ears.

"Oh, my God," Paul whispered in dawning horror. "I didn't realize it was Montgomery."

"It wasn't really," Molly managed from a faraway place. Then Paul was gathering her into his arms, crushing the bouquet of flowers between them. She froze stiff. She didn't want his sympathy. It made her feel dirty and wicked because it hadn't been like Tyler made it sound!

"When did you see Jordan?" Tyler demanded. "When?"

"I didn't know," Paul apologized again, smoothing back her hair. "Tyler's accident... I didn't know Jordan Montgomery was the one who... the man responsible."

Molly shrugged away from him, staring down at the bruised flowers. She was conscious of both of them staring at her: Paul with concern; Tyler with untempered rage.

"Jordan wasn't really responsible for—" she began.

"When did you see him?" Tyler interrupted furiously.

"The other day." Molly stepped back several paces. She didn't owe Tyler this. She didn't owe Paul an explanation, either.

"And you weren't going to tell me?" Tyler was working himself into a fit.

"Tyler, it was company business. I didn't want to—"

"He took away my legs, Molly!"

"I know what happened!" she bit out hysterically. "I was there, remember?"

"It's my fault," Paul tried to break in.

Molly held up an angry hand to stop him. Collecting herself with an effort, she gulped air and managed in a fairly credible voice, "Westwind and Montgomery Industries are doing business together, and that's okay. It has nothing to do with me." Turning to Tyler, she added flatly, "We all lost something in that accident, and Michael Montgomery lost his life."

The blood drained from Tyler's face. Molly ached for him, but she couldn't stand to listen to him deride himself and every part of life. He stared at her through red-rimmed eyes, then wheeled himself to the far side of the room, turning his back to her.

"I'll take care of things," Paul told her. "I don't want you to have to see him again."

"Jordan?" she asked dazedly.

"I don't know all the details, Molly, but it's clear he hurt your family deeply. I don't want anyone, or anything, around that can hurt my girl like that."

She shook her head impatiently, put off for no reason she could name. "Don't be ridiculous. It's part of my past."

"I'd tell you Westwind won't do any more business with him, but it'd be a lie. We're under contract, and pulling out now could be professional suicide if Montgomery chose to make things difficult."

"I wouldn't ask you to change your business practices on my account." Molly's tone was like chips of ice.

"Good...good..." Paul rubbed his hands together, trying to come to terms with the situation. "I'll just keep you two apart."

"Thank you for understanding," she added with pure irony.

Paul left a few moments later. Relieved, Molly squared her shoulders and tackled communication with her brother again.

"I'm sorry you had to find out about Jordan that way, but don't punish me for accidentally crossing paths with him."

"Accidentally?" Tyler sullenly refused to turn her way.

"It was no fun, and I don't plan on repeating the experience in this lifetime, if I can help it." She stalked around to stare him straight in the eye. "And we both know what really happened, like it or not. The truth came out in court."

"He hit the van with his car and look what happened!" He slapped his legs. Molly flinched. "He killed your baby, Molly!"

You were drunk at the wheel.

She didn't say it. She couldn't. He knew it, anyway.

"You weren't even going to tell me!" he cried suddenly, as churlish as a two-year-old.

Molly couldn't speak. She ached to her soul. The accident that had cost Tyler his legs had also cost him adulthood, for in many ways he was stunted. Emotionally he was a child, prone to rages, high drama and over-the-top reactions. Everything with Tyler was "the worst." The worst life, the worst boss, the worst luck. He wallowed in his misery. Sometimes she thought he actually thrived on it.

Molly had given up that particular competition years earlier. She'd learned never to tell Tyler a story of woe because he was bound and determined to prove that his life was a jillion times more horrible and so therefore she had no room to complain.

"What I would really like is for you and I to get along. Could we try to forget about the past for a while?"

He looked down at the wheelchair. "I never forget."

Molly gave up. Tyler might never be mentally well again, and it was time she started facing that unpalatable truth.

An eternity later Sharon came to pick him up. Tyler didn't even speak to her. He was too down and self-absorbed; this current trek into darkness was worse than most of the others. By the time the door closed behind him, Molly was drained through and through. Later, lying alone in her bed, she squeezed her eyes tightly closed and willed herself to sleep.

No such luck.

Pictures danced in her head. Pictures of her and Jordan and how they used to be. Pictures of Jordan now. Pictures of herself now.

Groaning, she dragged the pillow over her head. She hated picturing herself. Some deep inner part of herself always rebelled—a self-protective instinct that feared what she might see. It was as if subconsciously she knew she'd failed somehow. Failed to carve out a niche for herself. Failed to live up to her own modest expectations.

Since that terrible time with Jordan she'd been treading water, forging ahead in little ripples, slipping backward again to that same safe pool. Oh, sure, she'd made a career for herself of sorts, but her home, her personal life, her very existence had ended ten years ago.

Life's a bitch, and then you die.

Molly threw off the pillow, furious with herself. She'd succumbed to that negative philosophy without even realizing it. Staring at the ceiling, she determined it was time for a change. She wouldn't let Jordan get to her. She had some money in savings—enough to cover the check she'd written if she didn't eat, pay her rent or drive her car for the next three months. But she could refinance her car, and the money would come in time to take care of the worst of her overdue bills. It was a better idea than a salary advance. She couldn't even think of asking Paul to help her now. It went against everything she believed in.

And she absolutely refused to back down with Jordan.

A part of her knew she should ask Buzz—after all, the bill was really his. But she'd jumped in to protect her own sense of honor, not Buzz's, and so she'd damn well pay the piper herself. Knowing Buzz, he'd probably make it right to her someday. But even if he didn't, she would never back down with Jordan. The issue was just too important.

Snatching up the pillow again, Molly plumped it back into shape, feeling better now that she'd rationalized the situation to her satisfaction. To hell with the money, anyway! She wanted Jordan Montgomery to *know* she didn't owe him anything. No Capshaw did.

The sooner he recognized that fact, the better.

*   *   *

It was that eerie time between night and daylight, the sky a gray so dark it almost seemed black—but not quite— when Molly headed out for work the following morning. She felt stronger, better. Her night's reflections had left her more centered, relieved of a lot of nagging worries she hadn't quite faced.

As she drove, the sun became a blurry hint of gold on the horizon. Enjoying the moment, she detoured to an all-night convenience store for a cup of coffee, then headed for a few moments of peace at a neighboring park to watch ducks huddle on a pond, their heads tucked safely beneath their wings. With one hand stuffed into the pocket of her fawn-colored sweater coat and the other wrapped around the coffee foam cup, she hunched her shoulders against the nip in the air and tried to work up some enthusiasm for another day on the job.

Accounting might be her specialty, but she was truly not much more than a glorified bookkeeper at Westwind. Ron, the company's actual accountant, was a friend of Paul's father, Gerald Sheffield, and Gerald was Westwind's true owner. Since Gerald spent most of his time on golf courses and at racetracks, and therefore didn't have much of a hand in Westwind's day-to-day operation, there was the possibility that Paul would someday let Ron go and promote Molly. At least that's what she'd thought in the beginning, especially since Ron was something of an incompetent, and Molly was looking over his shoulder, fixing his mistakes.

But sometimes corporate life didn't heed the expected rules. Paul was a bit of a male chauvinist, and Ron was a friend of his father's. No advancement opportunity there. And in this case, being the boss's girlfriend was more hindrance than aid when it came to being recognized for a job well-done.

Girlfriend. Ugh. She wrinkled her nose as she walked back to the car. Her feelings for Paul had always been mixed, but right now she could honestly say she didn't want anything to do with him.

For reasons she couldn't later explain, Molly veered off the route to Westwind and drove instead to the strip mall that she'd inadvertently invested in. It was still too early even for the work crew, and the long, low building lay dark and hulking and cold-looking against the slowly lightening sky.

"What in the world are you doing here?" she asked herself as she pulled into one of the empty parking spaces. Pocketing her keys, she climbed from the car, took a deep breath and looked around.

There was a lone car at the far end of the mall, illuminated by a hanging, bare light bulb glaring from one of the store windows.

The car wasn't new. Vaguely, something clicked in her mind as she crossed toward it, her boot steps echoing hollowing against the pavement. The car was a vintage Mustang, dark blue; the light was reflected, warm and shining, on its glossy finish.

Memory connected.

"Oh, God..."

Jordan!

Instantly she whipped around, striding rapidly back toward her car.

"Molly." Jordan's voice was quiet behind her.

She stopped short, squeezing her eyes shut. *Oh, traitorous heart,* she thought half-hysterically as her pulse rocketed. She wanted to run like a rabbit, but it was too late.

Twisting on her heel, she offered him a tight smile of greeting. "I didn't know you'd be here."

"You didn't come to see me?" he mocked.

He was in a black leather jacket and a pair of worn jeans, his hair slightly tousled, his expression intensely focused on her face. Molly stared. She couldn't help herself. This was how he'd remained in her dreams. No, *thoughts.* How he'd remained in her thoughts, she reminded herself sternly.

The hair at the back of his neck just brushed his collar and the frisky little breeze that whipped the leaves in the dusty parking lot into frenzied circles teased at the black strands over his forehead. His eyes, shadowed by the dark gray morning light, assessed her thoroughly and without compassion. She remembered how sensually lazy and impossibly blue they'd been after lovemaking.

"Why are you at the job site?" she asked, tucking her hands up the opposite sleeves of her sweater coat.

"I make it a habit to stop by and check all projects."

"This one meet your expectations?"

"There are a few things that need to be addressed before we can go further."

"You mean Buzz's work?"

"Among other things."

"Buzz is an excellent workman," Molly said, compelled to defend him even though she knew it wouldn't make any difference to a man like Jordan.

"He's sloppy," Jordan countered flatly.

Molly was incensed. "No one's ever complained before. Maybe your standards are a little unrealistic. Buzz is one of the most well-liked subs Westwind employs."

Jordan uttered a sound of derision, shaking his head. When he moved, the leather creaked familiarly. Memories swelled on the wave of musky cologne the breeze threw her way.

"He may be a hell of guy, but he did a half-assed job." His gaze narrowed somewhere near her mouth. "You didn't have to pay for it, however."

"That's not what you said the other day!"

"Do you really want me to cash that check?" His brows lifted and he stared at her hard. "Maybe you think I won't. Maybe this is all just a lot of grandstanding."

Molly was so livid she could scarcely find her voice. Grandstanding, indeed! "As far as I'm concerned, you're paid in full! When I write someone a check, I expect it to be cashed. Go deposit it, before you lose any more interest!"

"All right, I will," he snapped. "But you're crazy if you think that sub'll make good on it. He screwed me, and now he's screwing you. You're just too full of indignation to face it."

"And you're just the person to make judgments on someone else's character!"

His jaw tightened, a muscle worked. He leaned toward her, eye-to-eye. Molly had to force herself to keep from backing up. "You didn't use to feel that way."

"I didn't know you then," she hissed.

"You *knew* me well," he stressed with unmistakable intent.

He couldn't have hurt her more if he'd tried. She fought it. She fought it hard. But a swelling, suffocating wave of emotion closed off her throat. Tears burned behind her eyes, but she forced them back. This was a battle she was determined to win.

His lips parted in surprise. He hadn't expected it to hurt, she realized. Not like that. Not that much.

"You evil, rotten bastard," she said in a low tone vibrating with emotion.

Jordan watched the tears well in her eyes. She wouldn't drop her accusing stare. The tears stood there, glimmering like diamonds. She refused to lower her gaze, and that made it a thousand times worse.

He hated himself.

"If I could change the past, I'd cut out that time when I knew you, even if it meant losing half a year of my life!" With that, she twisted to march away.

"Wait . . ."

Consumed by remorse and guilt and anger, he made the colossal mistake of grabbing her arm, connecting with the fuzzy warmth of angora and the steel of her tensed muscles. She jerked as if burned, whipping around to glare at him.

"Don't touch me!"

"I didn't mean that the way it came out."

"You meant it exactly how it came out!"

"Okay, I did," Jordan admitted recklessly. "I wanted to hurt you. I wanted to see if you felt *any*thing."

The tears still clung at the corners of her eyes, but there was no misty-eyed sadness simmering in those hazel depths. There was only anger and disgust and pure hatred. Pain stabbed inside his chest, turning into a deep, familiar throb.

"I don't feel anything for you," she said.

"Now who's lying?"

He knew he was pushing. Pushing hard. But it was important. Vastly important in a way he refused to define or analyze. For the first time in a long time, he was running on pure emotion, fueled by buried pain and anguish that had risen to the surface the moment he'd laid eyes on her again.

"All right, I feel angry when I see you," she told him in a tight, sharp voice. "It reminds me how stupid and impressionable I was back then."

"Back when we were lovers."

"Yes . . ." she hissed through her teeth. "Back when we were lovers."

Jordan ached to change the course of this conversation, but was goaded by some desperate inner need he couldn't seem to control. "I guess we were both impressionable."

"And stupid?" Molly raised her brows, daring him.

He lifted one shoulder. "Ignorant. Naive, maybe. I don't think either one of us is stupid."

"I can't tell if that's a compliment or not."

She was so gorgeous, he thought distractedly. Not like Julie. Not like the actresses and models seen in television and film. She wasn't perfect. Her brows weren't arched quite high enough, her chin was too strong, her mouth too set. And though her expressive, brown-and-green flecked eyes could grace the cover of any magazine, their intelligence and underlying suspicion weren't in keeping with today's obsession with youth and innocence.

Yet . . . Yet . . .

Jordan's senses reacted as crazily as they had ten years before when he'd seen her across a crowded gymnasium floor.

"It was merely an observation. Statement of fact." He answered her challenge in a quiet voice.

Molly's gaze narrowed. Something was changing here, and she wasn't quite sure what it was. She knew she didn't trust it. His tone had altered, turned more reflective.

Frowning, Jordan looked past her to the strip mall. "Why did you come here?"

Molly hesitated. "I wanted to see for myself what Buzz did wrong." It wasn't exactly the truth, but it wasn't exactly a lie.

He flicked a glance her way. Inside her sweater coat, she rubbed her elbows, focusing past him.

"Well, then, let me show you," he offered, gesturing toward the section of the building that was illuminated.

"Oh, no, that isn't necessary."

"You don't want to see?"

"I know Buzz. If you had problems with his work, it's probably not his fault." *Probably?* She was faltering and furious with herself for backing down.

Jordan walked a few paces away, pointing to his left. "Good old Buzz left his power saw and blades over there." She followed the direction of his hand. A temporary construction fence surrounded a section of the site. "That was after cutting through some power lines and nearly demolishing a key structural wall. Luckily, the power to that area was switched off at the time, so his stupidity didn't kill him."

Molly held back a hot retort. He knew more about the particulars than she did. He could make it sound any way he chose, and until she talked to Buzz, she couldn't refute him.

"He tried to do a slapdash job of putting a wall back together," Jordan went on, holding open the nearest store door and gesturing to a newly wallboarded section that divided this store from the next one. "I've had people fixing it. It's about finished now."

"Why didn't you ask Buzz to fix it?" Molly asked, reluctantly following him inside.

"I believe I did."

"And he refused?"

"He hasn't finished the job."

Molly looked around her, thinking fast. "You're not the easiest person to talk to. I don't suppose your attitude influenced Buzz to leave the job unfinished."

"A job is a job. You either do the work, or you don't."

Molly shook her head. "You sound an awful lot like your father," she murmured softly.

That hit a mark. Jordan jumped visibly, his expression swiftly changing, darkening. She suddenly hurt all over again, with the ache of something irretrievably lost, gone forever.

Clearing her throat, she suggested, "Why don't you give Buzz a chance to fix things to your satisfaction?"

"He's all out of chances," he bit out.

She gasped. "You are so hard! Worse, even, than my memory."

"Is that truly possible?" he asked in a coldly ironic tone.

She didn't answer. She didn't have to. The accusations she'd laid down with pen and paper crossed the screen of her mind and she imagined him reading them. No matter how much he may have wanted to end their association, they had to have hurt.

She was sorry now. Sorry she'd hurled her desolation and pain back in such an angry, terrible way. She wanted to apologize, but no words formed.

Jordan was squinting past her, gazing at some faraway point through the store's front window. For some reason, she recalled how he'd stared across the fields behind her house. She remembered the weeds he'd seen, and how embarrassed she'd felt that she wasn't as wealthy as he was. Ha! She was a thousand times richer in emotion and caring and human kindness. How could she have compared herself to him and come up short?

"I've been taken by a lot of people like Mr. Bentley," he said. "Half the time, they don't even mean to do it. They just put out their hand and ask, 'What have you done for me lately?'"

"You are beyond cynical!"

"My father's a first class bastard." He shrugged. "Maybe I am, too. But he was right about one thing—the world turns on money. It's all anyone really wants."

"Is it what you want?" she demanded, wanting to shake him.

"I've learned to look out for my own interests. No one else is going to do it for me."

"What happened to Jordan Montgomery, the idealist?" Reckless anger invaded her. "What happened to *him?*"

"Looks like he got a heavy dose of your realism," he shot back, and she thought she heard the underlying bitterness, though he tried to disguise it.

"That is such a cop-out." Molly shook her head. "I may be a realist, but I don't believe in that 'Gotta take care of myself, better stick it to somebody before they stick it to me' attitude."

"So, you think I should just smile and say, 'Don't worry, Buzz. You don't have to get the work done on time. It doesn't matter that your ineptitude delayed this project and therefore I can't rent out the space, collect payment and pay my employees' salaries.'"

"You're twisting this around."

"Oh, give it up, Molly. This whole damn thing isn't about Buzz Bentley, and you and I both know it!"

His sudden change of tactics drew her up short. "Buzz is a friend of mine. I just want to make sure—"

"Stop it. Just stop it."

She obeyed his harsh, angry command, then was furious with herself for buckling under. But Jordan swept on.

"If Buzz was doing work for a different company, you wouldn't have been so quick to come to his defense."

"Yes, I would."

"Liar. This is about you and me."

"I don't have to take this," she muttered, turning on her heel. She half expected him to grab her arm again, but he didn't. He did, however, fall in step behind her as she stalked back outside and into the gray morning light.

At her car door, she stopped, throwing a cold glare over her shoulder. "You know, I'm glad we met again."

He didn't hide his surprise.

"I'm glad, because a part of me always romanticized the past. I guess I always wanted to believe we were some kind of modern-day doomed lovers. It made the tragedy more palatable, somehow. Almost meaningful. But now I know it was just fate. People die from hurricanes and disease and they blame it on fate. Well, Michael's death and Tyler's crushed legs are fate's fault, too."

Jordan's mouth turned down at the corners. If she'd believed he had a conscience, she might have thought she'd seriously hurt him. "Nice try, Molly, but if that's how you really felt, you wouldn't blame me."

"I don't blame you."

"I could read you a letter that says otherwise," he replied in a low, throbbing voice.

Molly's breath caught. "I was only eighteen, Jordan."

"You said I killed our baby."

The gash in her heart that had never quite healed tore open. Molly opened her car door and slid inside, closing it behind her. She quivered from head to toe. Delayed reaction. He'd quoted her correctly, but she hadn't felt that way. Not then and not now. She'd just wanted to hurt him.

He stood with his hands in the pockets of his coat, watching her drive away. Molly glanced in her rearview mirror. He didn't move. With trembling fingers she touched the newly formed tears in the corners of her eyes.

No more crying. She'd wasted too many tears already.

"Damn you, Jordan," she murmured aloud, then wished she didn't feel so soul-wrenchingly guilty for making him believe she'd blamed him then, and for not having the courage to confess the truth now.

Chapter Nine

"Mr. Montgomery?"

The voice penetrated the fog of Jordan's brain and he realized dimly that it came through the intercom on his phone. Punching a button, he snapped out, "What is it?"

"Julie Huntington is on the line."

"I don't want any calls," he reminded her, irritated.

"I'm sorry, Mr. Montgomery. I couldn't put her off."

"Fine." Snatching up the receiver, he punched the button for the only flashing light. "What's up, Julie?" he asked curtly.

"Well, aren't you the grouch! I just wanted to remind you. We're supposed to meet Al and Gloria at eight. You didn't forget, did you?"

Jordan swore softly, answer in itself.

"Oh, Jordan! You've got to get away. Please, this is important!"

Al and Gloria. He'd be more comfortable on a bed of nails than in the company of Julie's dubious friends. "You said eight o'clock?" He thought fast, knowing already he couldn't turn her down again.

"Jordan!"

"All right, all right. I'll pick you up around seven-thirty."

"Good," she declared, relieved. "Don't worry. This is going to be fun!"

Fun.

Mumbling a goodbye, Jordan slowly replaced the receiver and swung his chair around so he could look out the floor-to-ceiling windows of his ground floor office. Montgomery Industries wasn't located in a high rise nor was it housed in a fancy new building. But the property was prime, with grounds any developer would die for.

Location, location, location. The most important three words in real estate.

If only life were so simple.

You are so hard. Worse, even, than my memory....

He shrugged, hating the depression his run-in with Molly had left him with. He knew what he had to do now, though he had resisted it all morning: go over the past.

The trouble was he'd spent an inordinate amount of energy and time recalling that period of his life already. For months, years, after Michael's death he'd found himself reviewing all the pieces, trying to make sense of something that could never make sense.

But sometimes it had helped.

Painfully, carefully, he picked through the layers of his own carefully laid self-deception to those repressed memories. They hurt too touch, like uncovering hot embers beneath cold ashes, but he searched through them anyway. He didn't have any choice, now that Molly had reentered his life.

Was he really worse than her memory? Her long-ago letter had been excrutiatingly clear about her feelings. She'd hated him then. She hated him now. Was he really *worse* than her memory?

Drawing a deep breath, Jordan turned the clock back to that time when he'd been arrested. To those hours and days spent in a cold cell where humiliation, regret and terror had reigned together, a terrible triumvirate of power. He'd spent his time thinking about Michael. And Tyler. And himself. But mostly he'd thought about Molly. Molly, hurt, broken and alone in a hospital. There'd been no way to contact her. No way to help.

But neither, he'd learned much later, had she tried to contact him.

Throughout the trial he'd been numb. Foster had bought him the best lawyers. He hadn't cared. He hadn't cared about anything but Molly. He'd learned she was out of the hospital; they'd told him that much. Out of the hospital and recuperating.

"Has she asked about me?" he couldn't help blurting out each day. *Does she hate me? Does she think it's all my fault?*

The answer had always been the same. No message. Nothing.

Still, hope is almost impossible to kill. He had his father to thank for finally managing to do it.

"I went to see her today," Foster had told him one particularly bleak afternoon when Jordan couldn't keep his mind on anything but what was going on with Molly.

Stunned, Jordan had been too eager for news to think of himself. "What did she say? How is she? Is she all right?"

"That whole family blames you, son," had been his father's cool response. "They don't give a damn about Michael, just their precious Tyler!"

"Did—Molly—actually say she blames me?" he'd whispered.

"She said a lot of things. Forget her and the Capshaws, and concentrate on the trial. That's all there is now...."

He'd argued, of course. Thrown down the ragged remnants of his pride and begged for more information. He'd told his father and mother he loved her. He'd shouted at the attorneys, who'd all frowned and shaken their heads.

He didn't want to believe the truth, but in all those weeks she'd never tried to contact him. Not once. And when his own emotions had finally settled down, he'd realized she never would. She blamed him for Tyler's crippling accident, just as much as he blamed Tyler for Michael's death.

It had taken the lawyers' combined efforts to save him. The tide of fury emanating from the jurors had nearly drowned him even before the case began. Tyler Capshaw's wheelchair-bound figure was a reminder of Jordan's guilt. Sometime during those awful days Jordan had recognized he was going to be sent to jail forever.

But he hadn't cared. He deserved it. He'd chased Tyler down with the intention of hurting him, and it didn't matter that he'd been crazed with fury and pain after witnessing his own brother's death. It didn't matter because he should have had more control.

Except...

An expert witness had been called to the stand. Tire marks proved that Jordan's bump with the Mustang hadn't been the reason the van turned over. Drunk at the wheel, Tyler had simply been going too fast to make the corner. The van would have turned over, regardless of Jordan's intervention. Also, witnesses had reported Tyler had ripped out of the Burger Hutt lot at full speed, negating the prosecution's contention that Jordan's pursuit had influenced Tyler's rate of speed.

There had only been conjecture about what would have happened had Jordan not been involved, but the expert had believed the van would have turned over regardless. The rest had been a bunch of maybes. Maybe Tyler wouldn't have been crippled; he could have been killed. Maybe Molly would have been killed. Maybe they both would have escaped unharmed.

Not bloody likely.

He'd read it on the jurors' faces. The evidence had been too clear. He hadn't really been surprised to hear the head juror announce, "Not guilty"; yet it hadn't erased Jordan's own guilt.

The verdict had brought Jordan out of his self-induced coma. It was clear Tyler had been as much at fault as anyone, but Molly's brother had already paid a terrible price.

Jordan had just wanted it all to stop.

Foster hadn't shared his feelings. He'd gone after Tyler with everything he had, obsessed with the need for vengeance. No one else, it appeared, had the stomach for revenge, however. Foster had wanted manslaughter and a prison term; Tyler's lawyers had plea-bargained, the judge had agreed and Tyler had been sentenced to community service. The only one who screamed injustice was Foster.

Sighing, Jordan rolled his pen through the fingers of one hand. His mind had traveled backward, and he was lost to the events of the past.

He'd written Molly a carefully worded letter of goodbye.

He'd written it seventeen times before he'd gotten it right. In the first sixteen attempts he'd sounded like a cry-baby, begging her to forgive him. By the seventeenth try, he'd pounded the emotion out of it, though upon finishing it he'd laid his head down on the letter, closed his eyes, and fought to still his frantically thumping heart, conscious of sweat on his brow and a scream of denial, way down inside.

Her answering letter had been cold, cruel sanity. The first contact in over a month, and it had been a doozy. The aimlessness of his life, the feeling that all was lost and he shouldn't go on, the wallowing in tragedy—it ended with a bang. She hated him. She wanted nothing to do with him. It was over with a capital *O*.

And she'd been pregnant and had blamed him entirely for the death of their child.

Jordan clenched his fist, pain shooting through his hand from the pen bowed between his fingers. He stared at it, releasing his grip slowly.

"Over with a capital *O*," he voiced. But the words sounded hollow. Because he knew in his heart it wasn't over—not for him.

"Veggie burger!" Heather shouted from the other side of Molly's desk, nearly deafening her. "Or today's special, a hot turkey sandwich with cranberries."

"Hot turkey sandwich with cranberries?" Molly repeated. "Really?"

"Yeah, but the turkey's kind of weird looking. You know, the pressed-together kind that's sorta green around the edges."

"I'll take the veggie burger," Molly said with a slight shudder.

Heather disappeared to go fill the order from Stanley Anderssen's lunch cart, and Molly finished transferring information to the general ledger. The weather had changed. Rain blew in fits and starts. It wasn't cold yet, but it was damp and gray.

A perfect barometer of her own mood.

Sharon had called. Tyler, it appeared, was not going back to school. He wasn't doing much of anything besides sponging off Sharon who, though she'd phoned Molly to ask for advice, seemed more than willing to bend to Tyler's iron will. It didn't seem to matter whether he was right or not.

Molly's advice had been to drop him off at registration whether he wanted to go there or not. This had elicited the news that Tyler had been equipped with his own specially designed van, which operated on hand controls. Molly had sensed this was what was really worrying Sharon. She wanted to deny him his independence. It frightened her.

"Maybe this is just what the doctor ordered," Molly had advised Sharon. "Tyler needs to feel worthwhile. Mobility could give him that."

"He's tried this before and gotten too frustrated," Sharon warned. "It's too hard for him."

"Sharon, you've got to let go a little. For Tyler."

"I can take him anywhere he needs to go. I'm happy to! All he does is complain about traffic, anyway. I don't see how driving is going to help!"

Molly had continued arguing with her but to no avail. Sharon wanted Tyler dependent on her. Anything else was too threatening.

Molly wasn't certain what the answer was, but, where Tyler was concerned, the status quo certainly wasn't working—that was for sure.

Heather returned with the veggie burger, which Molly ate at her desk. The afternoon wore on and grew dark, and her own mood deteriorated with the gathering gloom. At five o'clock she switched off her computer, grabbed her jacket and headed for the door. She didn't say good-night to Paul because she could hear he was deep in conversation with his father. Besides, she had no interest in seeing him tonight and really wasn't up to telling him she knew it would never work between them.

Running into Jordan again had shown her that truth, if nothing else, she realized with a grimace, as she pushed through Westwind's front doors.

To be honest, she hoped Jamie Lee was home. What she felt like was a bottle of wine and a heaping helping of Jamie Lee's oddball take on life.

"Molly," a familiar male voice said.

She stopped cold, jerked around. Jordan was leaning against his dark blue Mustang. He'd tossed on an overcoat but his blue jeans, open-throated work shirt and black leather jacket were visible underneath.

"What are you doing here?" she demanded, fumbling for her keys as she continued toward her car.

He shrugged, his hands in the pockets of the overcoat, and soft rain, almost a mist, coalescing on his dark hair. "I've asked myself that same question for the last hour. Twice I got back in my car."

"Maybe you should make it three times." Her pulse began the now familiar painful pounding generated every time she was near Jordan. She hated herself for it. "We don't have anything more to say to each other."

"I've been thinking a lot about the past. You might say I'm obsessed with it."

"I'm not," she lied. She twisted the key in the lock and snapped open her door.

"I need to get some things resolved."

"I don't want to talk to you!" she stormed.

"Too damn bad!" he snarled right back, crossing the distance between them in ground-devouring strides. Molly whipped around to face him, wary. "You want to stand out here in the rain, or go someplace drier?"

"I've got places to be, Jordan."

"So do I," he snapped. "I'm late for dinner already."

"Then go to dinner! This is just making everything a thousand times worse."

"Okay, fine." He lifted his hands in surrender. "There's no talking to you. I don't know why I bothered."

"I do." She slid into the car, grabbing the door handle to slam it shut behind her. Jordan moved with the speed of a jungle cat, grabbing the door, wedging one very masculine hip in the way, making certain she couldn't cut him off. His male scent filled the interior of the car, musky and compelling and, mixed with the rain, creating a powerfully seductive perfume. "What the hell do you think you're doing?"

"What did you mean by that remark?" he retorted.

"I asked what the hell you think you're doing."

"The remark about why I bothered," he reminded her icily. "Don't play games, Molly."

That irritated her. Partly because he didn't understand *anything* about her; partly because he was right.

"I know what you want. You want me to absolve you of guilt. Well, it's a little late, Jordan. A decade too late."

"I don't give a damn what you think of me. It's no worse than what I think of you." He stared her down, the rawness of his emotions communicating itself to her against her will. "Guess I made a mistake thinking talking about it might help both of us."

"What *you* think of *me*?" She latched on to the one comment that infuriated her the most. "Talking about the past isn't going to help either one of us!"

"Maybe not. But if you think you're fooling me by acting like it doesn't affect you, forget it. You're angry enough to sink yourself in debt just to make a point. You're not over this any more than I am.''

''It's not something you get over!'' she hissed.

''Exactly my point.''

They glared at each other, Jordan's scowl threatening against that gray sky, Molly's narrowed eyes a cover-up for her galloping heart.

''Get out of my car.''

''Damn it, Molly . . .''

''Get out of my car!'' She shoved at him with all her strength. Her hands connected with his hard, muscled chest. He didn't budge. She pushed again, wanting to pound some sense into him. She clenched her fists.

His hand shot out like a striking snake, clasping her right forearm. She struck at him with her left and he grabbed that one, too.

''Stop it,'' he commanded.

''Let go of me!''

''For God's sake, you're acting like a—''

''I don't care! I don't care! *Let go of me!*''

He flung her arms down as if she'd scorched him. ''Fine.'' In bitter fury he turned away. Molly slammed her door shut. Her lips trembled, and she pressed them together. He strode back to his car without looking back. She tried to switch on the ignition but couldn't get her hands to stop shaking long enough to accomplish the deed. Jordan flipped on his headlights and backed out of his spot with a sharp, abortive squeal of tires and was out of the lot before her engine caught.

''Damn,'' she muttered, infuriated and exhausted. ''Damn, damn, damn!''

She couldn't decide whether to screech out of the lot behind him, scream, or make a rude gesture with her hand.

She settled for dropping her forehead to the steering wheel, gulping air and laughing to keep herself from sobbing.

Her evening with Jamie Lee was all she'd hoped for, but by the time she'd worked her way through her second glass of wine she was nursing a throbbing headache and a tiny spark of remorse. She'd wanted to talk to Jordan. She hadn't wanted him to leave. Not really. She'd just wanted to—*hurt* him!

"Damn," she muttered again.

"What is it, honey?" Jamie Lee asked sympathetically. "You wanna just cry?"

"Yes," Molly hiccuped on a half-hysterical laugh. "How'd you guess?"

"You've been down in the mouth since you got here. What happened? Now don't lie to me. I really want to know."

"Oh, Jamie Lee. I want to just forget everything, and I can't."

"This man, again?" she guessed.

Molly hesitated for only a second. "I was in love with somebody who hurt me so bad. And now I've seen him again and I can't decide whether I want to hit him or—"

"Kiss him?"

"No!" Molly was affronted. "I just want to make some sense of all the terrible things that happened."

"What terrible things?"

Molly set down her wineglass. "It's a long story."

"I've got three packages of microwave popcorn."

"Bring it over," Molly said decisively.

The drive from Al and Gloria's to Julie's high-rise apartment was a disaster. A major freeway accident turned the twenty-minute trip into an hour and a half. An hour and a half when Jordan endured Julie's coldest fury. An hour and a half when he inwardly berated himself for making a fool of himself with Molly, as he'd been inwardly berating himself all evening. God, what an idiot he'd been! Expecting her to turn those huge, beautiful, drowning eyes his way and say, yes, she'd love to make the past right. Hoping she'd throw herself into his arms and cry out how it had all been a mistake. Knowing she had to feel the same way he did. *Had* to!

He groaned aloud. Julie sniffed and stared pointedly out the side window. He clenched and unclenched his hands around the wheel. The rage in his chest was mixed with dull pain. And self-disgust.

"Do you have to hurt me so badly?" Julie asked in a small voice.

"What?" Jordan threw her a glance, frowning.

"You said less than five words the whole night. You think I don't know why?"

Confused, Jordan shook his head.

"You don't want to be with my friends. And that's okay! I know it now. You don't like anybody I like. I didn't get it before, but I do now."

"I don't know what you're talking about."

"It's me, Jordan. Or more to the point—us. We're going in circles because you don't want me."

Jordan blinked several times, surprised by Julie's sudden insight. "I didn't mean to spoil your evening," he said truthfully.

"Well, you did." She drew a deep breath through her delicate nostrils and pursed her lips. "Are you ever going to ask me to marry you, Jordan? Or am I just wasting my time?"

Traffic was at a dead halt. Jordan thumped the steering wheel in frustration, then glanced at Julie. Earnest and vulnerable, she'd never looked so wonderful to him before.

Liar! She isn't Molly!

"You want to get married?" he asked seriously.

Her eyes widened. Gulping, she nodded.

A dull roar started in his ears, a faraway sound he recognized as a warning. He didn't listen to it. "Right now, I can't think of a single reason not to," he said with an underlying bitterness Julie didn't hear in the shriek of joy and disbelief that squeaked past her lips.

"You mean it? You really mean it?"

She threw herself around his neck, squeezing him and crying and shaking all at once.

He'd taken an irrevocable step. Away from Molly. Away from unhappiness.

His mouth was dry as dust; a sensation very much like fear crawled across his skin. He told himself he was doing the right thing, the only thing. But as he moved ahead, finding his place behind the ribbon of pulsing red taillights, he heard that rushing sound in his ears and wondered if it wasn't a death knell.

Instead of walking into her office the following morning, Molly parked her car in the lot and simply sat there, staring at the building, a line of concentration furrowing her brow. Her disclosures to Jamie Lee hadn't resolved any of her feelings, and as soon as she'd finished explaining, she wished she'd kept her problems to herself.

Not that Jamie Lee wasn't sympathetic. Oh, no. She'd practically broken down and cried at the telling, and that had made Molly feel like crying, too. But she'd shored up her emotions with those old, tired braces—anger and resentment—and managed to seem remarkably unemotional. After Jamie Lee had left and she was alone with her memories, however, those braces bent under the weight of self-recrimination.

She hadn't given Jordan a chance. Not the smallest chance.

He doesn't deserve a chance!

Doesn't he? Doesn't everyone?

"Blast," Molly muttered, yanking the key from the ignition. She closed her fist around it until it hurt. Slowly she unwound her fingers, staring down at the shiny bits of metal, seeing instead the Mustang logo—a galloping silver horse—on the grill of Jordan's car.

It was Saturday. She didn't have any reason to go to work other than to forge ahead on next week's business— not a bad idea but an unnecessary one. She just hadn't been able to stand the thought of staying home.

Jordan would probably be at the strip-mall job site. It wouldn't matter that it was the weekend or that it was early. He'd be there inspecting yesterday's job, anyway. And this early in the morning, he'd still be alone.

Isn't that why you really got up so early? So you could see Jordan? Be honest now, this has nothing to do with work.

With that last thought burning inside her brain, Molly crossly reinserted the key, cranked the engine to a roar and reversed out of the lot. She drove quickly, irritated over how *wrong* she felt about the way she'd treated him yesterday. It wasn't fair. Jordan had brought all this antipathy and hate on himself.

"You can't trust a Montgomery," she said aloud. "They're only out for themselves."

Her feet and hands didn't respond. They kept the car pointed in the direction of the job site and didn't heed any other warnings, though Molly reviled herself continually all the way to the strip mall.

He won't be here. This'll be the one day he doesn't show. You don't owe him anything!

His car was parked exactly where it had been before. A different light was on, in a section of the strip mall closer to where she herself had parked.

Apparently hearing her engine, Jordan came to the door, stood silhouetted against the bright interior. Molly sighed and climbed from her car. He didn't say a word or move so much as a single muscle as she approached. His hands were on his hips, his lips tight. When she was finally close enough to read his expression she almost turned tail and ran. In the early-morning darkness, his deep scowl looked menacing.

"I was kind of—abrupt—last night," she murmured.

"What do you want, Molly?"

"You said, umm, that you wanted to work through some things. I've been thinking about it all night. You were right. I need to, too."

"No, *you* were right." He drew in a deep breath, but the scowl never left his face. "We can't change anything. It's all part of the unfortunate past that we share, but history can't be changed."

She didn't like this role reversal. She didn't like hearing her earlier philosophy on his lips. It sounded so fatalistic. "I've spent ten years forgetting, and it hasn't worked. I'd like to try something else."

He was silent for so long, she was certain he was going to object. But then he inclined his head toward his car, silently inviting her to take a ride with him. When she didn't move immediately, he said, "We'll get breakfast."

They drove in silence. Her gaze wandered to his masculine hands wrapped around the steering wheel, then slid to the dark hair at his nape. Her impressions overlapped memory. She felt as if she were dreaming.

They pulled in at a small truck stop where the waitresses sashayed between tables, delivering coffee and wisecracks with practiced ease while workmen's talk buzzed like a constant engine. Several guys called out to Jordan, and he clapped hands with them and actually smiled in greeting.

His smile was nearly Molly's undoing. She'd forgotten it. Most of the time he looked so stern he was almost frightening. But the old Jordan had smiled a lot.

"Sorry," she said, bumping a waitress in her quick, self-protective turn away from Jordan.

"That's all right, sugar. Just grab a table. I'll be right back."

There wasn't an empty spot. Two men, recognizing Molly's dilemma, slid out of their booth and gestured grandly for her to take their place.

"We're outta here, boss," one announced to Jordan.

"Ain't you gonna introduce us to this lovely miss?" the other one asked with a cheeky grin.

Jordan had been listening to another man's complaints. Now he swung around, met Molly's eyes for a heart-stopping moment, then drawled, "This is Molly Capshaw... I think."

"You think?" she repeated.

"I don't see any rings," he explained with a slight shrug. "Doesn't mean you can't be married."

A shiver slid down her spine. "I'm not married."

"You're out with her and you don't know her marital status?" The cheeky workman's grin widened. "Whoa!"

They all laughed, and to Molly's amusement Jordan actually looked nonplussed. One of them clapped him on the back. Jordan finally found his tongue. "Molly works for Westwind. I wouldn't say this is social, would you?" he asked her.

"No." Her answer was too quick. Knowing looks slid their way as the men left.

Jordan let it pass, sliding opposite Molly in the booth and glancing at the chalkboard on the wall that listed the menu. "I probably shouldn't have brought you here."

"You'll get teased mercilessly?" She almost smiled.

"I'll certainly get asked a lot of questions."

"Do all of them work for you?"

"Most of them. They worked for my father until I took over the business."

Mention of Foster was certainly a cold dose of reality. Molly squinted at the menu, hiding her feelings. She could sense Jordan's eyes on her, and she ignored him. Being with him wasn't easy. It would never be easy. In fact, it hurt continually.

"What would you recommend?" she inquired in a voice she barely recognized.

"It's all pretty good. Better than anything at the Hutt, anyway."

She shot him a glance. "I'll just have a bowl of fruit and a muffin."

"Safe."

"What are you going to have?" she asked, reading more into that last comment than he probably meant.

"Eggs Tijuana." He gave her an ironic look. "They're made with Tabasco sauce and cilantro."

"Dangerous," she replied.

The corners of his mouth twitched. "Yesterday I had oatmeal, if it makes you feel any better."

"You did not."

Jordan's deep blue eyes stared her down in a way that rollicked her pulse. "All right. I didn't," he admitted quietly.

"Don't do that, Jordan," she warned him. "Don't lie to me."

"Molly, there are lies, and there are lies."

"Everything with you is a lie!"

It just burst out. She hadn't even known it was there, but as soon as the words were out she knew they were true.

Jordan knew it, too. His expression subtly changed, became harder. "I've got some things I want to say. I might as well say them before this conversation deteriorates into a slanging match. I'm sorry about the baby. I'm sorry about a lot of things, but I'm sorry about the baby most of all."

He'd knocked out her underpinnings with one blow. Speechless, Molly searched the chalkboard menu, the scrawled words blurring before her eyes. *I'm not going to cry!* she thought in horror. But tears burned, welled. She blinked them away unsuccessfully. They fell in rapid succession. She scrubbed her face, shocked.

"I didn't know you were pregnant," he went on unsteadily. "And I didn't know you were in the van."

"I know. I know." She nodded briskly, jerkily.

"I never would have chased Tyler. I was so angry and crazy. I can't change what happened. I wish I could, but I can't. And I'm...sorry."

"Don't...please. I don't want to..." She couldn't control herself. She had to get out. Get away.

"Molly," he murmured unevenly.

"Please, Jordan!"

She stared at him through a hot blur. The lines beside his mouth were deeply embedded. It had hurt him. It had hurt them both.

"I just want the pain to go away," she choked out, her voice cracking into a tiny sob.

He closed his eyes and inhaled sharply, deeply, holding it in for the longest ten beats of Molly's heart. Exhaling, he looked at her and nodded, his mouth twisting. "So do I," he admitted.

There wasn't a lot left to say after that. The waitress came for their order and neither of them said a word. They ordered, waited for the food, then left without eating. They walked in silence to Jordan's car, slipping inside by mutual, unspoken consent. Jordan drove back to the strip mall. Molly felt drained. She wanted to melt into the seat and never get out.

"I'm going down to San Diego tonight," he said. "Spending the night there. I'm leaving right now."

Molly looked at him, confused. "You're not working?"

"Not anymore. I don't think I can. I sure as hell know I don't want to." He shifted, the leather seats creaking beneath his weight, reminding her of the long-ago creak of his leather jacket when they'd first kissed, first touched. "Some things are happening in my life. I've gotta get some perspective."

She nodded. There was no need to comment. It had nothing to do with her.

His gaze narrowed on her face. He looked . . . intense. Molly couldn't help responding to his appeal. In a purely feminine way, she wanted just one more night with him.

Shock rippled through her. What was she thinking? God! She was nuts.

"Come with me."

"What?" she whispered, sure her ears had played tricks on her.

"Come with me. I want to work this out. I want to get over it, and maybe I'm crazy but I think it would help if we were together. Just to talk,'' he added quickly, apparently realizing his meaning could be misconstrued.

''I don't think so.'' She forced a half laugh.

''One thing I know, Molly. You and I never resolved what we had together, and it still makes a difference—whether you want to admit it or not. It's there. It's still there. It couldn't hurt like this if it wasn't there.''

''I am not in love with you,'' she bit out unsteadily.

''And I'm not in love with you,'' he responded brutally. ''And maybe we never loved each other. But whatever the hell it was, it was powerful. Powerful enough to matter *ten years later!* I want to get over it, Molly. I don't want to wait any longer.''

She gazed up at him, her eyes full of doubts. ''You think being together will really help?''

''Nothing else has.''

Could she stand to spend a day with him? Twenty-four hours or maybe a bit longer. And a night. ''Where would we stay?'' she asked cautiously.

''I don't care. We'll check into a hotel. You can have a room on a separate floor, if you like.'' He sighed. ''It's all been bottled up so long, I don't know if any of this will make any difference anyway.''

Something stirred to life inside her. She didn't like it. It was dangerous. Tempting. A sleeping tiger slowly stretching. She stared at him, into the depths of his eyes, into his aching, tarnished soul.

She saw her own reflection.

''Okay,'' she said.

Without a word, he started the engine and turned the nose of the Mustang south.

Chapter Ten

They drove straight to the hotel, a fabulous, sprawling mission-style resort crowned with pink tiles and surrounded by lush jade trees and bougainvillea. It was hot as they walked side by side, in shared silence, across the hexagonal tiles of the atrium, accompanied by the music of a tall, splashing fountain.

"Two suites," Jordan told the reception girl briskly.

"Just a single for me," Molly spoke up.

Jordan was terse. "I'm paying."

"No."

"Yes."

"*No,*" Molly insisted through a tight smile. Her eyes flashed warnings she had scrupulously kept to herself during the long trip to San Diego. However, Jordan wasn't about to heed them. He was glad she'd agreed to come, but sometimes a man had to do what a man had to do.

He handed his credit card to the woman, ignoring Molly. Her sharp hiss of breath told him the battle had just begun. With a start, he realized he looked forward to it. No. *Relished* it. He'd had yes-men surrounding him from the moment he'd joined Montgomery Industries, and it was refreshing and soothing—downright intoxicating, really—to be with someone who could do something besides blather corporate policy.

"I'll take the first bus back to Los Angeles if you try to pay my bill," she gritted in an undertone.

"Let's not get into an argument."

"Jordan."

He focused his full attention on her. Her hazel eyes were dark with suppressed anger. Her lips were set in a stubborn line. High points of color flamed in her cheeks, and her arms were crossed beneath her breasts. Her posture only succeeded in pushing her breasts slightly upward, drawing his attention, so that it was all he could do not to glance downward, to the soft, lush swelling beneath her plum-colored sweater.

"I don't know what the hell I'm doing here," she muttered for his ears only, "but it's not to be your expense!"

"Fine. You want to pay? Pay!" Yanking out his wallet, he pulled the weathered check she'd scratched out to him from where it had been carefully folded. He ripped it into tiny pieces in front of her nose. The yellow "confetti" floated and twinkled down to her feet. "But I'll be damned if I let you pay for Buzz Bentley, too."

"Fine," she snapped. "We don't owe each other anything."

Jordan growled beneath his breath.

"Any luggage?" the receptionist timidly asked.

"No," they barked back in unison.

In the elevator they didn't look at each other. Jordan punched the button for the fifth floor. They had adjoining rooms. He hadn't asked for them, but then again, he hadn't *not* asked. Molly didn't appear to realize it yet. Undoubtedly another fight in the making.

The elevator doors hissed open. Jordan led the way, stopping at his door. Molly's steps slowed and when she found herself at the door next to his, she glanced his way accusingly.

"So sue me," he said, banging his way inside.

Alone, he yanked off his coat and strode straight to the minibar at the end of the suite. Molly's suite was on the other side of the far wall. The connecting door was directly in his line of sight. He'd be damned if he unlocked his side. If she wanted to see him, it would be by the hall door. He wasn't issuing any invitations.

So what are you doing here with her?

"Damned if I know." He twisted open a beer and drank half of it in one gulp. A real beer, if you please. Forget that light stuff that was a halfway house to mineral water.

His bark of laughter sounded hollow in the empty room. Scowling, he finished the rest of the beer and strolled to the balcony. Dusk had fallen, and lights pulsed and glittered below, bright and soft in the warm night.

Sighing, Jordan sank onto one of the outdoor chairs, wishing the permanent weight crushing his chest would disappear. He closed his eyes and cradled his head with his hands. His senses came alive and lust grew into a hard knot in his stomach.

He wanted Molly.

"No," he gritted through his teeth, begging himself to listen. He couldn't have her. She hated him. He wasn't sure he liked her, either. Of course, his sex drive had never listened to reason. Why should he expect it to suddenly develop a conscience now?

Half an hour passed, and Molly made no attempt to contact him. A part of him—the still-marginally-sane part—didn't want to contact her, either. But he'd set the wheels in motion for this rendezvous, and avoiding her now wouldn't accomplish anything.

Julie Huntington is your fiancée....

Shaking his head, Jordan climbed to his feet and strode determinedly to the connecting door, rapping his knuckles loudly against the panel.

The noise jolted Molly from a half trance, and she gasped in surprise. "Oh, for God's sake," she muttered, annoyed with herself as she crossed the room to twist open her half of the connecting door. She'd been expecting him to call or knock. That's why they were here, right? To sort through this emotional baggage? So why was she ready to jump out of her skin?

"Ready for dinner?" he asked curtly.

"Yes."

He chose to cross her room on the way to the hallway door, and he glanced around briefly, as if expecting her room to be different from his. They left the room without closing the connecting doors. Molly was completely conscious of that fact, but she said nothing. Her glaring omission ruled her thoughts all the way to the dining room, stuck like some ominous vision in her mind.

Oh, for God's sake! Stop being an idiot, Molly!

To make herself feel better, she childishly ignored him. Now that they were finally together Jordan seemed reluctant to talk, as well. She ordered a salad. He had fresh seafood. Chasing around pieces of romaine lettuce with her fork, Molly wished she could work up an appetite. For no reason at all she recalled those long-ago sandwiches she and Jordan had shared on their backpacking trip. Tuna fish? She couldn't remember.

She hadn't been able to eat then, either.

"What are you thinking about?" Jordan ran his thumbnail over the label on his beer, peeling it back, his gaze focused intensely on his own action, as if it held all of life's mysteries. Her eyes followed the track of his thumb, too. It was easier than looking directly at him.

"This is kind of uncomfortable," she admitted.

He nodded. "I thought it might be easier."

"I wish we hadn't come here."

He glanced up at that. Startled, she met his gaze, then wished she hadn't. His eyes could see right through her, strip her bare. There was no way to hide anything from Jordan. They knew too much about each other.

"Maybe it wasn't such a hot idea," he agreed, surprising her. "They say confession's good for the soul, but it sure as hell isn't easy."

"Confession?"

His lips quirked, and for a moment she didn't think he was going to respond. When he did, he blew her away. "I was really in love with you. It wasn't puppy love. It was the real thing, and I don't think I appreciated it enough."

She released her breath with a shocked squeak.

"I would change a lot of it." He frowned, his expression harsh, almost forbidding. "Michael . . . Tyler . . . But I don't know if I'd change what happened between us."

"What do you mean?" She was scared to even ask.

"A lot of people never feel that kind of love. I'd say most people don't. But it was worth knowing it exists."

She knew how difficult this was for him. Only a complete social moron could miss the waves of emotion he was emitting. She struggled for some kind of answer.

"You've never felt that way since?" she asked lightly.

He turned his head slowly, assessing her frankly. "Did you feel the same way? I can't tell."

She was crushing her hands together so tightly they ached. "Yes."

"Have you felt the same way since?"

"No," she choked out.

"Do you think either of us ever will?"

There was a beat of silence. "No."

"Is it that rare?" he asked, curious.

It could be a philosophy class. A rhetorical discussion among interested students. But the resonance was too deep, the vibes she felt were too primal.

"Yes," she said with certainty. "It's that rare."

He nodded. She wasn't telling him something he didn't know already. He'd just needed her corroboration. Quietly, he remarked, "Then I don't know whether I'm sorry it's gone or not."

They lapsed into silence. Molly gave up trying to swallow another bite, and Jordan pushed his plate aside. He downed the rest of his beer, never bothering with the glass, then gave her a quelling glare when she made noise about paying the bill.

What next? she wondered nervously as they left the restaurant. Silently, she followed him outside and together they walked down to the harbor docks. The air smelled salty and musty and fishy. The sky was gray-black, the full moon almost blotted out by mist and fog. Stars that had been visible earlier were blanketed except for one or two sharp gems, dull pinpoints of light against a night so thick it felt like cotton.

"I'm amazed you say you really loved me." The words were out of her mouth before she realized she'd even thought them. Horrified, she stopped short.

"It's taken years on a psychiatrist's couch, but I can admit it now."

"You never went to a psychiatrist in your life."

"True. Sorry. I didn't mean to lie again." The moment of levity passed. "A bad habit."

"You never told me you loved me when we were together."

"I had trouble with those words. I still do. They sound trite, don't they? Like a parrot. Say the words, and wait for your partner to say them back."

He was speaking from experience, she realized with an uncomfortable jolt, but not experience with her.

"You're in love with someone else now, aren't you?" Molly said lightly. "And you're still having trouble saying you love her. You can tell *me* you loved me because it's over, it's safe. You just can't tell her."

Jordan hunched his shoulders and took a deep breath. "This doesn't feel safe."

"But it is." Knowing Jordan was involved with another woman empowered Molly even while it hurt. "I hated you for that letter you sent me."

"My letter?" He was surprised.

"You were so cold and clinical. I already knew it was over. You didn't have to write it down."

"I wrote that letter because it was what you wanted to hear."

She gazed at him in disbelief. "What I wanted to hear? Nobody wants to hear that! Do you know what kind of state I was in? I'd lost my baby. *Our* baby! And my brother was still in a hospital, fighting for his life. It nearly killed me, Jordan! You couldn't have hurt me more."

"You wanted that chapter closed," he insisted. "My father told me what you'd said."

"What I'd said?" Molly repeated incredulously. "The only time I saw your father was when he gave me *your* letter."

"No."

"Yes!"

Confusion and anger warred in his blue eyes. He dragged his gaze from her face and stared across the inky water. "You wanted it over," he insisted. "That's why you didn't contact me when I went through the trial."

"That's what your father told you?" To Jordan's slow nod, she said flatly, "I never talked to him about my feelings. He gave me your letter and made it clear it was over between us. I read the letter and sent you one back."

Shoving his hands through his hair, Jordan bit out, "Maybe it doesn't matter how it happened. All that matters is that it did."

"Your father lied to you," Molly whispered tremulously.

"Sounds like he wasn't taking any chances on my future," Jordan agreed bitterly.

Bittersweet understanding flooded through Molly. She could visualize it so clearly now. Foster had planted the seeds of doubt in Jordan's mind. He'd been the impetus behind the letter. For a shining moment, she considered what might have been, had she never received that letter. She would have gone on loving Jordan despite everything. There might have been a future for them, after all.

Jordan's cool, practical voice brought her back to the present. "Your letter summed up your feelings pretty clearly, so things would have turned out this way no matter what."

"No...no...you don't understand. I was really hurt and down," Molly apologized in a rush. She couldn't remember each and every accusation, but the bitter hatred she'd felt wasn't something she was likely to forget.

"It was my fault you lost the baby."

"No, it wasn't. I didn't blame you. I just wanted to hurt you. For hurting me."

"You blamed me," he argued. "I blame myself."

Molly shook her head. "Don't," she said softly.

"I wanted to fight Tyler. I wanted to tear him apart. I wanted to make him pay for taking my brother away from me." Jordan's voice was low and rough. "But I never meant to hurt you. I wanted to die when I saw you in that van...."

"Let's not talk about it anymore." She hugged herself, shivering deep inside.

"Okay." He inhaled several times and let each breath out with slow deliberation. "I've been over it and over it. At night. In bed. In time, it doesn't hurt so bad, but you never forget."

"Some people never let you forget."

That got his attention. "Me?"

"I was thinking of my brother."

Jordan was stunned. *"What?"*

"Tyler can't let it rest. He's just so bitter and angry. He won't get on with his life, and I wonder if he ever will."

"Does he blame *you?*"

"No!" Molly jerked in surprise. "No. That would be crazy."

But was it? There was no denying that Tyler always took a little piece out of her whenever he could. Disturbed, Molly walked away from Jordan to the end of the dock, hugging herself tightly, her gaze on some boats bobbing against the pilings. She felt, rather than saw, Jordan come up behind her.

"Has any of this helped?" he wondered aloud, sounding as if he seriously doubted it.

"I don't hate you anymore."

He made a sound somewhere between a laugh and a groan. "Good."

"Who is she?"

"Who?" he asked automatically.

"This woman you're in love with." Molly twisted to look at him. "You don't have to tell me if you don't want to, but seeing as we're being honest . . ."

She smiled, and Jordan suddenly found himself defenseless against that beautiful crescent of lips and teeth. Reason fled for a moment too long. He stared hard, wondering what would happen if he crushed his mouth against hers. He had to drag his gaze away. "I'm not in love with her."

"Another lie," she accused with gentle humor.

"No."

"Jordan—"

"I don't want to talk about her," he said tersely, focusing pointedly on the flashing red beacon atop a distant buoy. "I've seen a lot of women these past ten years—none of them worth telling you about. I've thought about marriage. I've thought about children. I want it all, but it just hasn't happened."

There was silence. Dead silence.

Sensing he'd said something dreadfully wrong, Jordan glanced at her. She was staring at the same buoy and wouldn't meet his gaze. "What?" he demanded.

"Nothing."

"Come on, Molly. This is about honesty, remember?"

"It's not pertinent to this."

"What did I say? Marriage? Children?" He watched her intently. Molly flinched at the mention of children, though she tried to hide it. "Children," he repeated. Then, more softly, "The baby."

Molly seemed to want to say something but couldn't get the words past her lips. Twice she opened her mouth; twice she closed it in acute distress.

"I'm sorry," he said, meaning it with all his heart.

"No, it's not the baby. Not really. I don't want you to feel bad, or guilty."

He waited, accurately sensing there was more.

She struggled. "It's unlikely that I'll ever have children."

He blinked. "Because of the accident? Oh, *God...*" Jordan staggered backward. Noise. Volumes of noise blasted inside his skull. He'd done that to her, too! It was his fault! He pressed his hands to his temples. "Molly," he choked out.

Her perfume enveloped him along with her arms. Shocked, he almost jerked out of her embrace. It took all his willpower to stay still, to accept her comfort. An ache filled his chest. Ballooning. Suffocating.

"Don't...don't..." she whispered. "I'm sorry I told you like this. It's not your fault. It's just something that happened."

"I've heard that enough times!" he gasped bitterly. He'd fallen into some black hole. He wasn't even sure he was standing. But her scent was strong. He breathed deeply, choking, strangling. He turned to her, his bent face to her neck. Pain pulsed. There was something violently wrong with accepting comfort from Molly. He'd hurt her too badly.

He tried to get a grip. "Molly."

Vaguely he realized her embrace was very circumspect. She'd reached for him because he'd needed it, but she didn't want to be close. He unclenched the hand tangled in her hair. He tried to pull back. His balance was off. He stumbled.

"No." He held up his hands when she automatically tried to help him. "No, don't. I'm okay."

"Are you sure?" She was very serious. In control.

"Yeah," he lied.

"You're not going to fall into the water or something?" she tried lightly.

He shook his head.

"Should we go back, do you think?"

He nodded.

He didn't remember the walk back. He must have acted reasonably normal, however, because Molly gave up asking if he was going to be all right.

He was never going to be all right. He'd lived with megatons of guilt over what he'd done to Tyler and Molly but had learned to accept it. Tonight she'd tipped the scales—a feather's weight more—and the whole damn thing had come crashing down.

He wanted to die.

"Jordan."

He jerked around. She was standing in the connecting door, still fully dressed. He'd been sitting on the end of his bed, staring into space.

"I've stopped hating you, okay? Don't make me feel sorry for you."

"Molly..." he began earnestly, but there was absolutely nothing to say to make things right.

She pulled a chair away from his desk and set it in front of him. "It's okay. Really." A strange look came over her face. Beauty and poignancy and regret. "You're making me remember why I fell in love with you, and I don't like it one bit."

Her expression was somber but sweet. He saw no anger. He couldn't understand it. He was angry through and through. At himself, at the fates, at Foster. He wanted to scream. He wanted to drag her beneath him and make love all night.

"Do you ever wonder what it would be like to start over?" he rasped, shocked yet not really surprised by the turn of his thoughts. He's always wanted Molly. Always.

"You can't start over."

"*You* can't start over," he corrected. "*I* can."

"Jordan, don't do this!" She jumped to her feet, but he reached out and grabbed her wrist. He couldn't help himself.

"Molly, I want a second chance. I want it so badly I feel sick."

"You feel guilt. This isn't what you think."

"Isn't it?"

He gazed up at her, and Molly felt herself drawn into those pain-filled eyes. It was a ploy. A trick. A checkmate in the Montgomery game of life. She was too smart for this. She'd managed beautifully until now, even though tears had burned in her throat when pain had nearly brought him to his knees.

He touched her. Her skin was hot. She slowly shook her head but he drew her closer, down to his bed. Her knee connected with the mattress. Her other leg touched his, tangled across his lap. She sat down in an ungainly heap beside him, her leg dangling over his.

He twisted to her, sliding his hands up her forearms to grip her upper arms. He'd expected her to leap away.

And, she wanted to! She was frozen, hypnotized.

"I don't want this," she whispered.

"Then make me stop."

"I will. I'm warning you. I really will."

His hands moved slowly, agonizingly slowly, across her shoulders and around her neck, drawing her face forward by inches. She could easily escape. At any moment she could be free. Yet, she couldn't move. She didn't want to. She was susceptible. So susceptible.

Blood rushed to her head. She focused on his lips. The last time she'd kissed him had been in the heat of love-making. It was years ago. An eternity. Only a moment ago...

His lips—warm, eager—touched hers. There was the briefest hesitation, as if he expected her to make good on her threat and stop him in some painful way, then with a groan his mouth covered hers with possessive abandon.

Molly emitted a squeak of protest, belated though it might have been. Jordan took no notice. He leaned over her, overwhelming, his kisses drowning her common sense. One moment they were seated, locked in a heated embrace; the next, Molly's back was against the mattress and he was half lying atop her, stifling any objection by the sheer potency of his kisses.

She moaned. What was she doing? This was the kind of lunacy that had created all their problems in the first place. And it had been years, *years,* since she'd made love to a man. Never mind that it felt like an instant ago. She didn't want to make love to Jordan.

He's the only man you've ever made love to.

There was danger in that thought, but the heat of the moment consumed it before Molly could sort it all out.

He kissed her neck, trailing his tongue against her skin. Warning bells rang, but she closed her ears. She wanted to touch him just as much. Taste him. Press herself close—so close.

His hand was at the small of her back, rubbing in anxious, tight circles. It moved over her hips and buttocks, cupping her bottom tightly against him. There was no doubt what he was feeling. The surge of his manhood against her made her head swim with dangerous delight. Yes, she wanted to make love. Right now. With no regrets and no strings attached.

She moaned and arched, dragging his mouth back to hers. Jordan's breath was expelled with a rush of relief. He kissed her hard, pressing her down, covering her body with his. His tongue thrust past her teeth, in and out, the rhythm firing her blood with its inherent demand.

Her fingers dug into his shoulders, slid down his muscled back. She wanted to rip his shirt off. *Careful,* some sane, distant voice warned. On the heels of that thought: *Please, please, hurry!*

He yanked off his shirt in fitful jerks that might have been funny if she wasn't in such a fever. He glanced down at her. Whatever he saw in her face made his jaw slacken.

"Molly," he whispered, his lips capturing the small moan of surrender she offered in response.

Free of the confining shirt, his back was rippled with taut muscles. Her fingers discovered every single one. She pulled him fully atop her. He moaned, then choked out a chuckle.

"Slow down," he murmured through silent laughter. "I can't take it."

Closing her ears, Molly disobeyed. Her hands roamed down to his belt, his hips. His spasmodic jerk told her she was playing with fire, but she didn't care.

"Take these off," she said, tugging on a belt loop.

"Wait..."

She gazed at him through heavy-lidded eyes. He unbuttoned her blouse, pulling it open. One finger traced the lace edge of her bra. His tongue followed, wet and hot against her skin. She moaned, her head tossing on the pillow.

He quickly dispensed with his clothes. A muscular twist, the rasp of a zipper, and the satin strength of his masculine form was hot against her. She wore jeans. He wriggled them over her hips. And then she was in her bra and panties and that was all that separated them.

To her shock he ran his hand lightly over her breasts, her rib cage, to the heat between her legs and back again. It was feather-light and teasing. She shifted, wanting more. It was embarrassing, too, the way he watched her, yet she gazed at him just as raptly. She couldn't believe this. Neither, apparently, could he.

He kissed her neck, then the dusky hollow between her breasts, unfastening the lacy slip of cloth and pulling it down her arms. She held her breath as his thumb lazily explored one nipple. Molly's fingers dug into the covers and she fought the moan of desire filling her throat. She shouldn't want this at all. She shouldn't want it this badly.

"Don't wait," she panted.

"I don't want to rush." He sounded out of breath.

"I do."

"No."

"Jordan, don't make me beg you to—"

His mouth swooped down, cutting off her pleas. She was past reason. She met his kisses eagerly. There was no sensual, slow session of lovemaking. It had been too long. Too much time had been wasted. She arched upward as his mouth closed over one nipple, drawing on it greedily. She writhed like a wild thing beneath him, and it shattered the last vestiges of Jordan's control.

He yanked off her panties and fell upon her, desperately trying to fight off the elemental need that roared over them like a thunderous wave. But it was too late. He covered her body with his own, pushing against her, driving into her. Her cry was one of ecstasy. She clung to him, stunned by the quick fierceness of her climax. Sounds of pleasure erupted from low in her throat. With a groan of release, Jordan poured himself into her, immersed in humbling, powerful forces that shocked his jaded senses.

He'd forgotten what lovemaking could be. He'd forgotten its strength. He'd forgotten what it was to make love to someone you truly loved.

They lay together, chests heaving in tandem, out of breath, spent and in complete denial of everything but this moment.

It was Molly who stirred first. Jordan pulled back to look at her sweet face. Her eyes were closed, their dark lashes resting against the creaminess of her skin. She lifted her eyelids slowly, staring at him through those wide hazel eyes he loved so much. An arrow of fear shot through him. There was no love there. Just a cynical, self-deprecating appreciation of her own weakness. He knew that look well. It too often mirrored his own feelings.

"Jordan," she whispered, a pink blush slowly rising in her face.

"I'm sure I don't want to hear what you're going to say." He kissed her cheek gently, then the curve of her jaw, the shell of her ear.

"I've lost my mind."

"Good." His lips curved into a smile against the soft waves of hair at her temple.

"Do I have to ask you to get off me?"

She wasn't really serious. Her voice was soft, drugged with pleasure. "Don't say anything," he whispered, refusing to let the moment unwind.

Sighing, she closed her eyes again. Jordan slowly, sensually, began re-exploring the areas he'd already plundered.

"Don't," she said, but there was no conviction in the demand. He kept right on kissing and caressing and holding her. She chuckled softly, her light, bright laughter surrounding him, reminding him of how much he'd loved her sweetness and joy.

"I can't help myself."

"Stop it, Jordan!" She was fighting an out-and-out belly laugh.

"My male ego should be irreparably damaged that you're laughing at me."

"You're right!" To his relief and delight she pulled his mouth to hers for a soul-stirring kiss, before pushing him gently away. "It's just so wonderful," she added with true Molly honesty.

"Yes," he agreed, disappointed to watch the gaiety leave her expression as she belatedly recalled the problems and the reality of their present. "It is."

Chapter Eleven

Molly awakened to a sense of foreboding. Her muscles protested as she stretched, then jerked to full consciousness, struggling upward with the sheet to her breasts.

Jordan! Oh, no!

Panicked, Molly snapped her gaze to the other side of the bed. He wasn't there. She collapsed against the pillows with relief so intense she could scarcely catch her breath. It hadn't been a dream. She was too realistic to harbor that hope for long. No, the painful truth was she'd spent the night making love with him, and it had been so incredible that she'd pushed aside every single reason to steer clear of a Montgomery, just so that she could wallow in pleasure.

The earth, she thought irritably, had definitely moved.

But he wasn't here now.

Quick as a cat she tossed back the covers, then was momentarily frozen at the sight of her own nakedness. Memories floated back like stardust. She clamped her mind fiercely shut, but it wedged open. She remembered his hair-roughened legs pinning hers down, the smooth, hard muscles of his back, his slightly salty skin, his haunting, male scent.

"Oh, no," she murmured, covering her face with her hands.

"Molly?"

He came in from the balcony wearing yesterday's clothes—the only clothes they'd brought. She stared at him, and his gaze drifted over her body.

Fighting a shriek of exposure, Molly snatched up her underwear and clothing, torn between an urge to run out of his room and the need to hang on to some modicum of pride and calmly sit down and get dressed. She chose the latter. Thumping down on his bed, she yanked on her clothes with more haste than sense.

He didn't say anything. She couldn't tell if he was watching her or not. It was nerve-racking. When she was safely in her jeans and shirt she whirled to face him. He was standing exactly where he'd stopped when he'd first walked in.

"Are you ready to leave?" she asked, glancing past him to the outside where the sun was shining high in the heavens. It was late. Noonish.

He shook his head. "No, Molly, listen—"

"*I'm* ready to leave."

"Wait a minute. Wait." He was struggling for control.

"Don't talk to me. Please. I just want to go home."

She almost crumpled at the flash of hurt that crossed his face. He wasn't taking this lightly, either. She didn't know whether to be glad or alarmed.

"I've got some things I need to say."

"Let me say them." Molly dug her hands in her back pockets, screwing up her courage. "Last night was a big, big mistake. We're both sorry it happened. Maybe it had to happen. I don't know. But it's over, and I don't want to think about it anymore. I'm sure you feel the same way."

"If I didn't, would it matter?" he snapped back.

"Our families don't get along. This is short-term. There's no chance it will be anything else."

"Are you trying to convince me, or yourself?"

His face flushed with anger. She was handling this all wrong, but she didn't care. Last night had been lunacy and even if he didn't realize it yet, she, Molly Capshaw, the realist, did!

"How do *you* feel?" Jordan demanded. "Can you stop long enough to tell me that?"

"I don't think that—"

"Damn it, Molly. How do you feel?" he roared.

"I don't know! *I don't know!*"

She wanted to cry. She bit down hard on her lip, fighting emotion with pain.

Jordan sighed, sounding exhausted. "Can we not worry so much about this right now?"

"Are you kidding? I'm worried sick." When he took a step toward her, she jumped away. "No, really. Please. I'm having a helluva time. I don't want to think about . . . last night."

"It's all I want to think about," he admitted with alarming candor. "I didn't know how much I wanted you until we were together. No matter what you say, it was wonderful. Better than wonderful."

She couldn't argue. Some inner voice warned her that she should, but she couldn't. He took another couple of steps her way, and Molly backed up until her shoulder blades connected with the wall. "Jordan..." she managed in a shaky voice.

Jordan crossed the rest of the distance in swift strides. Before she knew how to react, his hands were in her hair, his thumbs pulling her chin up, his mouth crushing hers. Fire leaped inside her. Spontaneous combustion.

"Damn you, I don't want this," she choked out, half-hysterically.

"You're the liar, Molly."

She squeezed her eyes closed, fighting her emotions, losing. "Yes," she admitted, digging her hands in his hair. "I am."

Within seconds they'd both fallen to the bed, and the joy and pleasure of the night before were being repeated in slow-motion ecstasy.

Halfway back to Los Angeles the doubts crept in again. This time Molly kept them to herself. There was no need to address them. Jordan had to feel them, too. Time, that ruthless friend, would take care of everything.

It was dusk when he dropped her at her car, still parked at the strip mall. They'd tarried in San Diego, dawdling over brunch, strolling along the pier, aimlessly watching the horizon. There'd been no more touching. An invisible barrier had arisen as soon as they'd left the hotel room—one neither of them was willing to scale or even approach.

Now, as Molly fumbled for her keys and climbed from the car, the weight of what they'd shared lay heavily on her conscience, filling her not with regret, exactly, but with something darned close.

She opened her mouth to thank him, then realized how ridiculous that would sound. The quirk of his lips made her realize he'd read her mind.

"It doesn't end here, you know," he said as she unlocked her car.

She glanced back at him without answering.

"It can't."

Molly slipped into the car, gently closed the door, then rolled down the window, looking up at him but feeling more in control now that she was safely inside. "We went away to talk some things out. Get past the past, so to speak." She laughed shortly. "I don't know if we accomplished that, but I do know this *is* where it ends."

"Why?" He put one hand on the doorframe, as if expecting her to quickly roll up the window.

"Our families will never—"

"To hell with them," he snapped fiercely.

"It won't work."

"You don't want to even try?"

"Now, you're getting it!" Molly shot back, rolling up the window.

"You're not afraid of what they'll think, you're afraid of yourself!" As the window slid snugly into its felt groove, Jordan pulled his fingers away in the nick of time. Molly refused to look at him. Turning the ignition, she backed out of the lot. He was right. She was afraid of herself. She'd never before let herself go like last night. She'd never been so reckless.

You were reckless when you were a teenager....

"Molly, you crazy fool," she half sobbed, unable to keep herself from glancing in the rearview mirror one last time, unable to stop the funny little kick of her heart at seeing Jordan staring after her.

By the time she reached her apartment she was in a blue funk capped by a simmering rage. Rage at herself. At the fates. At Jordan for being so damned attractive! Why was it other men couldn't hold that same fascination? Paul, for instance. Here was a man who wanted to marry her and was just waiting for her consent. But Jordan... Oh, no, he was *demanding* love from her, with no possible chance of it surviving.

Love? She shuddered as she stomped up the steps to her door. *That's really stretching the truth, isn't it?* Nowhere had there been any mention of love. Not that she was in love with him. She would have to be totally insane to still be in love with him; and if nothing else, she, Molly Capshaw, was eminently sane.

Before she could unlock her door it opened before her eyes. "What?" she cried in shock—before she remembered that Tyler had called earlier in the week and said he was going to be there.

"Where were you last night?" he demanded.

"Oh, Tyler!" She'd told him she was going to be home, had even left a spare key with the manager in case she was gone when he arrived. How could she have forgotten?

Blood flooded her cheeks, burning. "I'm really sorry."

"I stayed here all night! Where were you?" he repeated bluntly.

"San Diego. With a friend. Have you eaten? We could go out or order pizza or something?"

"Well, you weren't with Paul, since he called looking for you, too. And it wasn't your idiot neighbor, that Jamie-person."

"What do you mean by that?" Molly gasped, forgetting her own problems for a moment. "Jamie Lee is nothing but nice!"

"Not to me."

"To everybody," Molly insisted, tossing her purse on the kitchen counter. "If she wasn't nice to you, it's probably because you provoked her."

"Who were you with?"

"You are not my keeper, Tyler. As I'm not yours." Molly was utterly serious. "I'm sorry I forgot you were coming, but you didn't exactly give me a lot of notice."

"Well, next time I'll send a candygram!" he hurled at her. "Excuse me for forgetting my etiquette."

"What you forgot was that I'm a person with a separate life from yours!"

His face registered hurt. Molly didn't back down. She was irked and feeling more than a little guilty. She'd be damned if she took this from her brother.

"I had some good news to tell you, but if you don't want to hear it . . ."

Holding on to her temper, she asked, "What is it?"

"Nothing, really." He shrugged. "I registered for classes, winter term."

Her fury evaporated. "That's great! Where? In L.A.?"

"Yep." His lips were tight. "Got my own van so I don't have to rely on Sharon."

Dangerous territory. "You and Sharon aren't together anymore?"

"Thought I could bunk with you for a while. Mom and Dad think it's a great idea, as long as I don't interfere with your private life," he added with heavy-handed irony.

"You won't interfere with my private life," she snapped. A kernel of regret grew inside her. Regret that she was going to get her way: she and Jordan would never see each other again.

A knock on the door startled them both. Tyler looked askance at Molly, who shook her head. But her knees nearly buckled beneath her when she opened the door and saw Jordan on the other side.

"I didn't like the way things . . . ended. . . ." As his gaze fell on Tyler, he trailed off, his eyes glued to the wheelchair.

Molly didn't have to be a mind reader to understand and sympathize with his shock. She herself braced for the coming explosion.

Tyler blinked several times. "Montgomery?" he croaked out.

Jordan drew an aborted breath, came to himself, nodded.

Tyler swung around to look at Molly. He was shattered. Stunned. Childlike in his complete and utter betrayal. Her throat closed.

"Tyler," she whispered.

"You conniving tramp," he said in wonder.

Jordan tensed. Molly turned to him imploringly. "Don't! You'll only make it worse!"

"You've been seeing him all along. It doesn't matter that he sent me to this wheelchair or that he *murdered* your baby! You're still a Montgomery whore!"

"Oh, God," Jordan said on a breath. He stared at Tyler as if he'd grown horns.

"Jordan, just leave. Please." Molly pushed him toward the still-open door.

"I don't trust him not to hurt you!" Jordan was a wall of strength and purpose. He brushed Molly's hands away as if she were inconsequential.

"Call the police, Molly," Tyler growled in an ugly tone. "This is harassment, plain and simple."

"Tyler!" She glared at him.

"The man drove me off the road, put us both in the hospital. We'll get a restraining order, and if he still comes around we'll send him to jail where he can rot!"

Jordan was on the balls of his feet.

"Jordan, don't." She grabbed his arm, gazing at him through wide, appealing eyes.

"You killed my brother," Jordan reminded Tyler in a strangled voice. "When you were trying to kill me."

"Get out of here, you bastard!" Tyler screeched with wrath.

"Jordan, please, just go!" Molly pushed against him with all her strength. He staggered backward a couple of steps, his gaze pinning Tyler. Molly thrust against him again until they were both on the front walkway. She slammed the door behind them.

Jordan looked slightly sick. "I didn't know," he said in delayed shock.

"He's bitter."

Jordan hesitated. "He was right about one thing— I put him in that wheelchair."

"No, you didn't. You know as well as I do, the van would have gone over anyway. You can't fake that kind of evidence. Tyler knows it, too."

Jordan stared at her in amazement.

Molly made a sound of weary regret. "I wanted to hate you with all my heart. It's better than thinking my brother's a hotheaded killer, isn't it? And it made me feel better to direct all my anger and grief at you! You could afford it. You're a Montgomery, for crying out loud. And Montgomerys never play fair, so they deserve to be hated."

"Molly..." He reached a hand out to her, which she ignored.

"It wasn't fair I lost my baby," she went on fiercely. "And it wasn't fair that Tyler was hurt. And it wasn't fair that Michael was killed. But it had to be someone's fault, and it couldn't be *Tyler's!*"

He shook his head, denying what he was hearing.

"It was your fault. I wanted it to be your fault!" Tears slid unheeded down the curve of her cheeks. "And then you sent me that letter, and I knew I was right. So, don't think things can be different now, because they can't!''

Sobs racked her chest. Molly fought them, but they hiccuped one after another. Jordan started to move closer and she shook her head, knowing his comfort would only make things worse. But he grabbed her arm anyway, holding her so tightly it almost hurt.

''I'm . . . sorry,'' he said again.

''Please, just go,'' she whispered.

''All right. But it isn't over.''

Through a haze of pain and sorrow, she heard his footsteps retreating down the stairs.

Chapter Twelve

Dixie loped ahead of Molly, zigzagging and capering along the bike path, tongue lolling from her smiling dog's mouth. Molly, her expression as stern as Dixie's was friendly, jogged in a steady, straight line. Endorphins be damned. She didn't need a high; she needed peace of mind.

After two miles, she stopped, bent over and leaned on her knees, gulping down deep, lung-piercing breaths. Dixie gamboled all around her, leaping and barking and generally making a nuisance of herself. A high, thin whistle sounded. Dixie froze and stared in the sound's direction. The whistle shrilled once more, and the dog took off at full gallop.

"Benedict Arnold," Molly murmured, straightening her back.

That caught her up short. For the last five weeks *she'd* been the Benedict Arnold. Just ask anyone in her family: Tyler, who wouldn't deign to speak to her any longer; her father, who'd gotten so worked up he'd been prescribed a sedative by his doctor; and her mother, whose sad, silent gaze had been the worst of all.

She'd had no defense. She'd gone to San Diego with Jordan and spent the night with him; it hadn't taken Tyler long to put *that* scenario together. From there it had been a quick leap to the next damning conclusion—she'd made love with Jordan.

Tyler was right, up to that point, but then things got really crazy. He was certain she'd been sleeping with Jordan all along. Uncountable times over these past ten years. Yes sirree, Molly Capshaw had been sleeping with the enemy—a *Montgomery*, no less! A living, breathing monster. Quick, friends, break out the smelling salts! All the while she'd been professing to hate him, she'd been a fixture in Jordan Montgomery's bed.

It was a darned good thing Tyler had changed his mind about moving in with her. They would have been at each other's throats by now.

Groaning, Molly winced in real pain, both from the muscles in her legs and the knot in her chest. To her humiliation, she'd actually tried to explain. No one had listened. The truth was that she *had* been with Jordan. The particulars didn't much matter.

Worse still, however, was that she thought of Jordan constantly. After all the terrible revelations, she'd really expected that first weekend to be the end, no matter what he said. Maybe she hadn't totally blamed him all those years, but she'd wanted to, and she'd damned near succeeded in making herself believe it. If he'd admitted feeling that way about her, she wouldn't ever want to see him again. But Jordan was either a glutton for punishment, or more deeply committed to her than she would let herself believe.

He'd called her at home about a week after the scene with Tyler. She'd had such a terrible day at work, a lump had filled her throat as soon as she'd heard his voice. Luckily, she managed to hide her feelings. She told him not to worry about Tyler. He'd ranted and raved awhile but had finally gotten over it. A lie, naturally, but she wasn't about to tell him how full-blown this war between herself and her family had become.

But maybe he'd seen through her, because Jordan had then knocked her sideways with his own revelation.

"I told my father I'd been with you," he said in a voice laced with irony.

"How did he react?" Molly was breathless.

"Tyler should be given a medal for his restraint."

"Oh, Jordan!"

"Yeah, well, don't worry about it. Relations between us have never been great, anyway."

"But you run your father's business," Molly gasped, feeling completely guilty.

"The business is three-quarters mine. My father can disinherit me all he likes, but it's more bark than bite."

Disinherit . . . It didn't matter that it couldn't really be done. The fact that Jordan used words like that at all revealed a lot about how Foster had taken the news. He'd risked a lot by telling his father. Far more than he should have.

"I want to see you again," he said intensely before he hung up.

"No." She was definite.

"Tonight."

"No, Jordan. I can't."

"Molly, we've got something here. I don't want to lose it again."

Now, she drew a deep breath and opened her eyes. Of course, she'd agreed. He'd seduced her with his urgency. And her own needs were just as urgent, apparently, because her usually clamoring conscience had been easily defeated.

She'd met him at a secluded restaurant. They'd talked about nothing. All she could remember was the sensuality of his lips, the deep blue of his eyes, and the touch of his hand at the small of her back as he walked behind her out of the restaurant. At her door, he'd thrust his fists in his pockets and waited, staring at her silently, sexual tension crackling like lightning. Waves of desire had crashed over her. She'd taken one step toward him and *bang!*—the next thing she knew they were locked in a passionate embrace that moved directly to her bedroom where they'd made love until dawn.

"Oh, Lord!" She rubbed her hands over her face and began the long jog back to her apartment. That had been three weeks ago. Since then she'd kept him—and her own riotous desires—at bay. But she suspected it was already too late. To her amazement, delight and horror, the unthinkable had happened, and she didn't know what to do about it.

Her period was late.

Molly shook her head. She couldn't be pregnant. It was impossible. She knew it was impossible. She'd been *told* it was impossible! Her body was simply reacting to the sheer lunacy of her association with Jordan.

It couldn't go on. She would not see him again. She wouldn't.

Oh, yes, you will.

He'd called her again this afternoon. Her hand had squeezed the receiver, then grown moist with panic as Paul suddenly stepped into her office at that exact moment.

One look at her face, and Paul had known why she'd been so distant the past few weeks. Molly had hung up on Jordan without explanation.

"Who is he?" Paul had asked in a hurt tone. "I'm right, aren't I? There is someone else."

Molly had felt about an inch high. "It's kind of complicated."

"Are you sleeping with him?"

Her breath had rushed in. It astounded and infuriated her that everyone felt they had a right to know about her sex life. But then, she'd never slept with Paul. And when she hadn't answered that question, either, and realization had dawned, shattering him, she'd felt too guilty to work up much indignation against him.

"Molly..." he'd murmured, crushed.

"I'm trying not to see him," she'd answered unevenly.

"*Trying?* Don't do me any favors!"

He'd capped that with a slam of her office door just as Jordan rang back. "This isn't going to work, Jordan!" she practically screamed at him at the same moment Paul reopened her door to apologize for slamming it like a child.

They stared at each other. Jordan's name reverberated through the room. Molly quietly said goodbye to Jordan who'd warned her to not hang up on him again, then folded her arms on her desk and waited for Paul's recriminations.

There hadn't been any, of course. Too tacky for Paul. Perversely, she'd wanted a damn good row. And she'd still been in the same unsettled, angry state when she'd gotten home from work, which was precisely why she was jogging right now!

"This is too much!" she muttered, slowing to a crisp walk as she reached the parking lot on the west side of her apartment building.

Sweat dampened the front of her shirt and dried cold on her back. Swiping at her brow with the back of her hand, she stopped short upon spying a dark blue Mustang.

Confused emotions raged inside her. She didn't want to see Jordan. Not now.

Breathing deeply, she marched up the stairs. He was waiting for her at the top, watching her approach with deceptively lazy interest, one hip leaned against the rail, his black leather jacket creaking as he got to his feet. She wanted to yell at him. She hated the way he made her feel.

You love the way he makes you feel.

"What are you doing here?" she asked a bit breathlessly. It was from the run. Only from the run.

"When you hung up on me, I gave up using the phone."

"I told you I don't want to see you."

"Well, I want to see you. And I don't believe you."

Muttering under her breath, she unlocked the door, but then it stuck in its hinges. Shoving twice without success, she slammed it open with one swift, fierce kick. Jordan's sound of amusement drew her wrath, and she whipped around to glare at him as soon as they were inside. She wasn't going to let it be like last time. He was not following her to her bed.

"I don't want all the problems this is causing," she said, launching in reasonably. He was wearing jeans, and a blue chambray shirt peeked from the beneath the jacket. His throat was tan and arrowed downward to where a glimpse of crisp chest hair was visible. His arms were too muscular for a man who ran a company. That made her mad, too.

Jordan shook his head. "I don't care about the problems with your family and mine. I don't give one good damn about—"

"That's because you don't care what happens! This is just another—Montgomery acquisition!"

"Oh, Molly, come on!"

"I'll admit there's something sick and romantic about reliving the past. Look at me. I'm just as much to blame. But somebody's got to keep their head."

"Sick and romantic?" Jordan protested. "I care about you, and I want this to work. That's all."

Warily, Molly retreated farther into her tiny living room. She folded her arms across her chest and tried to ignore the sweet, delicious hope bubbling up inside her. "What are you saying?"

"I don't think it's impossible for a Montgomery and a Capshaw to be together. My father hasn't made any decisions for me yet, no matter how hard he's tried. I don't care what he thinks about this."

Molly had her own theories about that, too. "There have been times I wondered if maybe the only reason you started seeing me in Vernonia was to get back at your father."

His eyes narrowed. "It's been suggested to me that the only reason you saw me was because I was wealthy."

Molly choked. "Well, that's brutally honest. Thanks for sharing."

"The point is, neither one of those theories is right. I want to see you again. I want to make love to you. I want to be in love."

Molly's eyes were huge. She didn't doubt him. He was phenomenally serious. "With me?"

"Yes, with you," he said, impatient and amused.

"It won't work. It won't last. I can't do it!" She sounded as hysterical as she felt.

He had the audacity to smile. Worse, he started *laughing!* When he crossed the room to her, she took a half step backward, but there was no escape from the hands that slid up her arms and across her shoulders, then embraced her neck. His thumbs tucked beneath her chin, forcing her unsure gaze to his. "Don't you want to try? Don't you really?"

"Yes," she squeaked out.

When he kissed her she sighed in relief, choking on laughter when he succeeded in sweeping her into his arms, grinning down at her like a devil, and carrying her into her bedroom. Again.

"Well?" Jamie Lee demanded, arching one all-knowing brow, her dimples peeking out. "You're seeing the guy with the fabulous eyes, aren't you?"

Molly, who'd been chopping vegetables, humming tunelessly to herself, jumped about a foot and a half. "Don't you ever knock?" she complained.

"Honey, don't you ever lock your door?"

"I do when I think about it." She glanced nervously toward the bedroom, the room where she'd left Jordan sound asleep, utterly naked except for a sheet tangled around his lean, muscular limbs.

"I couldn't help but notice him," Jamie Lee revealed, plopping herself at the counter, her chin on her palms, innocent eyes turned to Molly. "I mean the man stood outside for *hours* waiting for you!"

"Hours?"

"It seemed like it." Jamie Lee eyed her levelly. "So, who is this guy?"

She opened her mouth to deny it—an automatic response, a learned reaction. She'd told Jamie Lee the whole heart-wrenching, bitter story, leaving her with the impression that she hated Jordan.

And now he was asleep in her bed.

"When I saw him waiting, I tried to talk to him, but it was clear he had one thing on his mind and he wasn't in a chatty mood. So, when did he leave?" She reached over and tried to grab a peeled carrot. Molly glared at her in mock, reproach which Jamie Lee blithefully ignored.

"He hasn't," she admitted.

Her friend's eyes widened. "Oh, my God!" She laughed. "He's *here?* In *there?*" Her gaze slid to the bedroom door. "Whoa, Molly! Things are progressing nicely."

Groaning, Molly crunched her teeth into a carrot herself, shaking her head as she chewed. "He and I have too much baggage to be doing this. It's nuts and it's juvenile."

"Oh, hell, it is not." Jamie Lee waved that away. "Life is too full of have-to's. You have to earn a living. You have to be nice to people you hate. You have to grow up. But you don't *have to* give up everything that feels good just because it doesn't fit into some stupid, narrow pattern of behavior that somebody else created for you."

"You sound like Jordan," Molly muttered.

"Jordan . . ." She frowned, thinking hard. It was only a matter of time before Jamie Lee put two and two together and came up with eight.

"Jordan Montgomery, of the Vernonia Montgomerys. And if you were listening closely before, you'll know he's the same Jordan Montgomery who—"

"Oh, my God." Jamie Lee couldn't contain her shock.

"Yes," Molly agreed.

For the first time since Molly had known her, Jamie Lee was at a loss for words. She frowned and Molly could practically see the wild connections being made in her brain. Finally, she just tossed up her hands and said,

"Well!" as if that were the definitive answer to all relationships.

"It's not me who's pushing this." Molly felt compelled to defend herself. "But I don't know what's wrong with me. I can't seem to say no!"

"I saw the man, remember? I bet there aren't a whole lot of women who *could* say no."

Molly didn't want to hear *that*. "Well, I should be the one woman who can," she snapped. "He hurt me so badly—well, his family did.... Circumstances were such a mess...." She sucked air between her teeth. "There's a part I didn't tell you. I was pregnant when the van went over, and I lost the baby. I wanted to blame Jordan even though I knew it wasn't really his fault."

"Oh, honey..."

"And I thought I couldn't have children. I was *told* the chance was almost nil." Molly's throat tightened and throbbed. She drew several deep breaths. "It's going to be tricky for me to go full term, but apparently I have no trouble conceiving."

Jamie Lee blinked several times, the information registering slowly. "You're pregnant?"

"Right again."

"Well, that's wonderful! Isn't it?" she asked after a beat, spying Molly's worried expression.

"I don't know." She set the makings for the salad aside and squeezed her shoulders in tight to her body, afraid she might burst with all these wonderful, scary, conflicting emotions.

"You haven't told him."

"Not yet. I didn't really believe it. I got final word this morning, but oh, God, this is déjà vu at its worst!"

"Well, I'm outta here." Jamie Lee slid off her stool and headed for the door. "Tell him now."

"He might think—"

"What?"

Molly heaved a sigh. "I told him I couldn't get pregnant. He knew that before we ever made love."

"You seriously think he's going to think you set this up?" Jamie Lee frowned. "Anyone who knows you would never believe that. Give him a chance. And do it *now*."

Her words of advice hung in the air, urgent and reasonable. What was she afraid of? She should have told Jordan the first time she was pregnant. She *had to* tell him now.

But the knowledge was too new, too fresh! She wanted to savor it, go over it with total wonder, hug it close to her soul. She was afraid he would destroy that. A few unkind words would tumble her from this pinnacle of hope to the abyss of despair. She couldn't trust him with her news.

It's his baby, too!

"What a disaster," she murmured, pressing her hands to her cheeks, not meaning one syllable. Jordan had asked for a second chance. No matter how she felt about the future, she had to give him one now. For the baby.

For you, you idiot! You want a chance for you!

The bedroom door squeaked open. Jordan, wearing only his jeans and looking sexily rumpled and sleepy, ran his hand through his tousled hair. Grabbing a chair at Molly's tiny kitchen counter, he wheeled it around and straddled it backward, smiling at her like a sated jungle beast.

"Want some dinner?" Her mouth was as dry as sand.

"Sure. Although I'm not all that hungry. Actually, I feel kind of..." He hesitated, meeting Molly's near-frantic gaze. "Satisfied."

She swallowed three times, each one worse than the one before, since there was no saliva in her mouth at all. Sensing her mood, Jordan looked at her expectantly, waiting. When she couldn't speak, he drew his own conclusions.

"Don't start giving me all the reasons we shouldn't see each other. Please." He held up a hand to ward her off. "I've heard all of them already."

"You said you wanted to be in love. Does that mean you think you're in love with me?"

"Where is this going?" he asked cautiously.

"Just tell me how you feel! I need to know!"

Her outburst drove him to silence. Molly felt new tears form. *Oh, no! Please, not now!* She gritted her teeth, furious with herself.

"I care a lot about you," he finally answered, picking his words. "I don't think that's any mystery."

She couldn't tell him. The words lodged in her throat. They stared at each other in mutual confusion, and Molly realized dizzily how much she loved him.

If she didn't care this much, it wouldn't hurt so much; it wouldn't matter so much. But her love was too new and tender to trust to the whims of fate. She could easily see what would happen if he learned the truth now: he would walk out, he wouldn't believe her; he would feel trapped, feel *she'd* trapped him.

It wasn't fair!

"Why don't you just say what's on your mind?" Jordan suggested.

She breathed rapidly. "I think we've got something here, something special."

His expression lightened. "I'm glad you're starting to feel that way."

"I don't want anything to ruin it."

"Nothing will, if we don't let it."

"Sometimes it's not that simple."

"Molly..." He shook his head and laughed softly. "You're the one who makes it complicated. It *is* simple. Just don't let all that other stuff get in the way." He came around the counter, drawing her stiff body into his arms, resting his chin on her shoulder, holding her. "I do love you," he said quietly in a low, throbbing tone that sent her pulse rocketing.

He'd said the words. Molly was mildly surprised, and Jordan was out-and-out amazed. He pressed a kiss to her temple, relishing the moment.

She wanted to tell him the same. Closing her eyes, she willed the words, but instead, emotion swept upward like a volcano, turning her mute and numb and hot. She fought tears, the easy tears of an expectant mother. Instead of answering, she swallowed back a sob.

Jordan gently twirled her to face him, studying the conflicting emotions ruling her expression. "Ease up," he told her softly. "It's going to be okay. Better than okay. Terrific."

For an answer, Molly offered him a trembling, uncertain smile.

"Today's special, Stan's Reuben, with three-month old sauerkraut and caraway rye. The corned beef looks edible, though—mostly pink, not too gray. Still, my vote's for the cauliflower-broccoli puréed soup. If I— Hey!" Heather shouted, as Molly bolted from her chair and raced headlong for the bathroom. "What about egg salad?"

Molly barely made it before retching her guts out. Finished, she trembled all over, laughing to herself as she rinsed out her mouth. Pregnancy. It was certainly real enough now. She'd forgotten what it felt like. Stan Anderssen's special delights were off-limits for the remainder of her pregnancy, she decided. Lord, just thinking about them made her stomach twitch in a fury of expected misery.

"Are you okay?" Heather shouted when Molly returned to her office, her decibel level making Molly's ears ring.

"Yeah, fine. I've got a headache, though. Make my apologies to Stan, but I think I'll go home."

The words were barely out when she heard a rap on her open doorjamb. "Can I come in?" Buzz Bentley tucked his head inside.

Molly hadn't seen him since his wrangle with Jordan. It all seemed so silly now.

"You look kind of pale," he told her with fatherly concern.

"How's Karen doing?"

"Great. The kid's an A student. Don't know where she gets it. It sure ain't from me!" he chortled with pride.

Molly smiled wanly. She really did feel awful.

"Sit down," Buzz told her, and she collapsed in her chair. "I came to thank you for what you did and pay you back as much as I can right now."

"Oh, no, Buzz—"

"Nobody pays my bills for me. I'll deal with Mr. Montgomery myself." He rolled Jordan's name over his tongue as if it had a bad taste. "You shoulda told me yourself," he chided. "I thought Montgomery had just forgotten. It wasn't till Jim wouldn't consider me for any more work that I got the whole story."

"Buzz, the reason I paid Jordan really had nothing to do with you. It was a—thing—between us. I used your fight with him to make a point. I'm sorry."

"I don't care what your reasons are." He dug through his wallet and started pulling out fifty-dollar bills.

"No, Buzz—"

"Here." He dropped a stack on her desk with a satisfied thump. "I'll getcha the rest real soon."

"Jordan ripped up my check! He wouldn't take the money."

Buzz pursed his lips. His graying brows drew together in heavy concentration. "He still thinks I owe him, though, doesn't he?"

"I—don't know."

"You give him this money. Show him a thing or two. And then maybe Jim and Paul will realize Buzz Bentley pays his bills, no matter whether he owes 'em or not."

He nodded at her with satisfaction. Molly stared after him helplessly. The pile of money mocked her. She'd used it as a tool, and the whole thing had backfired.

She wanted to laugh hysterically. Clapping her hand to her mouth, she fought back the urge, only to create a series of chest-aching hiccups she couldn't get rid of.

Snatching up her purse, she paused at Paul's open office door. He raised his brows at her in question.

"I feel like I look," she said.

"You're going home?"

Nodding, Molly added, "I can catch up tomorrow."

"Molly..."

She waited.

"I'm not interested in waiting around if it doesn't work out with Montgomery. But maybe we could be friends again. Someday."

It was an incredible olive branch for Paul to extend. Hearing himself, he flushed a dark crimson. "Thanks, Paul," she answered, touched. He waved her away in embarrassment, but Molly's step was lighter.

Paul's "blessing" gave her new courage, and without consciously deciding to do so, Molly turned her car in the direction of Montgomery Industries' home offices. There was only a slight chance Jordan would be there. He spent most of his time at various job sites, especially the strip mall since it was such a major undertaking. But she knew he had a lot of managerial business to take care of as well and he had to spend some time behind a desk.

Montgomery Industries was located in a black glass building about a forty-minute drive from Westwind. Molly drove quickly, making her way through traffic with practiced ease. But outside Jordan's building she felt a twinge of trepidation, and she lost courage with every footfall as she crossed the polished marble foyer to the reception desk.

She was sent down a hallway, around a corner, to a set of leather-faced double doors. Several desks were arranged in an open area—for Jordan's personal secretary and an inner receptionist, Molly guessed.

She twisted her hands nervously. She *had to* tell him about the baby. She was an idiot for not telling him already.

"Mr. Montgomery is in a meeting," one of the women answered her query. "I'm not certain how long it will be. Can I take your name?"

"Molly Capshaw," she said, clearing her throat. How intimidating! She found it strange that Jordan, who was idealistic and unprepossessing, employed someone to run interference for him. She should have expected it. An executive of his stature would undoubtedly have all the trappings. But it was still a surprise.

She took a seat on the cushy black leather couch near a bank of windows. Another woman, blond and serene, sat on one of the chrome-and-burgundy chairs clustered near the couch.

The woman eyed Molly curiously. "Are you with a company?" she asked.

"Westwind Construction."

"Ahh . . ." She looked relieved.

"Are you?" Molly couldn't help asking.

The woman smiled and her face turned from beautiful to breathtakingly gorgeous. "Oh, no! I'm Jordan's—Mr. Montgomery's—fiancée," she informed Molly. She gazed possessively down at the enormous diamond adorning her left hand, drawing Molly's shocked gaze to its glittering facets. "One of these days—soon, I hope—I'll be able to say I'm his wife."

Chapter Thirteen

"There's a young woman waiting to see you," Jordan's receptionist's disembodied voice echoed over his telephone loudspeaker. "Her name's Molly Capshaw."

Surprised, Jordan jerked his attention from the proposal Mac had delivered to him. "Tell her to come in," he replied instantly.

Mac's brows lifted at what he heard in Jordan's voice.

"Do you want to see her first, or Miss Huntington?"

Jordan inwardly groaned. Julie had said she was going to take him to lunch even though he'd done his damnedest to avoid it. He'd tried to break their engagement on more than one occasion, but she'd cut him off each time. The few social events she'd asked him to attend with her hadn't fit in with his work schedule. Their relationship had hit a stall, and though Jordan had phoned her several times, intending just to explain the truth, no matter how much it hurt, she'd been unavailable or so full of chatter he hadn't been able to follow through.

It was if she knew what he was going to say and simply refused to hear it.

But he was damn well going to make sure she heard it this time.

"Ask Molly to wait. I'd like to see Julie first."

"Two women?" Mac asked with feigned innocence when Jordan lifted his finger from the intercom.

"One woman," Jordan corrected. "One—" he grimaced "—problem of my own making."

The door opened and Julie strutted in, smiling like a Cheshire cat. Jordan groaned inwardly again. How could he have been so stupid? He'd led her on—not meaning to—but he'd definitely led her on.

"See you later," Mac said, sneaking out the back door.

Chicken, Jordan thought, hating himself.

His eyes were instantly drawn to the megadiamond on her left ring finger. Julie laughed, embarrassed, and shrugged a little. "It was my grandmother's," she explained quickly. "I just wanted something to show until you and I went shopping."

"Oh, Julie." Jordan felt sick.

"We can go right after you get off work. I know you've been busy. I've been busy making plans, too, and I just didn't want to bother you until everything was set."

"Julie..."

"Don't say anything until I'm finished!" Her tone was sharp, on the verge of hysteria.

She knows already, he realized. *She just hasn't faced it.*

"I called your father this morning and told him."

"What?"

"I know you two don't get along that well, but he really needs to know. I've been telling everyone!" she went on in a rush. "All my friends. Please don't look at me like that. I know you wanted to wait, but we can't now. It's all set," she babbled. "All set."

"Julie, it's not going to work," he said in horror.

"Of course, it is, Jordan."

"No..." He shook his head.

She finally heard him. Her face crumpled. She pressed a hand to her mouth and staggered into a nearby chair.

When Jordan whipped around his desk, reaching out a hand to help her, she slapped him away in a fury of sudden emotion.

"Don't you dare touch me!"

"I should never have let it go this far."

"You *bastard!*" Her blue eyes brimmed with tears.

He didn't bother to tell her he'd tried to break their engagement several times already. Julie was smart enough to know. Making an excuse for himself wouldn't ease her pain.

"I knew it was too good to be true. No woman is perfect enough for Jordan Montgomery," she pronounced bitterly.

Telling her how wrong she was was out of the question. In a way she was right: no woman had been perfect enough except Molly. And now that she was back in his life he'd move heaven and earth to make certain she stayed there.

"You're going to be a lonely old man, Jordan," Julie predicted, swiping at her eyes as she struggled to her feet. He made the mistake of offering help once more, but she scorned his outstretched arm. "I should have listened to Gloria," she added brokenly. "She told me you'd hurt me, but I wanted you so much. I wanted to be Mrs. Jordan Montgomery!"

That was closer to the truth, Jordan thought. Julie, like all the women his *father* had seen, before, during and after his marriage to Jordan's mother, had all been angling for the same thing: the Montgomery name. He'd suspected the same of Julie and her interest in him. He just hadn't wanted to accept that *he* might be anything like his father and consider marriage to a woman who merely wanted his name.

At the door, she glanced back. "It's really, really over?" she asked pathetically.

Jordan nodded.

"One of these days you're going to pay!" With that, she marched out of the office, crying bitterly.

Jordan turned back to the intercom. "Tell Molly to come in," he said urgently, more unsettled than he wanted to admit by Julie's parting shot.

"I'm sorry. She left. She didn't look very well."

"Damn it," Jordan said under his breath, severing the connection.

Cold gooseflesh broke out on his skin. Julie and Molly had been sitting out there together for a short while. Grabbing his coat, he sailed out of the office and past his openmouthed receptionist.

He'd be damned if he'd let Julie's prediction become a self-fulfilling prophecy.

"It looks like you'll be due around the middle of June," Dr. Matthews told Molly.

She'd guessed that much already, but hearing it made it seem so much more real. This was her first real appointment. She'd had a test but shied away from a consultation. Now, however, it seemed suddenly imperative.

"I was told I wouldn't be able to have children," she pushed past dry lips.

The obstetrician, a young man with a perpetually worried expression and prematurely gray hair, shook his head.

"It may be a difficult pregnancy. You have a lot of scar tissue, which I assume was from a previous pregnancy."

"Umm ... yes, I miscarried. There was an automobile accident that precipitated the miscarriage," she added reluctantly.

"Hmm. That may have added to the problem. But it doesn't mean you can't carry to term. There's just a higher risk."

"So, conception was never the problem," she choked out, wondering whether she would have taken precautions if she'd known that earlier. Undoubtedly. She wasn't crazy.

The doctor shook his head.

"I want this baby," she said in a low, urgent voice. "I'll do anything to make certain it survives."

"Taking care of yourself is the best preventative medicine."

"Okay." She smiled bravely.

She made a series of appointments on her way out of the clinic, then stepped into a dark wintry sky with a sharp, gusting wind. She would have this baby by herself, if necessary. She'd been given a second chance and she wasn't going to blow it.

Jordan's engaged!

She stopped at the store, bought some healthful groceries and drove like an automaton back to her apartment. She nearly turned tail and ran when she discovered Jordan waiting for her.

"Why did you leave?" he demanded without preamble.

Something caught in her peripheral vision. A gray van pulling into a nearby spot. Tyler's van.

She jerked away from Jordan as if caught in some nefarious act. The doors to the van slid open and the hydraulic ramp hissed down. Seconds later, Tyler expertly wheeled himself to the pavement.

"So," Tyler said.

He'd parked near the outside elevator. Instead of coming toward Molly and Jordan, he headed straight toward the elevator. He'd stopped by unexpectedly. Molly hadn't invited him. And truthfully, he was the last person she wanted to see right now.

"I met your fiancée this afternoon." Molly attempted a lightness she didn't feel, but her voice shook, betraying her.

Jordan looked pained. "Julie isn't my fiancée."

"She said she was. In fact, she was quite clear about it."

"Well, she isn't."

There was the sound of truth in his denial, but Molly couldn't forget the lustrous sparkle of Julie's engagement ring nor the joy and hope in her face. But she'd also sensed the woman's desperation and would rather die than appear that way herself.

"If you'd stayed, I could have explained it to you."

Molly shook her head. Glancing upward, she could imagine the fury building inside Tyler as he waited outside her door. "I've got to go. This is a bad time."

"Why did you stop by my office this afternoon?"

"I just—wanted to see you." She edged toward the stairway but Jordan followed.

"You've never stopped by before."

"I just—I know...." One foot was on the bottom step when his hand clamped around her arm.

"What is it?"

"Nothing."

"You look like a ghost. Are you sick?"

"No. I should be offended!" Molly half laughed.

"Molly!" Jordan was impatient.

"This is not a good time to talk!"

He glanced up. "I'll come in with you and—"

"No!" She yanked her arm free. "I don't want you to get in a fight with Tyler, and you *know* that's what would happen."

"Tell me what's wrong, then," he demanded stubbornly.

"I'm pregnant."

She was stunned. The words flew out from nowhere, angry and belligerent. Jordan was equally stunned. Whatever he'd expected, this wasn't it.

"I thought you said you couldn't get pregnant," he murmured dazedly.

She bit down on her lip, wishing she could call back the words. "That's what I was told, but apparently it's just that I'm bound to have a difficult time of it."

"What do you mean?"

"I've got some scarring—from the miscarriage. And the accident," she added quickly. He flinched as if she'd hit him. "I'll have trouble going full term."

"You came by this afternoon to tell me," he said, realizing the truth. "Oh, God. And then you saw Julie!"

"It's all right."

Her cool tone caught him up short. From shock and amazement, he was rapidly moving to acceptance and an emotion she couldn't immediately identify. A heartbeat later he made himself crystal clear. "It's my baby, too."

"If I'm intruding on your life—"

"Oh, God, Molly! I love you, and having a baby with you is a dream I never believed possible." He held her shoulders, gazing down at her with that intensity she'd grown to love and depend on. "This is our second chance," he said in a low, throbbing voice. "Don't you feel it?"

She wanted to. Her eyes brimmed with hope.

"Molly..." Jordan's voice was raw. He shook her gently.

"Yes," she admitted. "I feel it."

He gathered her close. She could feel the hard, reassuring beat of his heart. "We'll get married right away," he went on, the wheels churning in his mind.

"Wait."

He tensed. "What?"

"Tyler's upstairs. My family—they'll be devastated."

"Your family is the biggest reason you never told me about your first pregnancy," he said, picking the words carefully. "We both know how that ended. We can't let them interfere again."

"I know that. Believe me, Jordan, I want everything to be perfect this time. But I can't afford any stress, and so you've got to let me do this my way."

"Let me be there when you break the news."

"No, I—"

"Damn it, Molly. We both need to be there!"

His desperation caught at her heart. He was right. She knew it would be easier with Jordan by her side, but she dreaded the inevitable confrontations.

"Okay," she agreed reluctantly.

"Do you want to tell Tyler now?"

"Are you kidding?" She managed a choked laugh. "I don't want to tell him at all. He'll react the worst!"

"No, he won't."

His dry, positive tone spoke volumes. "Your father," Molly realized with a jolt of her heart.

"I want a family, Molly. I don't care what anyone thinks about you and me together. All that matters is that we're together."

With that he kissed her deeply, gratefully. It should have reassured Molly, but instead it stirred up an uncomfortable feeling she couldn't name. But then she was lost to the joy of his kisses and his love, and she pushed niggling doubts to the far recesses of her mind.

"Is he afraid to come up here?" Tyler demanded as he watched Jordan's Mustang pull out of the lot.

Molly unlocked her front door and pushed it open with one shoulder. "I asked him to leave. I didn't feel like hearing you get into it with him."

"You told Dad and Mom you're seeing him, didn't you?"

"Yes."

"How serious are you about him?"

Molly strode into her tiny living room and sank onto the couch. If she looked as awful as everyone said, she figured it would be best to rest. She leveled a warning look at her brother. "Very serious."

"Oh, God. *Marriage* serious?"

"Tyler," she said with hard-fought patience, "what I do with my life is my business. If you want to be a part of it, stop trying to ruin it."

"Ruin it?" He parked the wheelchair directly in front of her and leaned forward, affronted. "Jordan Montgomery ruined *my* life! And he'll—"

"He didn't ruin your life. You caused that van to turn over yourself!" A familiar, sour odor filled her nostrils. "Have you been drinking?" she demanded.

"He pushed me off the road! Killed your baby. Ruined our lives!" Tyler's face twisted with fury, and he slammed his fist down on the arm of the chair.

"You drove over here drunk," Molly accused, crushed by sorrow and amazement. *"Tyler!"*

"One drink. I had one drink." He whipped the wheelchair away from her, running a hand over his face.

"I don't know how you can tell me how to run my life when you don't know the first thing about running your own. You're not only endangering yourself, you're endangering others."

"You're sleeping with the man who crippled me!"

"I am marrying the man I love," she bit out tersely, too inflamed to honor her promise to Jordan. "And I'm calling Mom and Dad and telling them the same. I love Jordan Montgomery and I'm going to marry him, and there's not a thing you—or Mom or Dad or anyone—can do to stop me!"

With that she bounded to her feet and rushed to the phone, determined to take care of the matter once and for all. Tyler ground out some profanity and wheeled to the front door. Molly lunged for his chair.

"You're not leaving until I know you're sober!"

"Go ahead and tell Mom and Dad! I'm not going to be here to listen!"

"If you want to leave, I'll call Sharon, or I'll drive you myself."

"Sharon is dead to me," he snarled. "I live by myself."

His choice of words was a deluge of cold water. Molly got a grip on herself. "Let me take you home."

"I'm not leaving my van here."

"I'll drive you home in your van."

"And how will you get back, hmm? Call Montgomery to pick you up? Just leave me alone." He pried at her fingers like the child he was. Molly held on.

"I won't call Mom and Dad while you're here, but you're not leaving until you're sober unless I drive you."

"I'm not drunk!"

"Maybe not, but until I'm sure, you're staying here."

"If I had legs, you wouldn't be able to stop me," he said bitterly.

"Yes, I would. I'd call the police on you."

"Fine!" He tossed up his hands in surrender. "I'm your prisoner!"

"Good. I'll make dinner."

On that mutual note of discordance, they fell silent.

Jordan stood by the mantel in his living room, staring through the window. Rain—a deluge that had begun only minutes after he'd left Molly's—streaked down the pane, blurring his view, turning the lights to soft, glimmering sparkles, the gathering darkness to a velvety, inky illusion.

Molly was pregnant. *Pregnant!* She was going to have his child, and he felt dumbfounded, humbled and totally blessed. The way she'd told him bothered him, however: off the cuff; cool as ice; unconcerned with either his opinion or reaction. But what could he reasonably expect? Julie had informed Molly of their engagement, and she'd been wearing that outrageous diamond ring.

Groaning, Jordan wished he'd had the sense to explain the ring to Molly, but he'd barely begun talking about Julie when he'd stumbled on Molly's pregnancy. That news had certainly knocked everything else out of his head.

And he'd needed to bind her to him. He'd needed to know she would at least entertain the idea of marriage. Grimacing, he recalled their conversation. No romantic moment of discovery. No solemn promises and words of love. Oh, he'd told her he loved her, but thinking back, he knew he'd been about as emotional and giving as the Rock of Gibraltar. He'd sounded like he was making a business deal.

Still . . . she'd accepted.

Restless, he paced across the room. He wished she hadn't insisted he leave. He wished he hadn't listened to her. He didn't like her being alone with Tyler.

You don't trust her brother? Her crippled brother? Good God, man. Have you completely lost your mind?

The answer to that was, yes. When it came to Molly he was anything but reasonable. Emotions ruled his head. Passion ruled common sense.

It was because he loved her so intensely. How amazingly easy it was to say those words now. Once upon a time, he'd thought he never could. They'd seemed too trite. Too silly. Too meaningless. But with Molly, they filled his head, needing to be uttered. He'd fought them as a kid, but that was over. He loved Molly and he wanted to marry her.

He'd convinced her to wait and tell their families jointly but now, trying to imagine breaking the news to Foster with Molly, fragile as she appeared right now, he changed his own mind. He couldn't put Molly through that. His father had worsened with age, not improved. Telling his mother wouldn't be much of a problem; she'd removed herself completely from his and Foster's life. She wouldn't care a lot what he did. He'd faced that sad fact a long, long time ago.

But Foster...

And Julie had gone and told him *she* and Jordan were getting married! He groaned and clenched one fist. What a god-awful mess!

Crossing to the phone, he hesitated long moments while the clock steadily ticked and the rain poured down. He stood stiff and silent for so long that Carmella came looking for him, shrieking when she came upon him unexpectedly.

"Dinner ready?" Jordan asked, lifting one brow in amusement, to which she delivered him a look of suspicion, as if concluding he'd made her the butt of some joke.

"Yes," she said flatly and left.

Jordan punched out his father's home number, cowardly hoping for the answering machine.

"Montgomery household," Foster's cold, distinctive tones answered.

Jordan's mouth drew into a line of irony. So typical. Whenever his father deigned to answer the phone, he pretended to be some lofty servant. That way, if he didn't feel like speaking to the caller, he simply took a message.

"It's Jordan," he responded in an equally distant voice.

"Yes?"

It shouldn't have bothered him after all these years, but Foster's lack of warmth never failed to elicit some buried emotion he didn't want to feel. "I understand Julie called you."

"She told me congratulations are in order. Julie Huntington will make an excellent wife." His voice was full of satisfaction but he couldn't help adding, "You could have called me yourself."

"I'm not marrying Julie. I'm marrying Molly Capshaw."

"What?" he exclaimed acidly. *"No!"* he roared.

"I should have done it years ago."

"You're lying." Foster's latent fury bubbled upward, boiled over. "You've had your fun. Now tell the truth."

"I have."

Foster swore, bitterly and pungently. Jordan lifted his brows, a little surprised at such unseemly emotion from his unbending father.

"Are you marrying her to get back at me?" Foster asked tightly.

"No!"

"Is she pregnant again?"

Jordan choked on his next words, and Foster leaped to the right conclusion so quickly Jordan didn't have time to deny that Molly's pregnancy had precipitated his decision.

"Pay her off, for God's sake!" Foster bit out. "Don't think you're doing the honorable thing. This little war you've got going with me isn't worth throwing your life away on a woman like that."

"A woman like that is the only kind of woman I want!" Jordan shot back, so furious he was glad his father was safe on the other end of a telephone wire. He'd gladly have strangled the bastard.

"I bought you out of one mistake, Jordan. I'll be damned if I'll do it again."

Slam! The receiver hit the cradle so hard it cracked the plastic and the phone jumped off the counter and crashed to the floor. Jordan backed away from it, boiling with emotion. His father had *not* bought his way out of jail; his innocence was a matter of record.

But, oh, God, how he could twist the knife of guilt!

Molly, he thought, staggering toward the door.

The doorbell rang as she was putting away the last plate. Tyler, sober but still querulous, had left about fifteen minutes earlier. He hadn't stopped denigrating Jordan even for one moment. It had been a draining, nerve-racking meal. Since his breakup with Sharon, Tyler had become even more bitter. It didn't matter that he'd been the one to end their relationship; his downward spiral just continued. Slowly Molly had come to realize that nothing would change him. No miracle therapy lay around the next corner. Tyler's healing had to come from within, and it simply wasn't going to happen.

She swung open the door. "Jordan," she murmured, surprised.

He swept her into his arms, crushing her to him as if afraid to let her go. Sensing his urgency, she simply returned the hug but after long, long moments she asked quietly, "What happened?"

"I told Foster."

Molly pressed her face into his neck. A bad feeling settled deep in her bones—the same kind of bad feeling she remembered from all those years ago.

"It's not going to happen, is it?"

"Yes, it is." He was coldly determined.

"Jordan—"

"Shh." His hand wound in her hair possessively. "I will not let them keep us apart," he hissed, stressing each word.

Molly nodded, almost believing him.

A chill spread through her.

"We love each other," he reminded her. "I don't care what my father tries to do. We're going to get married, and we're going to have a family."

Molly nodded again, unable to speak. She wrapped her arms tightly around him. "We're going to get married," she repeated.

"Right."

"Right..."

She wished they both sounded more certain.

Chapter Fourteen

"When do you want to break the news?" Jordan asked solemnly the next morning.

Molly squeezed fresh orange juice, taking an inordinate amount of time and concentration as she twisted the oranges on the juice extractor. They were discussing her parents, of course. Jordan definitely wanted to be with her when she told them they were about to become in-laws with the Montgomerys.

"Umm...I'll tell them Saturday. Maybe I'll drive home for the weekend." She swallowed. "You don't have to come if you don't want to."

"I want to be with you."

"You told your father without me being there."

Jordan didn't respond. Molly shot him a look. Maybe she was glad she hadn't been there. Jordan had been particularly closemouthed about what had transpired between him and his father.

"I haven't told my mother," he said. "But we don't talk that much so it doesn't matter."

Molly's heart squeezed. For all her troubles with Tyler, Molly enjoyed a close relationship with her mother and father. True, they weren't going to handle the news that she was marrying a Montgomery very well, but they would get over it. They had to.

Frowning, she twisted another orange-half on the extractor, forcing the juice and pulp to squish out.

"You're killing that thing," Jordan pointed out.

"What kind of a wedding are you thinking about?"

"Something small and private."

"An elopement?"

Jordan shrugged. "Whatever you want, Molly. I just want you and the baby."

"I want you, too," she whispered.

"Then it'll happen." He came to her, and she fell into his open arms.

"I just have this feeling something's going to stop us from being together," she said in a small voice. "I'm not normally superstitious, but the feeling's so strong. It's like a weight on my chest."

Jordan rested his chin on her silky crown. He didn't reveal that he'd been feeling the same way. It was too weird—a kind of reverse déjà vu they were both experiencing.

It wasn't rational. It wasn't real.

But it was damn spooky.

"We'll go talk to them this weekend," he told her. "Together."

"Together," Molly echoed softly.

Saturday dawned gray and ominous, a harbinger of what was to come. Molly's mood deteriorated from anxious to downright scared as each mile passed beneath the wheels of Jordan's Mustang.

By the time they reached Vernonia she was cold to the bone and so sensitive to the atmosphere, she was certain some cataclysmic doom was going to visited upon them.

They drove past the Burger Hutt—now a fish-and-chips fast-food restaurant. But the parking lot was the same. The gravel area where Michael had been killed looked untouched, full of damp, rotting weeds.

Molly slid a glance at Jordan as they passed. Apart from a tightening of his jaw, he didn't acknowledge the place. For that, she was glad.

She hadn't been home in months. Almost a year, she realized with a distinct shock. Her parents' house, though freshly painted, had that settled-in look that only homes over twenty years old seemed to achieve. Developments had sprouted all around it, but it stood out, defiant in its quiet obscurity.

She wondered about Jordan's family home. They'd sold it long ago, and the last time she'd driven by, the hedge had been so overgrown even the tile roof was no longer visible from the road. An isolated fortress now. Whoever lived there was fanatically private and antisocial.

"They're not expecting you," Molly said on a dry swallow as Jordan cut the engine.

"Okay..."

"I couldn't tell them you were coming. I tried. I really wanted to warn them, but the words just froze inside me. Maybe I should go in first."

"No." He was adamant. "We'll do this together."

"Jordan, they're going to be so shocked."

"They already know you've been seeing me. They'll be half expecting this."

"Will they?" Molly almost laughed.

"Tyler acts as if he's been expecting it for ten years. He's bound to have let his feelings be known."

He was right. Tyler had not suffered in silence. Her parents were bound to know his every thought. For all she knew, he could have already told them she intended to marry Jordan. But based on her last conversation with them, she doubted it.

As they walked under the canopy of bougainvillea covering the front porch, Molly felt as if she were on the last march to a firing squad. The front door suddenly burst open and Tina Capshaw ran out, enfolding Molly in her arms.

"I'm so glad to see you," she declared, hugging Molly tightly. Spying Jordan, her smile slowly faded.

"Mom, this is . . . Jordan."

He extended his hand as the color slowly receded from Tina's cheeks. It was one thing to hear her daughter had been seeing him, Molly realized, but another thing entirely to meet him face-to-face.

"Oh..." she said expelling a faint sigh. She stared at his hand, hers trembling as she reached out and gave it a limp shake.

Molly held her breath so hard it hurt. "We're—we're planning to get—"

"Oh, no!" Tina's pallor turned as gray as the sky. She swayed. Jordan reached out to grab her, but she jumped back, bracing herself against the porch beam. "Oh, my God. Oh, my God."

At that fortuitous moment Molly's father opened the front door and walked on to the porch. He smiled at Molly, then looked past her, his smile fading, replaced by a frown of confusion that swiftly changed to dawning horror.

"What are you doing here?" he clipped out.

"Jordan's my—fiancé," Molly gasped.

John Capshaw pushed forward, fists clenched. Horror-stricken, Molly cried out at the same moment Jordan took several steps away from her, his gaze leveled grimly at John.

"Don't!" Molly screeched at her father.

"John," Tina cried faintly.

Every muscle in Jordan's body tightened. He prepared for the blow, expecting it, not sure whether to fight back or not. In a heartbeat he realized Molly's fears weren't unfounded. The Capshaws thought he was poison.

In a boxer's stance, John Capshaw shuddered and stilled. The moment spun out endlessly. "Get off my property," he ordered wearily.

"I'm marrying him," Molly clarified again. "We are getting married."

"Then don't come back here again," John said.

His rejection hit like a blow. She paled. She couldn't believe her ears, and the look on her face said so. Tina whimpered a protest. Her anguished eyes met Molly's.

"It doesn't have to be this way," Jordan said quietly.

"Yes, it does." Clasping Tina by the arm, John pulled his wife inside the house. The door closed. The lock scraped shut with chilling finality.

Dazed, Molly stood on the porch of her family home—the house she'd grown up in. Pain exploded within her chest. Jordan gathered her close.

Something cramped inside her.

"No," she whispered, shocked out of her misery. "Jordan, the baby!"

His gaze jumped to her stomach, then back to her eyes. "What?"

"Wait...wait..." She held out a hand, pulling away, fighting emotion. Nothing. "Wait," she said again as his expression grew grim and worried. "No, it's okay. I think it's okay."

"I'm taking you straight to a doctor."

"I think I'm okay."

Jordan was past listening. He drove straight to Dr. Rendell's clinic, the only clinic in Vernonia. Rendell wasn't an obstetrician, but he'd been the most respected doctor in Vernonia since Molly and Jordan were babies themselves.

Rendell wasn't in but his young partner was. Molly lay down on an examining table, the paper crackling beneath her. A nurse came in. Questions flew from all directions.

"Everything seem's fine," the doctor told her after the examination. "You're not miscarrying."

"I felt a cramp. I was worried that I'd lose the baby," she repeated for about the fifteenth time. "They told me I might have a difficult pregnancy."

"Keep the stress down, and I don't see why you can't make it full term," he assured her.

She didn't believe him. It was what they all said. A panacea. A soothing platitude.

Shivering, she wished Jordan were in the room with her.

Jordan paced outside the door, out of his mind with worry. He shouldn't have come back with her. He'd forced her to bring him without thinking about her pregnancy. God! Maybe he'd killed their baby again.

"Jordan."

He looked up anxiously. She stood in the doorway, fully clothed, her beautiful face pale and drawn.

"Molly." His voice was strained.

"I'm okay," she assured him. "And so's the baby."

"I'm sorry," he said.

"It's not your fault...."

But it was his fault. All of it. The drive back to Los Angeles gave him an opportunity for plenty of soul-searching. He'd pushed too hard. Wanted too much. Molly had been right in her premonition. Her parents and brother and his father would never condone this union. They would fight and harass and cruelly deny them their happiness.

And it would cost Molly the baby.

"What are you thinking?" she asked as he rounded the last corner before her apartment.

"The same thing you're thinking."

Molly's head lay limply against the headrest. All she wanted to do was curl up in a ball and go to sleep. "Well, I'm thinking about a long, long sleep."

"They're not going to make it easy," he said, ignoring her change of subject.

"No."

"Molly, you've got to avoid so much stress, or we'll lose this baby, too. You know it. I know it. Hell, every doctor you've seen says the same thing."

"I know."

"We can't fight them all. Not right now. We've got too much to lose."

"What are you trying to say?" she asked, but the answer came to her before the last word was even uttered. No more fights. No more confrontations. No wedding.

Not yet, anyway.

Not ever, a fatalistic voice warned.

"You think we should stop seeing each other for a while?" she asked timidly.

"What? No!" Jordan was adamant. "But I don't think we owe them any more explanations."

Relief nearly overwhelmed her. "I don't want to lose this baby."

"Neither do I. And you won't, if I have any say about it."

She smiled. He could almost make her believe things would work out. "Later," she said, scooting out of the car. Jordan made as if to follow her, but Molly shook her head. "I'm going to go straight to bed. Alone."

Jordan groaned before reluctantly agreeing.

Molly heard Heather's driving footsteps even before she crossed the threshold to her office. "Don't even tell me." Molly stopped her with one upraised hand. "I'm not interested in anything from Stan's lunch cart. My stomach can't take it."

Heather came into view, her mouth still open. She looked disappointed that she couldn't act the role of town crier. "Oh," she said, hesitated, then added hopefully, "He's got soup today. French onion and broccoli Cheddar."

Molly's stomach lurched. She quickly reached into her handbag, grabbed a cellophone-wrapped saltine, ripped it open and nibbled carefully on a corner.

"The flu again?" Heather asked.

Molly smiled faintly. "Pregnancy," she revealed, at which point Heather whooped with delight and started shooting questions at her at ear-shattering decibel level.

"A baby? When's it due? Aren't you just *so* excited? I can't stand it! Does anyone else know? Oh, my God! Is it Paul's?" Heather clapped a hand to her mouth, her eyes bright with excitement.

"No, it's not Paul's," Molly revealed, glad she'd had the foresight to deliver her news to Paul personally earlier that day. Not that it had been one of her brighter moments. Paul had turned an odd shade of gray and said in a shattered, bitter voice, "I wish I could say I'm happy for you, but I'm not the forgiving type. Montgomery's a lucky man."

A lucky man. Molly pondered that statement as Heather asked, "Does he know?"

"Paul? Yes, I told him."

"Then it's not a secret?"

She shook her head, and Heather clattered out of the office and began booming the news out. Her enthusiasm should have been infectious, but it just made Molly feel anxious. She'd overreacted about Saturday's cramping, but she still couldn't shake her sense of foreboding.

Pushing away the feeling, she followed Heather's path through the hallways, accepting congratulations from other Westwind employees who gazed at her curiously, clearly wondering who the father of her unborn child was. No one appeared shocked that she was a single mother, at least, and for that Molly was grateful. She was walking such a tightrope of emotions, she didn't think she could take any criticism, no matter how well-meant it might be.

"Maybe I'll try that French onion soup, after all," she said with a smile, catching up with Heather at the reception-room doors.

"Great! I'll get you a roll, too, and a glass of milk."

Amused, Molly's watched Heather race out the glass doors to the parking lot and Anderssen's deli lunch cart. Peripherally Molly noticed a sleek, black car—a Mercedes sedan—pull into a visitor's spot in front of the building, but it didn't seem significant at that moment.

It did five minutes later, however, when she was back in her office, cleaning off her desk for her anticipated soup, and the door flew open. Molly glanced up in surprise as Foster Montgomery strode across her office like a conquering Hun.

Memories speared through her, icicle-cold and sharp. Foster at her parents' house. *You're acquainted with my son, Jordan.* She could see him handing over Jordan's letter as if it were yesterday.

She hadn't laid eyes on him since.

"Miss Capshaw," he greeted her in that same acid tone.

No stress. No stress. No stress...

"Mr. Montgomery." Her heart thumped in her ears, deafening her.

"Jordan tells me you're pregnant and that he's duty-bound to marry you."

"Duty-bound?" she repeated dumbly, curling her fingers around her desktop. She breathed deeply, several times.

"Did you know he was engaged to Julie Huntington? They were planning to get married and start a family of their own. Until you swept into Jordan's life again and made it impossible."

No stress...

"He wanted to marry me before he learned about the baby," she said in a faint voice she scarcely recognized as her own. That was the truth, wasn't it? He'd told her he loved her. She knew he did. She couldn't let Foster confuse her. She couldn't do that to Jordan.

"My son's wanted a family for a long time. He'd finally met the right woman. I'll be damned if I'll let you spoil that for him now."

With that, he twisted on his heel and stormed out of her office, slamming the door shut so hard the overhead lamp flickered.

No stress. Molly lay her head on her desk and prayed the strange little cramping she felt wasn't what she thought it was.

Chapter Fifteen

"Your father called from Calloway Park Hospital. A friend of yours has been admitted, a Miss Capshaw?"

Jordan froze, his body half in, half out of his car as he'd impatiently grabbed for the ringing car phone. He was at the strip-mall work site and had ignored the damn thing the first two times it had rung.

His father? *Molly?*

"I'm on my way," he said.

The baby.

Oh, God!

The drive to the hospital was a blur of traffic lights and crowded streets, the beat of his heart a drum pounding the death knell. He screeched to a halt outside Emergency and blazed through the doors.

"Molly Capshaw," he bit out to the first woman in white he saw.

"Check with front reception," she answered automatically at the same moment Jordan's gaze collided with Foster's.

His first instinct was to slam his fist into his father's face. He managed to fight the impulse only because Foster didn't appear as smug as Jordan had expected.

"What happened?" Jordan's voice was a hoarse whisper.

"She hasn't miscarried yet."

His unemotional tone nearly destroyed Jordan's resolve to be civilized. Hands clenched, he demanded, "What are you doing here? I know she didn't call you."

For the first time in Jordan's memory, his father was at a loss. He cleared his throat several times, then said brusquely, "I went to see her at her work."

"Oh, my God."

"I wasn't the cause of this!" he hissed, watching the blood drain from his son's face. "She just collapsed."

"The hell she did. What did you say to her?" At his father's reluctance, he yelled, *"What did you say to her?"*

"I told her I knew of the pregnancy and that I understood you were planning to marry her."

"I'll bet you did."

Father and son faced off in a silent, blazing war of emotions that had been building from the moment Jordan had first dared to utter the word *no*. There had never been love between them; Foster neither understood, nor felt, the meaning of the word. But Jordan had been able to offer him a grudging acceptance—something close to respect but just missing the mark.

He didn't fully blame Foster for this. A lot of other factors had played parts in the drama. But his father was the director and sometimes lead actor. And for that, Jordan could never forgive him.

"If the baby dies, it's over," Jordan rasped, turning away, knowing he didn't need to elaborate. Foster was single-sighted and self-motivated, but he was far from stupid.

Fear had caved in her knees and brought the ambulance siren screaming to her rescue. She'd shivered uncontrollably, been barely coherent. But it was okay. It was going to be okay.

She still had the baby.

"This little one's a fighter," the doctor on call had assured her as soon as she'd been examined. "And babies in general are tougher than you might think. Just take care of yourself. Everything's going to be fine."

She'd smiled wanly, too weak in the aftermath of her relief to go into all the reasons why everything wasn't going to be fine, no matter how badly she wanted it to be. But though the cramping had been more severe this time, it was no more serious than before.

"Try to forget anyone ever told you this was going to be a difficult pregnancy," was the doctor's parting advice.

"And keep the stress down," she murmured with pure irony.

Jordan burst into the room before she was fully dressed. Molly gasped, clutching her blouse to her chest, then laughed at the ridiculousness of it all.

"How did you know I was here?" she asked.

"Foster called me."

She blinked, surprised. "He did?"

"What happened? Are you okay? Is the baby—"

"Yes, yes, the baby's fine. It's me. I feel like a total idiot. I'm jumping at shadows."

"So, you're okay?" he asked again, unconvinced. At Molly's nod, he folded her into his arms, resting his chin on her crown. In his warm embrace Molly felt safe. "If he comes near you again, I'll kill him," Jordan muttered emotionally.

"Let's forget about Foster for a while. I don't want to think about him, or anyone else. And everything's going to be all right now," she added with false cheer. "Everyone knows we're getting married. There's nobody else to tell and no one left to bother us."

"Your parents and Tyler don't know you're pregnant," Jordan reminded her.

"They don't have to know that yet." Determined to put things back to normal, she kissed him on the lips. Jordan's eyebrows shot up at her uncharacteristic initiative. Amused, Molly kissed him again and said, "Now, take me back to work so I can—"

"Back to work? Not a chance! I want you to go home and take care of yourself."

"I need to get my car," she explained. "I'm not an invalid. I'm just so afraid I'll lose the baby."

"Not if I can help it."

"Okay." She smiled at his determined tone. Maybe everything really would be all right. "Tell you what—I'll go back to work with you at the strip mall and then you can take me to pick up my car and we'll meet for dinner."

He frowned deeply and Molly added, "And I'm going to do my best to persuade you to rehire Buzz Bentley."

Jordan half laughed. "Okay, okay. I give up. But only because our being together's bound to be safer than being apart."

"Right," Molly said in relief. She had to get over this feeling of dread that seemed to constantly plague her. And she needed to get over her irrational fear. The more normal they acted, the more normal everything would be.

And she'd been telling the absolute truth that there was no one left who could hurt them.

"There's a Tyler Capshaw here to see you," Paul's receptionist told him.

"Send him in," Paul said instantly. He'd been worried sick about Molly ever since the ambulance had taken her away to the hospital.

When Tyler wheeled himself into the room, Paul demanded, "Is she all right? She's all right, isn't she?"

"What? I came to see Molly, and that girl outside sent me to you." Tyler scowled and ran a hand over his face.

"Molly's at the hospital! The ambulance took her away a couple of hours ago."

"Hospital?" he repeated blankly.

Belatedly Paul realized Molly's brother didn't know a damn thing about her. In irritation, he explained, "She was cramping. Afraid she was miscarrying. Why don't you go over to Calloway Hospital and let me know what's happening?"

Tyler's eyes were glazed. He blinked several times, as if he couldn't take it all in. "Miscarrying? She was pregnant?" Tyler shook his head. "Is Montgomery the father?"

"Maybe I've said more than I should have."

"That *bastard!*" Tyler shouted, whipping around and jerkily wheeling himself back out the door. A sour odor trailed through the room after him.

Paul hesitated, slowly identifying the smell. Alcohol. Tyler had been drinking. Disturbed, he crossed to his office window and watched Tyler unlock his van and lower the hydraulic ramp. He seemed okay, but . . .

Worried, Paul strode out of his office toward Westwind's glass entry doors but before he could push through them, Tyler's van had backed out and was heading for the main road.

"Seems to be driving okay," he muttered to himself.

"He said he was Molly's brother," the receptionist revealed.

"He is."

She chewed on the end of a pen. "He also asked about the strip-mall site. Said he knew Jordan Montgomery and wanted to talk to him. I told him its location. It's not a secret, is it?"

She wanted reassurance. Paul wanted to give it to her. The front doors rattled against a chilly, determined wind.

"No. It's not a secret." With an effort he dismissed the feeling of foreboding that had settled under his skin. Molly Capshaw and her bitter, drunken brother were not his responsibility.

Molly leaned against Jordan's Mustang, inhaling deep, gulping breaths of the biting fall air. Wet leaves lay in damp yellow, orange and red piles across the parking lot, blanketing the asphalt.

Hearing tires spin and squeal, she was amused to see one of the workmen trying to gain traction for his vehicle in the slippery carpet of leaves.

Glancing back, she looked at the strip mall with pride. The renovation was moving right along. Most all of the stores were newly wallboarded now and plate-glass windows adorned every storefront. Jade trees and birds of paradise had been planted along the brick walkway. Wires hung down from the eaves where neon signs would soon advertise each small business, and every shop door sported an old-fashioned bell that would ring each time the door was opened. The overall feel of the place was charming and welcoming.

Jordan was inside the nearest store, talking with one of the finishing carpenters who needed assistance. Molly had assured him she would be fine. It felt good, in fact, to be standing outside, drinking in the cool, faintly musty outdoor scents. She turned her face skyward, realizing with a distinct jolt that she felt fabulous. Jordan loved her. She loved him. And they were going to get married and have a baby.

In that moment of crystal clarity Molly realized she hadn't told Jordan how much she loved him. Not in words. He'd pushed her to give their relationship a chance and she'd fought him all the way, each step reluctant and cautious.

She hadn't told him she loved him since those long-ago days in Vernonia. He deserved to hear the words.

"I'll tell him tonight." She smiled to herself.

The finishing carpenter walked outside and into the next storefront to pick up some tools. Jordan was still inside the original store, backlit by the bare hanging light bulb, his form so familiar and appealing that her breath caught. He looked up, met Molly's gaze and shrugged an apology for taking so long. She shook her head to tell him it didn't matter.

The roar of an engine penetrated somewhere in the back of her mind. She glanced down the row of storefronts, expecting to see another vehicle start up and try to burn through wet leaves to get to pavement.

But none of the cars, trucks and vans was moving. Someone was coming.

Molly glanced backward. The van was gray, traveling fast. It squealed around a corner. Molly blinked. Her heart lurched.

"Tyler?" she whispered, disbelieving.

She whipped around. Jordan was still standing behind the plate-glass window, illuminated brightly. Spotlighted against the slowly darkening afternoon sky. "Jordan," she called. "Jordan!"

The van screeched and turned, shimmying. It jumped a corner and tore straight for the strip mall. Straight for Jordan!

Oh, God!

For a moment Molly was frozen. She couldn't see Tyler's face, but she knew with sudden insight that Tyler had learned about her marriage and the baby. He was out for Jordan's blood. She could almost hear his need for revenge in the throbbing engine of his van. Her heart hammered painfully, and fear sliced through her body and soul.

Molly screamed and reached out an arm—a useless, pathetic attempt to stop her crazed brother.

The van thundered forward and crashed through the front window. Glass shattered, exploding in crystal-like shrapnel. Molly didn't have time to duck. She raised one arm as glittering shards sprayed all around her. White dust billowed outward from pulverized wallboard.

Please, God! No... no...

She stumbled forward, legs numb. "Jordan! Jordan!"

He lay on his side, eyes closed, thrown against the back wall. For one terrible, soul-shattering moment she thought he was dead and her world collapsed. "No!" she cried, sobbing, falling down beside him. Her hands clenched in his shirt, dragging at him. "No, no, no! Please... Oh, God..."

Through blurred eyes she saw movement, the shallow rise and fall of his chest.

Thank you, she prayed silently, swallowing hard.

Workmen poured into the store, choking and shouting. "Call an ambulance," Molly yelled to one of them, holding on to Jordan's wrist, feeling for a pulse. He couldn't die! He couldn't! She wouldn't let him.

"Don't do this to me," she warned him. "I won't let you. I won't let you."

Jordan's breath escaped on a sigh. "Molly..." he moaned.

Someone pulled her up, tried to drag her away. She fought like a wildcat, but he wouldn't let go. When she focused on his dust-covered face she realized it was Buzz. Jordan had already hired him back.

Breaking into body-shaking sobs, she counted the seconds until the ambulance sirens screamed their approach.

The waiting room was hell. Molly sat like a stone. Hours slipped by, and then her parents were there. Tyler had survived injury but was under lock and key somewhere in another part of the city. Molly had scarcely been able to look at him when he'd been helped from his van. She'd clapped her hands over her ears when he'd started screaming how he'd found out about the marriage and the baby. This time she knew there would be no leniency, and she was glad.

Her mother held her hand. Her father sat hunched in chair beside her, twisting his hat, his eyes closed in sorrow. Sorrow for Jordan, or sorrow for Tyler? Molly was too numb to know or care.

"We're praying for him," Tina whispered, squeezing Molly's hand.

"I'm marrying him. I'm pregnant," Molly answered unemotionally.

Her father heaved a shaking sigh. Her mother embraced her, her warm tears dampening Molly's cheek when she pressed a kiss to her skin.

And then Foster strode in, white as death. He spied Molly and her parents instantly and switched directions without slowing down, pushing his way around an elderly couple to stop directly in front of them.

His tall, distinguished frame shook with anguish and fury. "Your son tried to kill him!" he hissed at Molly's father. "He tried to kill him!"

Molly trembled all over. Foster was out of his mind with rage and fear. He turned his wrathful eyes on her.

"It's you," he snarled. "It's your fault."

"Leave my daughter alone." Her father slowly got to his feet.

"Stop it. Both of you! Stop it!" Molly cried. The fighting and blame were pointless. All that mattered was Jordan.

Oh, Jordan. Please. I love you so much.

Footsteps sounded. A young woman doctor crossed toward them. In the confusion, Molly thought she was flanked by two officers, but then realized the policemen had simply arrived at the same time to speak to her.

"Miss Capshaw," the taller man in uniform greeted her.

"Could I speak to her first, please?" the doctor interrupted. Her tag read Dr. Geddes. The officer seemed to want to argue, but then looked at Molly and nodded. He turned his attention to her parents, and Dr. Geddes focused kind eyes on Molly.

"Would you mind coming to my office?" she asked.

Molly tried to speak, and couldn't. She managed a nod, but her legs had ceased to offer support, and only Dr. Geddes's helping arm kept her from falling over.

The doctor led her to a small office with a desk and two patient's chairs. Molly glanced around but all she could see was her last vision of Jordan being strapped on to a stretcher, his face covered with bleeding lacerations.

"I'm Jordan's admitting doctor," Dr. Geddes explained. "He's out of surgery."

"Is he all right?"

"We'll know more when he wakes up. He suffered a concussion, a broken leg, broken collarbone, some internal bleeding, and we had to remove his spleen."

The blood drained from Molly's face. Her knees buckled, and Dr. Geddes gently eased her into one of the chairs. "He came to right before surgery and asked for you. He said you were pregnant and he was worried about the baby."

No stress.

Molly opened her mouth, but her throat closed, hot with unshed tears. She pressed her lips together, fighting back small sobs. "I think the baby's okay. I'm just—so scared."

"I want to make sure you're all right before you have to talk to the police. Or..." She looked down at her desk. Molly followed her gaze, feeling helpless. There was nothing on the smooth desktop except a cassette recorder. "Or you could talk to me and we could tape you. After you feel better."

"How long will it be before Jordan wakes up?"

"Could be a while. It's hard to tell."

Dr. Geddes was leaning over her, examining her face closely. Molly lay her head back and drew several calming breaths. "I think I'd like to talk to you now, while I'm waiting for him."

"You're sure you're ready?"

"As ready as I'll ever be," Molly said tiredly.

"Can I get you a cup of coffee? Tea?"

"Tea," Molly requested in a cracked voice. She glanced at the cassette recorder and realized if she was going to tell the story, she was going to have to tell the whole entire tragedy.

Their love deserved that much.

Chapter Sixteen

*C*lick.

Dr. Geddes depressed the stop key on the cassette re corder, bringing Molly out of her reverie.

"Sorry," the doctor said with an apologetic grimace "We were getting near the end of the tape. Were you fir ished?"

Molly gazed at her a bit dazedly, the last image of Jor dan's accident still burning brightly on the screen of he mind.

"Yeah. I guess."

There was a foam cup of untouched cold tea in he hand. She vaguely remembered Dr. Geddes placing it be tween her palms. Now she set it on the desk, still deepl absorbed in her own thoughts.

"Your brother will be facing criminal charges," D Geddes said quietly, rising from her own chair and sho ing her hands in the deep pockets of her white lab coa

"Drunken driving, vehicular assault..." She hesitated, shooting a glance Molly's way. "You realize he'll probably be convicted and face a jail sentence, don't you?"

Molly nodded jerkily. She swiped her bangs from her eyes and drew a long breath. She felt numb where Tyler was concerned. Later she would be angry; she already sensed her anger building somewhere deep inside. But she was too worried right now to think of anything besides Jordan—how extensive his injuries were, how soon he would recover. He had to get better. He *had* to. She'd damned well make certain of it!

"Would you like anything else?" Dr. Geddes asked.

"No, thank you." Molly smiled faintly. "I was told I could have a difficult pregnancy and I've been sick with worry, but now I'm not worried anymore. Nothing could be worse than this, and the baby and I are fine. You'll probably think I'm nuts, but I know I'll deliver without complications. Sometimes you just *know*."

Dr. Geddes had witnessed too many minor miracles to dismiss Molly's conclusion as wishful thinking. Maybe she was right. Time would tell.

"I need to know about Jordan," Molly said now, her voice catching. Swallowing, she added, "I love him. He is my whole life."

"I understand."

"Do you? Do you really?"

This was no idle question. Dr. Geddes looked into Molly's intense hazel eyes and read her feelings. Molly wasn't searching for reassurance. She really wanted to know if anyone could possibly understand her deep, abiding love for Jordan Montgomery.

Dr. Geddes had never experienced it herself, but once, maybe twice, in her career, she'd witnessed something similar.

"I believe that your love for him will pull him through," she responded bluntly.

"I don't care what they all think anymore," Molly said reflectively, searching to the roots of her soul. "My mother and father, Tyler, even Foster...especially Foster. Do you know, I don't think he's told Jordan's mother that her son is in the hospital? He's that selfish and unforgiving. If I knew how to get hold of her, I'd call her myself."

"Surely she's been contacted, given the seriousness of Jordan's condition?" Dr. Geddes frowned, compelled to defend the hospital.

"Oh, he'll notify her when he gets around to it. If I had the energy to hate anyone, I'd hate him," Molly added matter-of-factly. "But all I want is Jordan. I want him to live." Her composure fissured, a stab of pain darkening her face. "That's all I want. Is it too much to ask?"

"No."

"Will the police let me see him?"

"The police—yes. But we'll have to wait and see how he feels."

"I can't stand this waiting much longer." Molly paced across the room. "If we're done, I want to go wait outside Intensive Care."

Dr. Geddes's phone buzzed. They both jumped. Picking up the receiver, the doctor spoke softly and discreetly to whomever had called. Molly could only eavesdrop on half the conversation, and Dr. Geddes's monosyllabic replies gave nothing away.

But then the doctor came around her desk and stopped directly in front of Molly. "They've moved him to his own room," she said, unable to hide her own delight. "He's awake and asking for you."

Molly stared at her. Then she raced for the door and down the hall, ignoring the floor nurse's sharp admonishment.

Foster was already outside Jordan's door. Molly wanted to cheer with joy when she saw that a bulky orderly was guarding entry to the room. Doctor's orders, she'd bet. Jordan had no more wish to see his father than she did.

"You can't go in there!" Foster barked at her when Molly laid her hand on the door.

She glanced at the orderly who asked, "Are you Molly?"

"You got it."

She sent Foster a sweet smile. He stepped sharply forward and she whirled around, matching him glare for glare. The orderly bristled.

"That's my son in there!" Foster's voice trembled. "This woman is no relation!"

"He's asking for her." The orderly, whose tag read Bruce, rocked back on his heels, deceptively unconcerned. "Doctor wants to speed his recovery, and this patient's medicine looks to be right here!" He smiled at Molly.

Molly was too eager to see Jordan to savor this small victory. She pushed open the door. The room was dimly lit; the rain that had been threatening all afternoon was now sheeting against the windows.

Jordan lay flat on his back, his head bandaged in a tight white wrap. One leg was splinted, too swollen for its cast yet, and a series of nasty cuts crisscrossed his left cheek— cuts from the glass that had shot at him when Tyler's van burst through the window.

He turned his head. Recognition dawned in his blue eyes and Molly wanted to cry out with relief.

"You look like hell," she said, scooting a stool to his bedside.

"Feel like it, too," he mumbled.

"You gave us quite a scare."

He struggled to raise himself up. "The baby...?"

"Lie back," she insisted firmly and when he collapsed, she assured him, "The baby and I are great. No problems. We've been too worried about you to get in trouble ourselves." She hesitated. "When I saw Tyler's van jump the curb—" Her breath caught and she switched directions. "I've been so worried about you," she said roughly.

He reached for her fingers, clasping them in the warmth of his palm. Molly lay her cheek against the back of his hand, summoning up her own strength to battle the tears that wanted to fill her throat and spill down her cheeks. He was going to be all right.

"I love you," she whispered. "I *love* you. I should have said so earlier. I love you so much."

"Molly..."

"No, don't say anything. You were the one who believed we could have a second chance. I should have believed. I was so afraid. But I'm not anymore. I love you and I want to marry you and I don't care what anyone else says."

She looked up and saw his eyes were closed. Fear grabbed her heart. "Jordan?" she asked sharply.

"I'm here," he said so softly she could scarcely hear him. She leaned closer, anxious and worried, when she saw his lips move and couldn't make out the words. She squeaked in shock, when he suddenly reached out and pulled her close, drawing her down for a kiss.

The kiss was sweet and light.

"God, that hurts!" he groaned.

"You shouldn't—"

"Oh, yes, I should. I feel like I've waited a lifetime to hear you say those words. It's been pure, unadulterated hell. So, I want to hear them again."

She smiled with pure joy. "I love you."

"Again."

"*I* love you."

"Again."

She kissed his curving mouth. "I *love* you."

"Again."

His teeth gleamed white, as his smile broadened. She kissed him harder this time. "I love *you.*"

"Again."

"Jordan . . ." she warned.

He opened his eyes to gaze in wonder at this beautiful, brave, unique woman who loved him and would soon be his wife. "Again," he said.

"*I love you!*"

And with a swooping, silencing, aeons-long kiss she put an end to that silly game once and for all, while Jordan broke into laughter, punctuated by complaints about how much it hurt. Molly reveled in the totally new sensation of being able to express her love without fear that it would somehow end in tragedy.

* * * * *

It takes a very
special man to win
That
Woman!

She's friend, wife, mother—she's you! And beside each Special Woman stands a wonderfully special man. It's a celebration of our heroines—and the men who become part of their lives.

Look for these exciting titles from Silhouette Special Edition:

August MORE THAN HE BARGAINED FOR by Carole Halston
Heroine: Avery Payton—a woman struggling for independence falls for the man next door.

September A HUSBAND TO REMEMBER by Lisa Jackson
Heroine: Nikki Carrothers—a woman without memories meets the man she should never have forgotten…her husband.

October ON HER OWN by Pat Warren
Heroine: Sara Shepard—a woman returns to her hometown and confronts the hero of her childhood dreams.

November GRAND PRIZE WINNER! by Tracy Sinclair
Heroine: Kelley McCormick—a woman takes the trip of a lifetime and wins the greatest prize of all…love!

December POINT OF DEPARTURE by Lindsay McKenna
(Women of Glory)
Heroine: Lt. Callie Donovan—a woman takes on the system and must accept the help of a kind and sexy stranger.

Don't miss THAT SPECIAL WOMAN! each month—from some of your special authors! Only from Silhouette Special Edition!

TSW3

OFFICIAL RULES • MILLION DOLLAR SWEEPSTAKES
NO PURCHASE OR OBLIGATION NECESSARY TO ENTER

To enter, follow the directions published. **ALTERNATE MEANS OF ENTRY:** Hand print your name and address on a 3"x5" card and mail to either: Silhouette "Match 3," 3010 Walden Ave., P.O. Box 1867, Buffalo, NY 14269-1867, or Silhouette "Match 3," P.O. Box 609, Fort Erie, Ontario L2A 5X3, and we will assign your Sweepstakes numbers. (Limit: one entry per envelope.) For eligibility, entries must be received no later than March 31, 1994. No responsibility is assumed for lost, late or misdirected entries.

Upon receipt of entry, Sweepstakes numbers will be assigned. To determine winners, Sweepstakes numbers will be compared against a list of randomly preselected prizewinning numbers. In the event all prizes are not claimed via the return of prizewinning numbers, random drawings will be held from among all other entries received to award unclaimed prizes.

Prizewinners will be determined no later than May 30, 1994. Selection of winning numbers and random drawings are under the supervision of D.L. Blair, Inc., an independent judging organization, whose decisions are final. One prize to a family or organization. No substitution will be made for any prize, except as offered. Taxes and duties on all prizes are the sole responsibility of winners. Winners will be notified by mail. Chances of winning are determined by the number of entries distributed and received.

Sweepstakes open to persons 18 years of age or older, except employees and immediate family members of Torstar Corporation, D.L. Blair, Inc., their affiliates, subsidiaries and all other agencies, entities and persons connected with the use, marketing or conduct of this Sweepstakes. All applicable laws and regulations apply. Sweepstakes offer void wherever prohibited by law. Any litigation within the province of Quebec respecting the conduct and awarding of a prize in this Sweepstakes must be submitted to the Régies des Loteries et Courses du Quebec. In order to win a prize, residents of Canada will be required to correctly answer a time-limited arithmetical skill-testing question. Values of all prizes are in U.S. currency.

Winners of major prizes will be obligated to sign and return an affidavit of eligibility and release of liability within 30 days of notification. In the event of non-compliance within this time period, prize may be awarded to an alternate winner. Any prize or prize notification returned as undeliverable will result in the awarding of that prize to an alternate winner. By acceptance of their prize, winners consent to use of their names, photographs or other likenesses for purposes of advertising, trade and promotion on behalf of Torstar Corporation without further compensation, unless prohibited by law.

This Sweepstakes is presented by Torstar Corporation, its subsidiaries and affiliates in conjunction with book, merchandise and/or product offerings. Prizes are as follows: Grand Prize–$1,000,000 (payable at $33,333.33 a year for 30 years). First through Sixth Prizes may be presented in different creative executions, each with the following approximate values: First Prize–$35,000; Second Prize–$10,000; 2 Third Prizes–$5,000 each; 5 Fourth Prizes–$1,000 each; 10 Fifth Prizes–$250 each; 1,000 Sixth Prizes–$100 each. Prizewinners will have the opportunity of selecting any prize offered for that level. A travel-prize option, if offered and selected by winner, must be completed within 12 months of selection and is subject to hotel and flight accommodations availability. Torstar Corporation may present this Sweepstakes utilizing names other than Million Dollar Sweepstakes. For a current list of all prize options offered within prize levels and all names the Sweepstakes may utilize, send a self-addressed, stamped envelope (WA residents need not affix return postage) to: Million Dollar Sweepstakes Prize Options/Names, P.O. Box 4710, Blair, NE 68009.

The Extra Bonus Prize will be awarded in a random drawing to be conducted no later than May 30, 1994 from among all entries received. To qualify, entries must be received by March 31, 1994 and comply with published directions. No purchase necessary. For complete rules, send a self-addressed, stamped envelope (WA residents need not affix return postage) to: Extra Bonus Prize Rules, P.O. Box 4600, Blair, NE 68009.

For a list of prizewinners (available after July 31, 1994) send a separate, stamped, self-addressed envelope to: Million Dollar Sweepstakes Winners, P.O. Box 4728, Blair, NE 68009.

Silhouette®

SPECIAL EDITION

WILD RIVER TRILOGY

by Laurie Paige

Come meet the wild McPherson men and see how these three sexy
bachelors are tamed!

In HOME FOR A WILD HEART (SE #828) you got to know
Kerrigan McPherson. Now meet the rest of the family:

A PLACE FOR EAGLES, September 1993—
Keegan McPherson gets the surprise of his life.

THE WAY OF A MAN, November 1993—
Paul McPherson finally meets his match.

Don't miss any of these exciting titles—only for our readers and only
from Silhouette Special Edition!

Silhouette Books has done it again!

Opening night in October has never been as exciting! Come watch as the curtain rises and romance flourishes when the stars of tomorrow make their debuts today!

Revel in Jodi O'Donnell's STILL SWEET ON HIM—
Silhouette Romance #969
...as Callie Farrell's renovation of the family homestead leads her straight into the arms of teenage crush Drew Barnett!

Tingle with Carol Devine's BEAUTY AND THE BEASTMASTER—
Silhouette Desire #816
...as legal eagle Amanda Tarkington is carried off by wrestler Bram Masterson!

Thrill to Elyn Day's A BED OF ROSES—
Silhouette Special Edition #846
...as Dana Whitaker's body and soul are healed by sexy physical therapist Michael Gordon!

Believe when Kylie Brant's McLAIN'S LAW —
Silhouette Intimate Moments #528
...takes you into detective Connor McLain's life as he falls for psychic—and suspect—Michele Easton!

Catch the classics of tomorrow—*premiering* today—
only from ❦ *Silhouette*